KT-151-022

PENGUIN BOOKS

UNDER MY SKIN

'Dazzlingly self-contained ... Hannah Wolfe is tough, feisty, with a delicious line in wisecracks at the many moments of high drama ... As well as a cracking plot we are in for a thoughtful investigation of women's self-images' – *New Statesman & Society*

'PI Hannah Wolfe goes down to a women-only health farm to sort out some nasty sabotage ... well-researched and wonderfully written' – *Sunday Times*

'A laid-back, wisecracking style shows Sarah Dunant at her talented best ... This is Dunant's third Wolfe novel, and Hannah is now a character to be reckoned with' – *Sunday Express*

'An assured performance from Dunant – one which must put her among the top three or four women novelists in the female private-eye field' – *Daily Telegraph*

'The perfect English response to the tougher American divas' – *Literary Review*

ABOUT THE AUTHOR

Sarah Dunant was one of the founding presenters of *The Late Show*, BBC2's cultural magazine programme. She is the co-author of two political thrillers and a BBC television thriller serial, *Thin Air. Snow Storms in a Hot Climate* was her first solo novel, and she is the editor of *War of the Words: The Political Correctness Debate* (Virago). Her first Hannah Wolfe novel, *Birth Marks*, was shortlisted for the 1991 Gold Dagger Award and her second, *Fatlands*, won the 1993 Silver Dagger Award presented by the Crime Writers' Association. Both of these are published by Penguin.

Before she began writing, Sarah Dunant spent many years travelling and working as a radio and print journalist. She now lives in London with her young daughters.

Sarah Dunant

UNDER MY SKIN

PENGUIN BOOKS

PENGUIN BOOKS

Published by the Penguin Group
Penguin Books Ltd, 27 Wrights Lane, London W8 5TZ, England
Penguin Books USA Inc., 375 Hudson Street, New York, New York 10014, USA
Penguin Books Australia Ltd, Ringwood, Victoria, Australia
Penguin Books Canada Ltd, 10 Alcorn Avenue, Toronto, Ontario, Canada M4V 3B2
Penguin Books (NZ) Ltd, 182–190 Wairau Road, Auckland 10, New Zealand

Penguin Books Ltd, Registered Offices: Harmondsworth, Middlesex, England

First published by Hamish Hamilton 1995
Published in Penguin Books 1996
13 5 7 9 10 8 6 4 2

Printed in England by Clays Ltd, St Ives plc

Chapter One

It had come through the latest Comfort and Security addition to office technology: the portable phone. Any time, any place, your employees can get the message. So said the blurb. Except it didn't allow for the volume of the sound system in the Holloway Road Odeon. Not to mention the kids. Beside me Amy was stuffing another fistful of popcorn into her mouth, eyes big as saucers, transfixed by the sight of a humungus blue genie strutting his stuff for Aladdin. But she still heard it before I did.

'Hannah, why's your jacket beeping?'

Think of all the things we miss being cloth-eared adults. Maybe it's just children who believe in fairies because they're the only ones who can hear them chattering away at the end of the garden. I sacrificed the pleasure of Robin Williams for the sound of Frank. Not a fair contest really.

'Sorry?'

'What? Hannah? Where the hell are you?'

'Hold on a minute.'

On screen there was some serious magic going on. No point in asking Amy to come back later. 'I'm just going out into the corridor,' I hissed. 'I'll be right back, OK?' Another automatic hand to mouth and the scrunch of popcorn. The slightest of nods.

I slid out of the row and through the doors down by the edge of the screen. I kept one of them propped open so that I could still see her head halfway along the row. It could wreck a private eye's reputation – losing a five-year-old to child molesters in the middle of a Disney film. I slid up the aerial.

'Hi, Frank.'

3

'What's the racket?'

'Aladdin's trying to impress Princess Jasmine.'

'What?'

'Half-term. Forget it, you're too old. So, you called, master?'

'Yeah, congratulations. You got the job.'

Bad sign. The ones I get are always the ones Frank doesn't want. 'Which one was that?'

'Castle Dean health farm in Berkshire. They've got a problem with their Jacuzzi.'

'So call a plumber.'

'Not that kind of problem. Someone dumped a dozen dead carp in the frothy bits. Probably the same someone who put spikes in the massage brushes.'

'Nasty.'

'Not the kind of thing you'd pay two hundred quid a day for, that's for sure. They want you there pronto.'

'Frank, I'm baby-sitting, remember?'

'So give it back. You know how it is, Hannah. Crime never sleeps. It'll be a stay-over job, so you'd better get home and pack a bag. I'll fax you the details. Oh, and remember to take a tracksuit.' And he laughed. Which is cute considering Frank's the one with the weight problem. I told him as much.

'You're absolutely right. Except I'd be a distinct liability in a women-only health farm. You should be grateful, Hannah. This way you get paid for being a guest. I got you a hundred and fifty a day, plus all the lemon juice you can drink. Nice, eh? You can kiss my feet later.'

Sabotage in a health farm. Not exactly life at the cutting edge of late-twentieth-century law enforcement, but then who am I to turn down a free massage?

'Good. So when do I say you'll be there?'

I looked at the screen. Princess Jasmine was psyching herself up to kiss the villain. Yuk. Even in Disneyland the course of true love doesn't run that smooth. 'After the happy ending.'

*　　　　*　　　　*　　　　*

4

I had promised Kate I'd keep Amy till 4 o'clock, so I took her home with me. She sat on my bed eating Rice Krispies and reading the cereal packet out loud while I packed. Then she read the labels on my suitcase, then started in on the title page of the Raymond Carver book by the bed. A little learning can be an awesome thing. Good job I wasn't a Bret Easton Ellis type of girl.

Although it was traditional that I should bitch at Frank I wasn't unhappy to be on the road. The last couple of weeks have been too quiet and I haven't been sleeping that well – a case of a vicious man I once met in a country lane coming back to haunt me (now you know why Bret and me don't get on). Maybe a little exercise would release the toxic wastes in my imagination, help me to work up a few hot sweats instead of cold.

From the details waiting on the fax machine Castle Dean would be the right place to do it in. A brochure showed a photo of a stately house with some snazzy ad-copy and a price list to make your eyes water. There were also some notes from Frank. I shoved everything in a bag, along with a manky body suit and a pair of trainers that smelt fine as long as you never took them off. In the kitchen I threw out anything more than a week past its sell-by date and checked the calendar for any engagements I might have to cancel. It wasn't an arduous task. I crossed off the next week. Well, no case paying a hundred and fifty quid a day should be solved that quickly.

At Kate's I had to ring the doorbell twice. When she opened it, she looked so zonked I could have sworn she'd been asleep, except it was hard to imagine anything sleeping through the racket coming out of Ben's room.

'Hi, Mum.' Amy marched straight in past her. And was marched right back again.

'Excuse me, young lady. What do you say to Hannah?'

'Thank you, Hannah,' Amy chanted in that sing-song tone that children perfect when the relatives demand thanking. I gave her a wink. She screwed up both her eyes in reply and disappeared into the noise beyond.

'What's up with Ben?'

'I wouldn't give him the kitchen scissors to play with. He'll get over it. You want a cup of coffee?'

'Uh-uh. Gotta go. A job's come up.'

'Ah, well, thanks, anyway. How was it?'

'Great. She held my hand all through the scary bits. I wasn't frightened at all.' Kate smiled. But it seemed more duty than pleasure. 'You all right?'

'Yeah. Fine.'

'You sure?'

'Yes. I'm tired, that's all.'

Tired. Of course. I should have guessed. Kate's been tired for the last five years now. Five years. During that time I've been a lot of things: in despair, in trouble, in pain, even briefly in love. But Kate – gorgeous, energetic Kate as was – has just been shagged out. For every time I want to put my sister to bed and let her sleep for a week, I also want to kick her up the backside and tell her to snap out of it. She says it's children. I say it's life. But then we both know what I feel about the partner she picked to share it with. Better not to bring it up. Better just to agree to disagree.

'When's Colin back?'

'Er . . . Thursday, probably.'

Just like him to be out of town during half-term. 'Well, I'll give you a call when I'm clear. Maybe Amy and I could take in another laser game at that place in Archway.'

'Fine. I'll try and get her to let you win this time.'

I used the portable to let them know I was on my way. The client's name was Olivia Marchant, owner and supremo. But my contact at the farm was the manager, one Mrs Waverley. She told me I should come to main reception and she'd see me there. She also offered further directions from the motorway. In the early days of my career I would probably have

6

turned them down, worrying about the image of a private investigator who couldn't read a map. Now I know better. Now I take all the help I can get.

The brochure said Castle Dean was just over an hour from central London. Which it may well have been in another car, but I've got the kind that stops at traffic lights and obeys the speed limit, so it took me an hour and a half. Not bad, though. In terms of fat breakdown you could probably still make it from the city in time to counteract the effects of a big lunch.

Off the motorway the landscape was scarcely 'Beautiful Berkshire'. More the tame home-counties variety; prissy little fields and painting-by-numbers hedgerows with the villages in-between so tidy they might have been in a theme park. There certainly didn't seem to be anyone living in them. Too expensive, presumably. When the antique shops and wine merchants close down, you know the commuter belt set are in real trouble. Ah, this pesky recession. I drove on, imagining myself into the role of a Tory-heartland voter searching for the recovery that is just around the next corner. But I must have been on the wrong road, because the only signs I saw were For Sale ones.

Castle Dean seemed to be doing all right, though. At least, you wouldn't know any different from its entrance: two massive stone columns topped with proud English lions and some imposing ironwork with a Latin inscription. 'Beware all excess weight that enters here'? I squeezed the top of my thighs to reassure them. As luck, or rather genetics would have it, mine was not a major problem. In our family even the hamster was thin. Which is just as well, because I'm not that crazy about exercise. I see myself more as the Gene Hackman sort of investigator. *French Connection I*. Remember? That gut-wrenching finale when he and his extra fifteen pounds chase the bad guy right the way across the Marseilles docks? In homage I once pursued a shoplifter all the way down the Edgware Road and into Paddington Station. I caught him too. Just couldn't get enough breath to lift myself off him for the next half-hour. Since then pride has forced me into a passing acquaintance with the local gym, but we're not talking a serious love affair here.

The drive curved round to offer up a big house and an even bigger sign. CASTLE DEAN – HEALTH WITH STYLE. One hundred and one things to do with a stately home. Very nice, assuming you had the money. The place reminded me of a certain French château it had once been my pleasure to solve a crime in. But it's not wise to rest on old laurels when new triumphs lie ahead.

Close up the house turned out to be younger than it looked – the façade a rather crude fake Gothic, probably late nineteenth century.

The entrance lobby kept up the illusion: baronial William Morris with a lot of help from the Sanderson's catalogue. The girl at the reception desk looked fit but not invincible. I felt heartened. I gave her my name. In return she gave me a key, a welcome pack and a place to sit while she looked for Mrs Waverley. Once she'd disappeared, I leant over the desk and checked out the reception book. Whatever problems they'd been having, the guest list still looked healthy enough. I sank into an overstuffed floral print settee. A couple of long-legged ladies in white towelling robes strolled by, hair wet from the shower. One of them smiled at me. I smiled back. Let's be nice to the new girl. On the coffee table among copies of *Good Housekeeping* and *Cosmo* I spotted last week's *Hello!* Well, we all have our guilty secrets. I was heading for the centre spread on Ivana and her new Trump card when Mrs Waverley arrived.

'Miss Wolfe?' She was average height and in better than average shape, with slightly troubled skin only partly disguised by clever makeup. Age? Thirty something probably, like me. But with more poise. And no doubt a more coherent career plan.

'I'm Carol Waverley, the manager. Welcome to Castle Dean,' she added for the benefit of anyone who might be listening. No one was. Which was a bit of a shame, because she'd made a real effort with the diction: sweet and crisp, and a considerable way from wherever it was she'd been born.

She ushered me across the hall towards a door marked 'Private' and into a small office overlooking the guest car park. Not the greatest view, but at least the place was healthy, with its own water machine and a set of herb teas where the serious caffeine equipment should have been. She offered. I took a rosehip. She made it herself. I watched her as she poured the boiling water into the mug, carefully crushing the tea-bag with the spoon and depositing it into the bin with the precision of a patriot missile. I bet you're the kind that irons your underwear, I thought. Interesting how quickly you can take agin someone. Come on, Hannah, it's hardly her fault that you're not out busting international drug smugglers.

The tea arrived with a dry biscuit. I nibbled delicately to make it last while she sat and told me what I needed to know. When it got interesting, I took notes. Good I didn't do shorthand, or I might have had trouble remembering I wasn't her secretary.

Castle Dean was, apparently, a very successful health farm catering for a middle- to top-notch clientele and offering a range of high-class health and beauty treatments with value-for-money prices. I nodded vigorously. On the video I fast-forward through the adverts, but it was a little too early in the job to offend the client.

The picture, however, had got decidedly less rosy twelve days ago when a client had gone into the sauna, only to find that she couldn't get out again. 'Fortunately one of the other guests came in to use the shower and heard her banging. A chair had been pushed up against the door just under the latch, with a big box of fresh towels on it. She called a member of staff and together they managed to unwedge it and let her out.'

'How was she?' I said, writing the word 'Parboiled' in my notebook.

'A bit panicky, but all right. Technically speaking, we were in the clear, since we expressly ask guests not to use the equipment unless there are staff on duty.'

'And you're sure it was deliberate?'

'Not at the time, no. The chair could well have just been pushed against the door by mistake. At the time that's all I thought it was – just a careless accident.'

Not three days later though when a Marks & Spencer's senior buyer emerged from her morning peat bath to find herself a less than fashionable shade of indigo.

'Then, of course, I knew. Only one of the baths had been affected. Out of four made up from the same batch by the same person.'

'Who was?'

'Oh, one of the senior beauticians. She's been here since the place opened. But after she'd done the baths, she'd been called away to take a phone call. She was gone about ten to fifteen minutes. Anyone could have got in then, and the water's such a dark colour you wouldn't notice anything was wrong until you were in it.'

Or rather out of it again. 'Was it permanent?' I asked, finding something mildly irresistible about the idea of a blue Marks & Spencer's buyer.

'No. But it took a long time to get it off.'

'So what did you do?'

'A mixture of soaking in a clean bath and rubbing with cleansing cream.'

Once a beautician always a beautician. I smiled. 'Actually I was thinking more in the way of an investigation.'

'What? Oh, well, of course, yes. I talked to everybody who'd been on duty. But no one knew anything.' She sighed. Caught up in the drama of the story the real Carol Waverley was starting to slip through the cracks, certain carefully rounded vowels flattening out as they moved further north in search of their homeland. At least it was more natural. 'After that it was just a question of waiting for the next thing to happen.'

'Which was?'

'The nails in the G5 pads.'

'The what?'

'G5. It's a massage system. Electrically operated. The sponge heads vibrate and whirl round. Then you press them down into the flesh. It's very popular. We were lucky the operator spotted them. At that speed the nails would have ripped the skin apart.'

'Have you still got them?'

She moved to the desk near me and opened a small drawer. She took out a small envelope and emptied its contents into my hand. A set of tiny little nails no bigger than new fivepenny pieces lay glittering there, sharp and eager. Could have been bought at any hardware store, I thought. Like finding a needle in a haystack. And probably as painful.

'Your girl must have had sharp eyes.'

'Not really, but she did have some nasty little wounds on her legs. In the circumstances I could hardly criticize her for using the equipment.'

G5. Must be pretty nice if the operators do it to themselves. I made a note to try it out sometime.

'So, you think the equipment was tampered with during the night?'

'I have no way of knowing. The treatment rooms are locked at night, but until recently there was always a key in the supervisor's office. Anyone who knows the place could get hold of it. I've had it removed now.'

'But when you found the nails, you knew you were in trouble. What did you do?'

'I called Mrs Marchant in London.'

Ah, ah. The elusive client. 'And what did she say?'

'She gave me permission to close down the whole treatment area. I told the guests there was a fault in the heating system and did an inspection on my own. Since then I've double-checked everything in the building myself before it's used. Which means I know for certain that it was between midnight last night and 7 this morning that someone took the carp out of the fish pond in the garden and put them into the Jacuzzi, then switched the heating on. They were dead when I found them, oily, slimy, floating on the surface.' She shivered. 'That's when Mrs Marchant called you.'

'She was still in London?'

'Yes. She'll be back tonight or tomorrow.'

'Is that usual, her being away so much of the time?'

'Yes . . . no . . . I mean Mr Marchant works in London, so she spends some of the week up there with him and some down here.'

'What does he do?'

'He's a consultant.'

Isn't everybody these days? 'But from what you're saying she's not a particularly hands-on owner?'

'It depends. At the beginning she was very involved. But since I've come, she's taken more of a back seat. Left it to me.' She paused. 'She's a good employer,' she added, as if I needed to know it.

'And neither you nor she have had any contact with the saboteur?'

'I don't understand . . .'

'No notes, no threats, no demands for money or anything like that?'

'No. Nothing.'

Either they were biding their time or we were looking at a malice over profit job. More interesting psychologically, but for that reason harder to crack.

She picked up a pile of files from the desk in front of her. 'Mrs Marchant told me to give you a copy of the employees' records. She said you'd probably want to see them. We have twenty-four girls altogether. Twenty live on the premises, the other four in the local village. Then there are two visiting nurses and a doctor, but they're only part time. I've included details of everyone's work shifts over the last two weeks so you can see who was where at what time.'

'Thanks. Yours are here too, are they?' I said casually.

'Of course. Right on top,' she said, her diction sharpening up again at the hint of trouble.

'Good.' I paused in case the silence made her feel uncomfortable. It didn't. 'I'm assuming that none of the staff knows who I am?'

'Absolutely not. You're booked in as a regular guest.'

'Even though I'm here talking to you?'

'It's nothing out of the ordinary. I often make it my business to meet new guests.'

'And if I need to contact you urgently . . .?'

'You can dial me direct from your room. I've added both my office and room numbers to your notes.'

'Fine. OK. Well, I'll need a plan of the place, a list of the clients who have been here in the last two weeks and someone to show me round. Oh, and I think I forgot to bring a swimsuit.'

From under the desk she picked up a large bag with CASTLE DEAN written in big fluorescent letters. 'I got you this in case you didn't have time to pack. The suit is size 10, but it stretches. If it doesn't fit, let me know. I've booked you in for a full day's treatment starting tomorrow morning at 8.15 with water aerobics in the pool.'

I could feel my muscles twitching in anticipation. I got up. 'Anything else?'

'Not really,' she said, and then with admirable aplomb, 'Although you might start by concentrating on the waist.'

Any more like that, lady, and you could find yourself the victim of a fit-up.

Chapter Two

Despite Carol Waverley's taunt the good news was the costume fitted. The bad news was the body hair it revealed. The legs I could probably get away with, the pubes were another matter. Designed with beauty-salon profits in mind, the suit was cut high enough into the hip to call for some serious waxing. Unless, of course, you had the nerve to go without. Given my natural aversion to masochism, I would normally not even have considered it. But in this case I was being paid to fit in, and what if the girl who did the waxing also did the sabotage? You know what the pundits say about small acts of violence leading to larger ones. I decided to sacrifice myself for the cause. I dialled an appointment at the beauty parlour, then slipped into my old but happy tracksuit and went downstairs for the guided tour.

After a quick zip around the dining-room and lounges (more catalogue décor) we moved on to the serious stuff. The health section was in the new extension behind the main wing. The heart of the complex was the pool, a glistening tropical blue under a vaulted glass ceiling and surrounded by some clever trompe l'oeils of exotic seascapes. Through arches of fake palm trees, a series of corridors led off to the treatment rooms. Our tour guide, Marianne, otherwise known as the Client Liaison Officer, whizzed us round the facilities. I loitered a while in the doorway of the G5 massage parlour. The machine, which looked like an elaborate vacuum cleaner, stood by the massage bed, its sponge heads lying limply over the top. I closed my eyes, the better to imagine the screams and the walls splattered with blood.

On the floor above, the last aerobics class of the day was

coming to an end with some frenzied jogging to hype up the heart rate. I looked through the doors at the backs of some twenty women bopping up and down like a clutch of overage cheerleaders practising for the big game. The sight much reassured me. Despite all the ad talk, Castle Dean was clearly not the kind of health farm which doubled as a finishing school for super models.

On the other hand, as the gym next door showed, it did have its health freaks. In a corner two women were pumping serious iron on the chest and leg machines. One of them was more or less a normal shape, but the other was built like a piece of flex. You could almost feel the electricity pulsing through her. They both looked some way away from climaxing. Know how you feel, I thought. I have the same problem with working out as I do with sex. Low boredom threshold. Whatever's pumping. Near the door an older woman was cycling slowly to nowhere, overshadowed by her Olympic companions. I gave her a reassuring smile.

In the heat treatment area the figure in the sauna looked hot but voluntarily so, while the six or seven women in the steam room – well, I've already waxed lyrical about the Cezanne bathers.

I was ready to take my clothes off then and there, but apparently that wasn't allowed. Not yet, anyway. Before the treatments you needed to have a treatment plan, and that meant seeing the nurse.

She turned out not to have quite the customer charm skills of the lovely Marianne. No doubt she had learnt her trade in the National Health Service, and was having trouble adapting to the private sector. After a tight little smile and a few brisk personal details, she had me 'popping' off my clothes and on to the scales. The weights danced between the eight- and nine-stone mark, coming to rest nearer the latter. It was the kind of revelation that might have driven Naomi Campbell to suicide, but I gained comfort from a more historical perspective: if Naomi and I had both been naked in front of Rubens it would not have been her who would have made it to the National Gallery.

Staff nurse Ratched, however, was more of a Giacometti fan. The treatment she worked out for me involved rigorous daily exercise and a week on the reduced-calorie diet. She made it sound like a penance.

Back in my room I used up my first day's quota of calories on a hefty slug of scotch from my hipflask – that's the great thing about Catholicism, after penance comes further sin – and hit the staff records. I looked at Mrs Waverley's first. It made aspirational reading. Carol Waverley, née Clacton and born just outside Rugby, had left school early and gone into the beauty business. Four years later she went to college to do a business diploma, and Castle Dean was her first big break after qualifying. En route somewhere she had acquired and then lost Mr Waverley. There had been no children.

No one else on the team quite came up to her aspirational or academic standards. The average age was around twenty-two, and their track records painted a picture of casual labour, six months here, six months there, with the odd stint on cruise liners or in the big stores. Most of their references were good. All of them had been checked out either by Carol or the owner herself (the odd signed comment in a fine italic hand).

A little time-and-motion study successfully narrowed the field. Out of the twenty-four of them, eight had been off duty (although that didn't necessarily mean off the premises) during the key times. I put them to the bottom of the pile and went through the remaining sixteen again. There still wasn't an obvious suspect among them. But then if there had been, they'd hardly be wasting a hundred and fifty quid a day on yours truly. Thinking about the money, I decided to do a little research among the guests.

Downstairs dinner was in full swing. Nothing so crude as a gong to summon the faithful, more a communal rumbling in the stomachs of a hundred underfed souls. Let's hope they didn't smell the scotch on my breath. Luckily the panelled dining-room already had its own prevailing aroma – that of low-cal salad dressing. It reminded me of the lunch I'd missed.

At candlelit tables, each with its own bowl of flowers, sat little groups of women, heads bowed over plates of green beans and glasses of iced water. A soundtrack of low chatter echoed to the ceiling. The effect was positively devotional. 'For these and all the calorie-controlled food of our lives may the Lord make us truly grateful.'

I picked a table with four others. In beauty terms they ranged from beyond hope to the 'who needs a health farm anyway?' I have to admit I was ready to dislike them, ready to find them too rich or too idle, or just too self-obsessed. But it wasn't like that. Whoever they might have been with their clothes and makeup on, without them they were pleasantly ordinary, there as much for the rest as for any miraculous transformation, and with few illusions about the state of their bodies.

My favourite was the most recalcitrant image-wise, a lady whom I recognized from the sauna. She must have been in her fifties. Her long black hair, streaked with grey, was held up in an untidy bun and she wore the kind of housecoat that one sees only at jumble sales. I got the impression she knew that and didn't give a damn. Her stay at Castle Dean was a thirtieth wedding anniversary present from her daughter, an attractive TV producer sitting next to her. The family that gyms together slims together. As mother–daughter relationships go they were doing better than I ever had.

To the mother's left was someone who owned her own travel agency, in for a 'retread' (her words not mine), and next to her a well-preserved woman called Katherine who worked in the city and advised people with too much money what to do with it. In spite of my prejudices even she seemed OK. Maybe it was the diet, the absence of E numbers reducing aggression levels. Theirs and mine.

I used my newcomer status to ask some dumb questions,

but got little back. Carol Waverley had done her job well. Neither the nails nor the blue Marks & Spencer's buyer had entered Castle Dean folklore. After a while the conversation reverted inexorably to food and the culinary fantasies that come with all calorie-controlled diets.

Coffee – decaf, of course – was served in the lounge, accompanied by a short talk by a local expert on the wines of the Languedoc region – an extra-curricular activity of some sadism, I thought, for a place under prohibition. I gave it a miss and went to check out the servants' quarters.

The girls (or the beauticians, as the brochure insisted on calling them) lived at the far end of one of the wings of the house, their rooms carefully segregated from those of the guests. I went via the outside, across the immaculately mani-cured lawn through a small gate marked PRIVATE. The grass on the employees' side was decidedly less green, but then these ladies weren't paying two hundred quid a day to stare at it. I looked up at their rooms. Only a few still had their lights on. The morning shifts started at 8 a.m. Tough business, beauty. On the top floor there were a couple of windows open. From one a tinny stereo was pumping out house music, the volume too muted for the choice of music to make sense. Bedsit land. I've always had a sneaking fondness for the simplicity of it. Kate thinks it's the Peter Pan in me, never wanting to live in a real adult house. I'll leave you to guess what I think of what she thinks . . .

I wondered what they made of their lives, boarding-school girls by night and handmaidens by day, massaging, pummel-ling, waxing and cosseting an endless stream of women who spent more in a day than they probably made in a week. Presumably they were all paid-up members of the church of health and beauty. But even the faithful can be tempted. Maybe one of the bedsit windows concealed a recent convert to Living Marxism dedicated to exacting vengeance on the complacent middle-classes. I could hardly wait till morning.

Back in my room I washed down some leftover popcorn

from *Aladdin* with a couple of hits from my hipflask. I tried to think full but my stomach wasn't fooled. More than a couple of days of this and I'd be ready to sabotage the place myself. I channel-flicked until there was nothing left but night-owl trash, then changed into my new swimming costume. It seemed pretty unlikely that the saboteur would strike again so quickly, but I was being paid partly to let Carol Waverley sleep more easily in her bed, and, anyway, it's one of my favourite activities, midnight swimming.

Someone, however, had beaten me to it. As I entered the atrium, the moon emerged from behind clouds and bathed the pool in a cold, foggy glow. I saw a figure moving cleanly through the water, a lovely smooth breaststroke, up, down, up, down, the ripples flowing out like cut silk behind her. I stood watching her, counting the laps, envying her elegance and her ease. Then, just as I was in danger of becoming mesmerized, she stopped and stood up. She put her hands up to her face, pushing off the water, and let out a long gasp of tiredness, pulling herself up over the side of the pool. In the moonlight I could see she had a beautiful figure: long legs, high, rounded breasts and slim waist in a simple black swimsuit. I did not recognize her from any of the staff mug shots and certainly nothing that lovely had been in the dining-room earlier. From a chair near by she picked up a long, dark bathrobe and pulled it round herself, sliding her feet into a pair of slip-on shoes.

She was still oblivious of my presence. Since I was standing directly between her and the exit, she was about to get the fright of her life. I braced myself for her shock. But it never came. Because she didn't leave that way. Instead she walked round the pool to the back of the atrium and out through what should have been a locked door.

I went after her the second it closed, but by the time I reached it it was locked again. I knew from the plans that it led not to the treatment rooms but to the garden, and from there one could reach the girls' block. I tried the other doors.

They were still locked. Someone who had a key to one could well have the key to others, but if I had been doing something naughty in the steam room I would hardly have stuck around for a leisurely swim afterwards. I dug out my torch to check the time. Ten to two. Even if I did wake her, it was unlikely Carol Waverley would feel like getting up to search the premises in the middle of the night. I decided to leave her to her beauty sleep and get up early.

*   *   *   *

As it happened she didn't feel much like searching then, either. 'Oh, I don't think we need to worry.'

'Why? D'you know who it was?'

'Yes, I think so. I think it was one of the beauticians.'

'Which one?'

'Er . . . Patricia Mason. From your description it sounds like her.'

'Is it allowed, the staff using the pool?'

'Not strictly, no. But it does happen.'

'And what if it was more than a swim?'

'Well, I'm pretty certain it wasn't, though of course I'll check. Thanks. I'm grateful for you telling me so promptly.'

Liar, I thought. Nobody can be grateful for being woken at 6.30 a.m. – I certainly wasn't when the alarm went off in my ear after less than four hours' sleep. And I wasn't that certain that she would check, either. Interesting.

Half an hour later I was the second one down for breakfast. By then I was so hungry that I could have eaten anything. I almost did. I was on my way to the buffet table with its tempting choice of bran or grapefruit when the woman ahead of me started screaming. Food deprivation and hysteria – an interesting medical phenomenon. I pushed past her. There, in pride of place in the centre of the table, stood an enormous bowl of yoghurt. 'Live', I believe, is the technical term. In this case it was a precise use of language. I watched fascinated as its thick white surface heaved and squirmed with a mass of drowning maggots.

For a moment nobody did anything. Then I picked up a napkin and flung it over the bowl. Next to me the woman's screams had transmuted into panicky, yelping little hiccups. 'Don't worry,' I said calmly. 'They're protein. Very low in calories.'

Sabotage. It comes in all shapes and flavours.

Chapter Three

Of course neither of us felt much like eating after that. Indeed my breakfast companion felt more like going home. Don't blame her, really. I sat in reception with a cup of red zinger pretending to read a magazine, while Carol Waverley placated and charmed her over the bill. I thought on balance it was probably better that way. At least if she went, there was more chance she could keep it quiet.

'So?' I said, after she had waved her goodbye. 'Do you want to give me the records of the kitchen staff?'

She gave a desperate little shrug. 'The supervisor says they laid out the cold table at a quarter to seven, then all the girls went back to prepare the hot meal in the kitchen. Anybody else could have walked into the dining-room during that time.'

Down the snake back to square one. Time to start getting to know some of the anybodies.

By lunchtime I had done aerobics in the pool, a round in the gym, fifteen minutes in the steam room, a sojourn in a peat-coloured peat bath and half an hour under the glorious G5. I'd also met Mary, Karen, Flosie, Nicole and Martha. None of them smelt of fish bait, but between them I learnt more than a person should ever need to know about the beauty business: how it took anything from one year to three to get your diploma, and how, once qualified, many girls chose the health farms first because you could make the salary stretch longer and it was good experience before moving on to London or the big wide world.

They were all living in. Flosie was straight out of college,

Nicole and Karen on their second job, and Mary, lilting and shy, just over from Ireland. The accommodation wasn't bad. They either had their own room or shared, and there were communal kitchens. Half a dozen girls had cars, so there was always the chance of getting the hell out into Reading for a night off. From the sound of it, Reading was clearly the most exciting thing that had happened to most of them. They were not so much boring as unformed. Oh, to be that young again.

Finding out that much proved easy. But when it came to casual inquiries about problems, all I got was the occasional whinge about schoolgirl bitchiness in the dorms and missing their boyfriends.

Luckily Martha, with the notorious G5 massage machine, was more forthcoming.

Take away the nails and I have to tell you G5 rates as one of life's great experiences: the human equivalent of those carwashes where huge pillars of vibrating fluff rub your bodywork all over. By the time we got to the polishing stage I was rendered almost inarticulate with pleasure, but as mine is a vocation as well as a job, through it all I kept talking.

So, bless her cotton socks, did Martha. She was a handsome woman, with black hair and soft olive skin, probably in her mid to late twenties, and with a nicely tuned sense of humour. That she was good at her job was proved by the selection of thank-you cards Blu-Tacked to the wall: 'Thanks for helping me relax,' 'A week was not enough!' . . . I had read them while I was supposed to be undressing. I had also checked the massage head, just because – given all the trouble with the worms – Carol would not have had time to.

'Sponge,' Martha said. 'I think you'll like it. Most people do.'

I lay on my front first and she spread powder over my back and shoulders and down my legs. She had good hands – confident, not at all tentative. I was pleased to have them on me, even if they did remind me of how long it was since anyone else's had been there.

My stomach grumbled softly, just to draw attention to its continued bad treatment.

'Hungry,' she said softly. A statement rather than a question.

'Mmm,' I murmured, wondering if any of the popcorn had maybe fallen into my coat pocket.

'That shows it's doing you good,' she stated with what I thought was admirably concealed irony.

She worked for a while in silence. But once given the cue was quite happy to chatter more, both about the place and herself. She'd been there for almost a year. It was her third job and she was looking to move on. She'd already done the see-the-world stint on the cruise liners only to discover that all that glitters isn't gold – I mean where's the glamour in spending twelve hours a day in a room without a window while the Caribbean sun shone on the rich folks out on deck? Anyway, she was more ambitious than that. Wanted to run her own salon. And to do that she was going to have to move to London. She had sent off a number of applications already, so presumably she didn't feel the need to be that loyal any more. Whatever the reasons we were getting on famously.

'You couldn't stay here and climb up the ladder, then?' She was halfway across my back with the sponge attachment and speech was becoming an effort.

'Hardly. There's only one pair of shoes I'd like to be in here. And I don't think she's planning on taking them off.'

How right you are, I thought. 'So, you'll go?'

'If I can get the right job. I certainly don't intend to spend the rest of my life in an overage girls' school.'

'Are you talking about the staff or guests?'

Martha laughed. 'Do you have to sleep in shared rooms?'

'I got the impression they treated you quite well.'

'Oh, it's not bad. We're just not taken that seriously.'

'And you think you should be?'

She shrugged. 'I think it's probably our skills and relationships with the clients which make this place really work. I mean' – she lowered her voice – 'would you come here for the food?'

I twisted my head to see whether or not the remark might have maggots in it, but she was concentrating hard on the machine, moving into my shoulders with a particularly deep stroke of the massage head. Maggots or mange-tout. Who cares? I thought limply.

'The fact is we're just taken for granted,' she said after a bit. 'Unless things go wrong. And then we're the ones who get the blame.'

'What kind of "wrong"?' I prompted to see if I could tempt her into further indiscretion.

'You wouldn't want to know,' she said mischievously. 'It might make you defect to the competition. Right.' She lifted the sponges off my back. 'That's one side finished. Why don't you turn over now and I'll do your tummy and your front.'

I did as I was told. She poured more powder on to her hands and then rubbed it along my arms and over my breasts and stomach. At some point I must have flinched. She stopped. 'Sorry. Are my hands cold?'

'No, they're fine.'

'You feel a bit tense. I noticed it on your back. Why don't you try and relax?'

But I already had. Had begun to like the feel of her hands on me. I let myself think about it some more. Once again her touch brought back another's. How long had it been? Eight, nine months? That had been its own kind of therapy too. Nick going out of his way to prove that not all men were the kind you meet in country lanes. Nice thought. Nice man. Wrong adjective for a lasting relationship. Shame really. I was about to start playing with other ones when I remembered how much I was being paid to keep my mind on the job. Martha had put aside the powder and started in with the sponges. I climbed back on to the end of the plot.

'I'm sure you're right,' I murmured. 'About the workforce being important. In my experience people only do stupid things if they're unhappy or angry about the job.'

'Absolutely,' she said, busy with the sponge-head on my thighs, 'but if management don't notice who's upset or why, then what can you do?'

'So should I be prepared for a mutiny or just the occasional individual act of violence?' I asked, keeping it as light as I could.

She laughed. 'Oh, nothing like that.' But she realized that she had probably gone too far. She worked in silence for a little longer, then ran the sponge-head evenly down my left leg and over and along the bottom of my foot. A feeling to die for. I got the impression it was also a little added extra. She lifted the massage head off me. For a second she left me there, lost in my own pleasure. Then she said quietly, 'OK. That's your time up, Mrs Wolfe, I'm afraid.'

Oh no, please, say it isn't so. I dragged myself reluctantly from the bed and started to dress. I could have done with another hour, or maybe a day. 'That was fantastic,' I said, for the first time since I arrived really meaning it. 'Is this your speciality?'

She was busy detaching the sponge-heads, not looking directly at me. 'No, not really. We all have to do everything. I think I'm probably best on the massage table, though. I like it.' She wiped her hands down on a towel and smiled. 'You know you can always ask for me again at the office. If, that is, of course, you want to,' she added, and this time her look had just a touch of the coy. Behind her the thank-you messages joined in the chorus of approval.

Are the Kennedys gun-shy? 'Thanks. I will.'

*   *   *   *

My deforestation was booked in for 4, which left me a couple of hours in hand. The treatment rooms were closed between

1 and 3 for lunch. I had a quick gourmet repast – two bowls of lettuce and half a dozen crispbreads – then slipped back to see if I could spot any unauthorized activity. In the sauna a tall girl with cropped black hair was picking up towels and pushing them into a black plastic sack. She looked pissed off, but that could have been the menial nature of the job, and she gave me polite, but short shrift when she saw me there.

I retreated to the poolside. Counting the girls I had seen but not talked to, I'd probably come into contact with twelve or thirteen of the twenty-four staff, but still as yet no sign of my mermaid, Patricia. I had to admit to a certain disappointment.

The atmosphere in the atrium was relaxed and sleepy. I watched a group of middle-aged women enjoying the Jacuzzi, chattering away to each other like young girls. After a while one of them got out and made her way to the pool. I recognized her from lunch. She smiled and nodded at me. She was a museum administrator from Oxford, due to retire in a few years' time. Over the fruit course she had been great company – funny, intelligent, with a quiet confidence about who she was and what life had meant to her. But some of that confidence seemed to have come off with the clothes. She hurried across the tiles, aware of my gaze, a little less graceful in the way she carried herself. Of course a health farm isn't the world's most compassionate place to show off one's body, but even so . . . I thought of my night swimmer with her perfect body silhouetted in the moonlight and found myself guiltily fascinated by the contrast: the older woman's arms, the way the loose flesh underneath wrinkled and sagged into her armpits, the lumpy body and the weight of her thighs pitted by mini moon craters with purple veins running like mineral deposits under the surface. I tried to see it all as a testament to a life well lived: to children, husband, job, all those years when she had just been too busy to care for herself. That and the inexorable pull of gravity on older flesh. I understood the process but the deterioration still made me a little sad, like visiting a handsome old house where the effects of age and neglect have combined.

I tried to imagine myself at her age. Would I mind? Or would I just accept it? Maybe age would bring its own surrender from the burdens of image and sexual attraction. Or maybe it just altered the threshold. Just as I no longer fancied 22-year-olds, finding them too baby-smooth and un-lived, maybe she only got the hots for men with double chins and crêpe paper round the eyes. Could be I was mourning my own loss of youth. I tried to see it all as sexual politics, the tyranny of an aesthetic based on young flesh and beauty, but underneath there was a harsher, more democratic truth. Everybody sags, everybody wrinkles. Everybody dies. Of course nobody ever said nature was kind, or even fair. But given the havoc it wreaks, no wonder we're so scared of it.

Across the pool Katherine, last night's city broker, was flicking through a copy of the *Financial Times*. From the treatment area Martha came out and called her name. 'Miss Cadwell, G5.' I looked at my watch. It was 2.25. Lucky Katherine. She would get an extra five minutes under the sponge. I felt almost jealous.

She folded up her newspaper and walked to where Martha was waiting. And as they entered the corridor, I saw the beautician put her hand lightly on the woman's sleeve and say something. Katherine laughed and then they were gone. I could just picture another thank-you card on the wall. Did they say it with flowers? In the pool my museum director was half submerged, playing with the pleasures of reduced gravity, while the Jacuzzi was filling up with other bodies. Outside real life was no doubt still in progress. But stay here long enough and you could be forgiven for forgetting it.

The wax strips brought it all back to me. Poor legs. They'd never had so much attention in one day. First the pleasure, then the pain. On the other hand I would have been hard-pressed to say which was more excruciating – the waxing or the conversation.

Julie was nineteen, newly plucked from the suburbs of Southampton and a born-again beautician. She had nothing but praise for Castle Dean, which she saw as some kind of high temple to beauty and self-improvement, with herself presumably as vestal virgin. And marketing manager. By the time the first leg was finished, she'd told me of three separate beauty products to prevent new hair growth and recommended a facial particularly good for tired skin, i.e. mine. Either she was a consummate actress or I could cross her off my suspect list right now.

To try and stop her talking I pretended to be interested in the décor. The walls sported a curious selection of posters advertising new and wondrous treatments designed to take on nature and stop the march of time. I thought back to my formidable wrinkly from Oxford. Not a lot of comfort here for her, although one picture showed somebody who seemed to have had the puffy bits of skin lifted from her eye sockets.

In the forty to fifty age range there were apparently more drastic transformations to be had from face peels and collagen injections. Collagen: there had been a time when I had thought it a new term for Tory higher education. But even I have had enough contact with women's magazines to know that what it really means is Barbara Hershey's lips exploding into Mick Jagger's. The woman in the photo I was looking at had not only puffed up her smile, but also doctored her eyes. Not a laugh line to be seen. It was all so weird and alien that I could not resist asking Julie about it. Curiosity, after all, is meant to be one of the tricks of my trade.

'Are they for real, those pictures?'

'Of course,' said Julie, tearing a strip off the back of my right leg, a strip which may or not have included the skin. 'Sorry, did that hurt? You really ought to have them done more regularly, you know. Your hairs are just too long to lift off easily. Yes. I've met a number of ladies who've had collagen implants. It's been a great success.'

'How old do you have to be?'

'Oh, any age. The skin starts to lose its elasticity from your mid-twenties on. You'd notice a difference if you did it, although you probably wouldn't actually need it for a couple of years.'

Well, that's a relief. 'So what would you recommend for someone like me, then?' I said it half in jest. I should have known better.

'Well, we do a collagen-based face mask. That's marvellous. Really pumps up the skin. And a peel is always beneficial.'

Good word, beneficial. Probably exactly the right word for a peel. 'What does that do?'

'It's like a kind of chemical scrub. Takes a layer of skin off.'

'Did they use it in the Gulf War?'

'What?'

'Nothing. Anything else?'

She hesitated for a moment, and I could see she was a little embarrassed. It answered my question, really. Not that I'm vain, it's just over the last year I've grown so used to seeing it in the mirror that I sometimes need to know how much other people notice it too. I helped her out by winking the eye.

'Well, you could always have something done about that little er . . . scar.'

'Do you think so?'

'Oh, certainly. It's marvellous what they can do nowadays. I could recommend a clinic if you're interested.'

'Thanks. Maybe. I'll get back to you on that one.'

She hesitated again, as if she was going to say something else, then decided to let it go. I let the conversation lapse. Just as well really, since a few minutes later she started in on the bikini line. I found myself digging my nails into the palms of my hands for a little light relief. It probably hurt less to have your stomach tucked.

From Julie I moved to the gentler ministrations of Lola, who, from the brief glimpse I had of her before she smothered egg white over my eyelids, looked like a girl in need of what she was selling; she was a short, plump little chicken with a smattering of angry spots around her chin. Her fingers were deft enough, though – a nice line in temple massage and then flick-flick-flick with the face mask before leaving me alone to let it harden. After ten minutes the egg white felt as if it had been bonded with quick-drying cement. As my skin stretched tighter than God ever intended, I had a moment of pure panic that I might have inadvertently come across the saboteur. But then she returned and did something enormously soothing with a warm flannel and what she described as an ampoule of hydro-active moisturizer. I was so grateful I forgot to ask her if she had any grievances.

I was duly dispatched from the beauty parlour half an hour later, with legs and upper thighs a delicate shade of lobster and my pores cleaner than they'd been probably since birth. At the desk I signed a chit for forty-eight pounds. That didn't include the recommended creams which, had I so chosen, would have set me back at least another fifty. In any other business tough women would be out on the street shouting fraud. I tell you, there's something about beauty that affects the brain.

The treatment rooms were taking their last clients for the night. I had a quick browse, then went to my bedroom to see if I still recognized myself and to make my notes on the day.

The mirror told me curtly that I had wasted my money, but at least the postman had been: an envelope under the door containing the guest list I had asked Mrs Waverley for. It made a dull read, except that is for the junior government minister with the asterisk by her name and the scribbled note from Waverley emphasizing the need to respect the clientele's confidentiality. But this particular client was already too busy wrecking the country to waste time on a silly little health farm, and none of the other names had stayed long enough to be suspicious. Disappointed, I went back to the staff.

I could now more or less confidently cross off six names, although two of those – Lola of the face mask and Julie, my born-again beautician – were already at the bottom of the pile since they had been off duty at certain key times. Martha, she of the G5 pleasure principle, remained a question mark. I reread her file more carefully and discovered a Bromley girl who'd left school at sixteen, then gone back to college to get O-levels and a beautician's diploma, supporting herself by running the bar at a local disco. Since her arrival at Castle Dean, her conduct had been impeccable, even winning a nice comment in Mrs Marchant's italic script about her rapport with the guests.

I also dug out Patricia Mason's photo to try and match her up with the pool beauty. But it was a head-and-shoulders snapshot and without the body it was a impossible to tell. I put it to one side and went through the other files again, looking for any sign of dissatisfaction: a reprimand or warning that might have gone septic. But all I could find was a note on the lovely Irish colleen's file about punctuality, and it just didn't seem enough to warrant such a sustained campaign of violence.

Indeed that was part of the problem. Someone so deliberately trying to destroy the place without the financial incentive of blackmail must have had one hell of a grievance. Either that or be a pretty disturbed personality, something which the management had failed to spot. For that reason – among others – I needed to have Martha's hands on me again. Until then all I could do was damage control. And given that the intervals between the incidents were getting shorter, that meant some serious night patrolling.

I had dinner (you don't want to know about it), then phoned home to check my messages. There was one from an old friend who'd got tickets for a Leonard Cohen concert that night and wondered if I was interested, for old time's sake. Rumour has it that Leonard is less depressed these days. The same, however, can't be said for his fans. Since the concert had already started, I didn't bother to ring back. Next came a somewhat distracted monologue from Kate, wondering if I was back yet, but, since I wasn't, it didn't matter anyway. Except it sort of sounded like it did. I dialled her number. Bad timing. She was putting Benjamin to bed. For the third time.

'Colin isn't back yet?'

'No.'

'Sounds like you've had a day of it.'

'Amy fell off the climbing frame. She's got a suspected fracture in the lower arm. We've been in casualty all afternoon.'

'Oh, Kate, I'm sorry. Is she OK?'

'Yeah, she's fine now. Can't believe her luck. Ten days off school and everyone fussing over her.'

'Is that why you called?'

'Yes. No. I just . . . er . . . Listen, I can't talk now, Hannah, I've got my hands full here. Maybe I could call you back?'

'No can do. I'm still away.'

'Where are you?'

Well, what words would you have used to try and make it sound like hard work? After I put the phone down, it struck me that this was probably exactly what Kate needed: a regime of enforced self-indulgence without even the echo of a child's voice to be heard. Maybe if I lucked out on the plot, I could trade in part of my fee for health farm vouchers.

Since it was probably still too early for prowlers, I lay on the bed and watched a bad action movie. The car chases alone were enough to send a girl to sleep. The hipflask called to me from the top drawer. I've always seen myself as a girl who can take her alcohol, but thirty-six hours of exercise and green beans and it wasn't so much my body that was feeling lighter as my head. I had a hefty slug and I decided on a little fresh air to wake me up for my night tour of duty.

I went out through the back door and stood on the lawn,

peering into the garden beyond. In daylight this was a fabulous view down through a set of graduated terraces to a lovely ornamental pond (home of the unfortunate carp) and an old brick wall at the bottom covered by a vigorous spring clematis in full bloom. Maybe if you got close enough, you could see the flowers glow in the dark.

I moved out of the pool of light thrown by the house and felt my way along the path and down the first flight of steps. Last night's moon was obliterated by heavy cloud and within fifty yards or so the night enveloped me, bringing with it that peculiarly intense alive country blackness which is always such a shock to us urban types.

I turned and looked towards the house. What's the problem? Don't tell me you want to go back, Hannah? But it was already too late. Already I could feel a small thump going stereo at the bottom of my chest. I walked deeper into the dark, deliberately goading it further. Welcome back to the beginnings of fear. Well, hello, I said softly, I've been expecting you.

It was almost a year since I had walked through a similar country blackness into someone's malevolent fists. There are certain things about that period of my life that are already hazy or half-forgotten. But not that night. That night remains stubbornly insistent – so much so that it still doesn't take much to resurrect the threat of him in a night silence, to feel the heat of his breath on my face, to smell the sweat of his excitement. I put up an involuntary hand and traced the thin, white line under my right eyebrow where his fist had split open too much flesh to heal properly, marring my beauty, but sparing my eye by an inch. Even the memory of it made me scared.

Except there was nothing to be scared of any longer. This is now and that was then, and the thug can't bother you any more. That was the point. I had won. I had been the victor. No country lane would see him again. So how come I still have such vicious palpitations of memory? Occupational hazard, Frank would say. What had been his advice that night in the hospital? Don't fight it. Let it bury itself. Sensible man, Frank, and one with experience. And I had done what he told me. Am still doing it. Even so, it's a cause of some shame for a private eye to be waking crippled by nightmares so long after the event. Do the boys suffer this, I wonder, finding the hangover from the violence nastier than the one from the booze? Sometimes I think I'm in the wrong job, trying to fit the myth to the reality. But only sometimes.

'Hi, Joe,' I said out loud this time, turning slowly around on the spot, daring him to scare me further. 'How is it with you?' But now I had named him, he wasn't there any more. Coward. Him or me? The flutter eased and the darkness became benign. I walked on further just to prove my point, right down to the wall and the pond and the clematis climber. I felt, if not saw, the white of its big flashy flowers, dipped my fingers in the cool water, and only then when I was satisfied with myself, did I turn and go back to the house.

And as I did so, I saw someone move across the lawn ahead of me and go in through a back door. See. If I hadn't spent so much time indulging my fear, I would have missed it. Sometimes the girl's way of doing things pays off.

I waited a while to make sure whoever it was wouldn't hear me following and then slipped back across the lawn in after them. Question was, which way were they heading? I did a quick tour of the dining-room and the kitchen, but they were both dark and empty. Then I made my way down the corridor through to the atrium. This time the pool was empty and there was no moon. The beam from my torch played around the space, exposing an edge of a palm tree, and the slick black of the water. Silence everywhere. I moved methodically round the treatment area, starting with the steam rooms and then the gym. All the doors were locked.

Then I heard a sound from the other side of the pool – a single sharp metallic noise, like something clattering to the floor. I snapped off the torch and stood in the dark, listening and waiting. Nothing. When the next sound came, it was less clear but almost certainly human, a sort of low moan or a gasp for breath. I risked the torch again. This time the beam found out a closed door leading to the massage rooms. When I got to it and turned the handle, it fell open.

As my torch lit a river of light up the passage ahead, I saw the thinnest gleam seeping out from the bottom of the door at the end. My heart did a quick aerobic work-out without the help of the gym teacher. I tried to remember the layout of the rooms. Slender tone or G5? Surely not more nails? They – whoever they were – had to have more imagination than that.

I moved on tiptoe until I was standing opposite the line of light. I heard a small grunt, again like someone clutching for breath. I took a few deep breaths of my own and put my hand silently on the door handle.

I turned it quickly and pushed. It rattled, but didn't give. Inside there was a sudden noise and the light snapped off. Shit. I shot myself back against the wall, then lunged forward using my foot as a battering ram. The lock splintered under the force of the first blow and gave entirely with the second. And as it did so, I let out a huge warrior wail, the only really useful thing that the Holloway Road Adult Institute self-defence class ever taught me.

It worked. A woman's voice screamed in terror as the torch beam lit up a section of massage table and a flash of face. My fingers connected with the light switch. The neon strip zapped on and off twice, then flooded the room. It is, I think, fair to say that I could hardly believe my eyes when I saw what it revealed.

Before me there was not one but two women. The figure on the table was lying naked on her back, the face twisted towards me recognizable now as that of Katherine Cadwell, the dapper city broker. While sitting astride her, uniform pulled up above her bare thighs, was the very talented

Martha. Near by, the sponge head of the G5 machine dangled forlornly by the table leg. Nothing so useless as a used sex aid. I was instantly reminded of a certain infamous one-word headline in a tabloid newspaper after the British navy had sunk an Argentine battleship. Gotcha. But I managed to hold my tongue.

'Oh, my God.' Katherine was already pulling herself up, trying to get Martha off her at the same time as she lunged out for her bathrobe. For her part Martha was still staring. I studied her face. It was flushed and wide-eyed, an adrenalin of sex as well as fear about it. And I thought back to those hands, so capable and tender. No, I thought. Not so much business as personal. Then I looked past her to all those dinky thank-you cards pinned up on the wall behind. And I had to smile.

'Sorry,' I said as I pulled the door closed behind me, or at least as closed as the broken lock would allow. 'Sorry. I must have got the wrong room.'

Chapter Four

Breakfast was an early affair in Carol Waverley's office: grapefruit segments and brown toast. She didn't eat anything. But then she already had a number of other things on her plate. The first was her further diminishing guest list. Katherine Cadwell was no more, which was a shame given how regular a customer she'd been. The early receptionist had arrived down at 7 a.m. to find her packed and ready to leave. She'd paid by cash, asked for her registration details to be taken off the files and wanted to receive no further information about Castle Dean's special offers. You could say that she'd already had them.

'I can't believe it. I just can't believe it.'

It was hard to know which particular bit Carol was having the most trouble with: the fact that there was some gay nooky taking place in her clean and health-obsessed establishment, or that she'd just kissed goodbye to another of Castle Dean's regular pay cheques.

One thing she was certain of, though. Someone was going to pay for it. So she was even more disappointed when I couldn't tell her exactly who. 'I'm sorry, but I just can't believe you didn't recognize the second woman. Or at least enough to give me some description to go on.'

I shook my head. 'I'm sorry, too. But I've told you it was dark, and as soon as I realized what I'd stumbled into, I assumed you'd prefer me to use tact rather than inquisition. The other woman had her face turned away from me. It could have been anyone.'

She stopped pacing and turned to me. 'Well, I hope you

realize this puts me in an impossible position. How can I carry on when one of my staff is soliciting the guests?'

It wasn't the verb I would have chosen. But let that pass. 'And what if it wasn't one of the staff?'

'Of course it was the staff. How else would they have got into that room?' She was trying hard to be tough, but the voice behind the words was getting a bit tremulous.

'You tell me. I thought you said that none of them had keys any more.'

'Well . . . Well, they don't, now. Oh, my God.' And all of a sudden she was a lot less poised. 'What am I going to tell Mrs Marchant?' she said, shaking her head.

'When does she arrive?'

'Er . . . probably later today.'

'She doesn't seem very eager to get here, does she?'

'She's a busy woman.'

'Well, I don't think you should tell her anything.' She looked at me angrily. 'Listen. What I saw were two women making love with the help of a sponge massage. And I don't mean to be crude about it, but it looked to me like they were both consenting adults. So, unless you've got a problem with that, I suggest you check out the steam and sauna areas for possible faults while I get on with finding the saboteur before anything else happens. And that we leave the rest until we're in a position to know more.'

'And when will that be?'

'Well,' I said gaily, although I'm not sure she would have appreciated the use of the adverb, 'every day's a new day.'

      *   *   *   *

You'll think me mean, perhaps, not to have told her. You'll think me even meaner when I say it wasn't anything to do with saving Martha's skin. No. My silence had a more pragmatic subtext. Nasty word blackmail, but in a job like mine sometimes the end justifies the means.

In the pocket of my dressing-gown was my treatment schedule for the day. I had already established from the office that Martha was on massage that morning. I wasn't booked in till the afternoon. But the good lady from Oxford had a morning appointment. I caught her in the pool during early water aerobics. We had a few laughs about trying to jog backwards under water to the sound of the Three Degrees, and then I mentioned that a work problem had come up and I was going to have to be on the phone for a consultation at exactly the time of my afternoon massage, and that they couldn't fit me in any other time. And of course, being someone who understood the pressures of work, she offered to swap with me.

So it was that when 9 a.m. came around I didn't wait to be called but instead walked across the poolside to the massage room, knocked, entered and closed the door firmly behind me.

Martha was washing her hands at the sink, and looking at herself in the mirror in that casual way people do when they think they're not being observed. When she saw me, suddenly reflected by her right ear, her face registered a definite shock. She turned. 'I'm sorry, I –'

'I swapped with Mrs Graham,' I interrupted smoothly. 'Didn't they tell you?'

She shook her head and I saw her swallow slightly, but she held my gaze. For a while we just looked at each other. My, you're very cool, I thought. Then she seemed to relax. She gave a little nod, carefully laid down the hand towel and walked across to the massage table. And when she spoke, there was a certain quiet confidence in her voice. 'So, do you want to get undressed, then, Mrs Wolfe?'

And the instant she said it I realized how it must look to her. After all, she didn't know I was a private eye. From where she was standing I was just a regular guest who had waxed lyrical about her fingers, colluded in a certain humour and provocation and then, seeing it for what it was, gone to some considerable trouble to get myself back for more. For my part, I'd been so busy with my own agenda I'd obviously missed hers. Courtship rituals. Fact is I've always been a miserable failure at them.

Except ... Except maybe it hadn't been such a total misunderstanding. Maybe I'd been giving out some ambivalent signals of my own without realizing it. I felt again her hands on my stomach; how tense and then how good they had made me feel. How easily they had triggered memories of matters sexual. I saw her almost coy smile as we parted and then her face in the night, flushed and open, confident in both the giving and the taking of pleasure. Oh my, Hannah. What a great moment for sexual ambiguity to raise its mischievous little head. I took a deep breath, cuffed it soundly about both ears and got on with the job in hand.

'I'm afraid you're mistaken, Martha,' I said quietly. 'I haven't come for a massage.'

'Oh,' she said. And she was bright enough to register the depth of my retreat. This time her voice had a touch of defiance in it. 'Why are you here, then?'

'I need some information,' I said. 'And I think you're the one who could give it to me.' And then I told her who I was.

She listened in silence, standing very still with her hands deep in her uniform pockets. When I was finished, she bit at her bottom lip and laughed a little. 'Christ, how stupid. I ought to have guessed when you asked so many questions. So, I tell you what I know, and in return you don't tell them. Is that it?'

'More or less.'

She shook her head, then walked past me over to the door. For a moment I wasn't sure, for a moment I thought she was actually going to leave. Instead she flicked the catch below the handle, tested to see it was locked, then turned to face me. 'Seems I don't have much option, do I?'

And from there it just fell into my lap, really. She was a smart cookie, of course. Somebody looking to be a manager herself. When it had become clear that Carol Waverley was

41

getting her knickers in a twist about something, it hadn't taken Martha long to work out what it was, particularly since she'd been one of the girls assigned to the retinting of the Marks & Spencer's buyer. It had just been a question of using her ears and eyes. Especially her eyes.

'You want a name, I suppose. Let me tell you about her first. She's not happy here. Not that that's enough to convict her on. Half the girls in this place have had a run-in with management one way or another since Waverley took over. But her problem is more basic. She's got a kid, an eighteen-month-old daughter by some guy who walked out on her. The baby lives with her mother in Swansea. She goes up there every third weekend. There are no jobs there. She needs the money, but, of course, she doesn't want to be separated. She tried to persuade the piranha to let her work longer one week and then have extra days off the next, but Waverley said no. They had a bit of a ding-dong about it.'

'Jennifer Pincton,' I said, my mind racing through the files, putting facts to images. 'Tall, dark-haired girl, quite big.' She was the one who had given me a hard time for being in the heat area yesterday afternoon. She'd also been in all the right places at the right times. 'But this row with Mrs Waverley. That's not on her file.'

'No, well, it wouldn't be, would it? Not worthy of note, I expect.'

'I still don't see why you think it's her.'

'Well, I'll tell you. Because she's recently become very flush has our Jennifer, flashing around a lot of unexplained cash. I noticed it the night after the steam-room incident, although I didn't think about it much then. A few of us went out to the local that evening, had a game of darts and a few drinks. She didn't usually join in that kind of thing. Too careful with her money, sending everything she had home to Mama. But not only did she come that night, she also bought a round, and paid for it with a fifty-pound note. I'd been to the loo and was coming back when I saw her at the bar.

'A week later she had a new pair of trainers on. Label ones. Must have set her back fifty or sixty pounds. And on Saturday when one of the girls was going into Reading and she was on duty, she gave them a package to post for the baby. It was heavy. The postage alone came to seven quid.' She paused. 'I was curious. So, last week I searched her room.'

I must say her timing was immaculate. She left another pause then glanced up and registered the amused admiration in my eyes.

'You took a chance,' I said.

She smiled. 'Yes, well, I do, don't I? It wasn't just the money. She'd been jumpy recently, not quite herself. I spend a lot of time watching people.' And she kept on looking at me. 'After a while you get a nose for who's giving off signals.'

It was more a dig than a come on, but a gentle one. I found myself wanting to smile. 'Ever thought you were in the wrong profession, Martha?'

'No. As a matter of fact I think I'm in absolutely the right one. Don't you?'

And despite myself I laughed. 'So what did you find?'

'Cash. Lots of it. Her room is on the ground floor. She shares it with Lola March . . .'

'Small, plump girl, quiet?'

'Yeah, that's her. Anyway, I picked a time when they were both on duty, went round by the garden and fiddled the window lock. I found the money in the bottom drawer of her chest under some uniforms, a big brown envelope with ten fifty-pound notes in it. Five hundred pounds. You tell me where a junior beautician gets that kind of extra cash?'

Offering night massages to the right kind of guest, I thought, but didn't say. I played Frank for a moment. It often helps. 'It still doesn't prove anything.'

'Doesn't it? The very next morning Kylie Chantner took a couple of lumps out of her legs testing the G5 machine. When

I looked up the log, I found that Jennifer Pincton had been one of the last G5 operators the night before.'

'So why didn't you tell all this to Mrs Waverley?'

'Why should I? Seems to me a good manager should make it her business to check out those employees who might be tempted.'

'You really don't like her, do you?'

She gave a little shrug. 'She's too interested in making it look good. Thinks that's the way to keep it under control. She misses what's underneath.'

And it struck me that Martha probably would make a good manager. As long as she could keep her hands off the clients. Back to the couch.

'So, tell me about last night.'

'What do you want to know?'

'How about starting with why you took the risk of the G5 room. You must have realized that security would have been tightened up.'

She gave it a little thought before answering. 'It was Katherine's idea. I thought it was a risk, yes, but it wasn't one I could really tell her about. I suppose you could say I'd just got used to it.'

'How did you get in?'

'I've got my own key. Had it duplicated months ago before all the fuss started.'

'So when you got down there last night, was it locked up?'

'My section was.' She paused. 'The beauty salon was open, though.'

The beauty salon. Interesting. A lot of tender skin going through there every day, a ripe area for damage. 'How do you know?'

'Because I needed some body lotion. And I didn't have to use my key to get it.'

'Did you see anyone?' She shook her head. 'Hear anything?' She gave me a funny look, maybe yes, maybe no. 'Well?'

'Maybe.'

'But you didn't stop to look?'

She shrugged. 'Katherine was waiting. I had other things on my mind.'

She was good at the insolence. No doubt there were those for whom it held its own attractions. But I could feel myself being pushed somewhere I wasn't sure I wanted to go. I dug my heels in. 'So, how much did Katherine Cadwell pay you?'

'That wasn't how it was,' she said angrily, for the first time showing a glimmer of vulnerability. 'Not at all.'

And I thought of the number of other times she must have been on that couch. And how many others she would have shared it with. 'But it is sometimes,' I said quietly. '"Thanks for helping me relax"? "A week was not enough"? Come on, Martha, you're not that good at your job.'

She looked at me steadily. 'Maybe not. But right now I'd say I'm better than you are at yours.'

And in a way she was right, of course. It's been a while since I've been professionally and sexually upstaged in the same encounter. It seemed only gracious to admit to at least one of them. 'Very possibly,' I said getting up. 'Although it wouldn't do either of us any good to go public about it.'

'No,' she said quietly. 'It wouldn't.'

I got up and went to the door. As I flicked the lock, I turned to her. 'Well, thanks, Martha. You've saved me a lot of time and trouble. And don't worry. My lips are sealed.'

She nodded. 'I know that.' She smoothed out the towel on the massage table. 'You know, your hour isn't over yet, Mrs Wolfe. I could always do a bit of work on those shoulders for you. They look awfully tense.' She let the second linger. 'Straight and narrow,' she added with a quiet seriousness.

'Maybe at the end of the job,' I said thinking about it. 'Oh, and by the way it's "Ms".'

*   *   *   *

45

The beauty salon didn't open till 10 o'clock. Carol Waverley must have been pretty pissed off when I rang to tell her that on further consideration I thought I might have heard a noise in there too, but she was worried enough not to make a thing about it.

We went in through the back and worked fast. Hair, face legs, hands and feet. My, my, what a lot of lotions, creams and ointments it takes to make a girl look lovely. Luckily Carol Waverley hadn't got to where she was today without knowing her way around a beauty parlour. She used her nose primarily, and when she wasn't sure the back of her hand. So it was that when she came to a particular massage cream used for softening up the hands and wrists after a manicure bath, she inflicted a small but noticeable skin burn on herself.

What exactly it had been doctored with neither of us knew, although there was a faint whiff of something DIY about it. As I watched her trying to make light of the pain caused by the angry red welt, the word acid sprang to mind. But whatever she felt, it didn't stop her from checking everything else, just in case. What she lacked in intuition, Carol Waverley certainly made up for in dedication.

While she was testing, I was thinking. There were four manicures booked in for that day. The girls in the beauty salon were Margaret on hair, Flosie on waxing and feet, and the born-again Julie on faces and hands. The jar in question was new and full, sitting next to an almost empty one on the trolley. At some point during the treatments the first one would certainly have been finished and the second one opened. All Jennifer Pincton had to do was to sit back and wait for the screams.

What I had to do – if I was going to keep my promise to Martha and not expose her as my source – was to trap the culprit red-handed, if you'll excuse the expression. Which meant finding a way to make her return to the salon to check the manicure jars.

As plans go, it wasn't a great one, but at least it convinced Carol. We pulled another full pot of cream down from the shelf and (after checking it) put it next to the doctored one, which we marked with a large black X on the bottom. Then Carol took the young Julie aside and, swearing her to secrecy on pain of instant dismissal, told her which cream to use and which one to avoid.

I wish I could have been there to see Julie's face, but I was already round the back of the girls' block, sharpening my Abbey National cash card ready for a little breaking and entering. With Jennifer supervising peat baths and Lola Marsh on Slendertone for the rest of the morning I had the place to myself.

It went just like the movies. I didn't even scratch the card. Inside, the room was warm and stuffy, the curtains closed. It was also a mess. Mind you, it wasn't really big enough for two people to live in. The beds were pushed against opposite walls. They both had stuffed toys at their head, but there was no mistaking Jennifer's: the wall next to it was covered with snapshots of a cute little baby; close enough to touch, but not to hold. You know the problem with real life? The baddies are never quite the ones you want them to be.

Come on, Hannah, leave the bleeding hearts to the social workers. Thank you, Frank. Always there when you need him. I looked around. Two beds meant two chests. I went for the one nearest to Jennifer's. Bottom drawer. Just as promised, there it was, stashed in between white starched cotton, a bulky plain brown envelope with a wad of fifty-pound notes inside.

The only thing different was that there were more of them now. Fourteen instead of ten. But then half a dozen goldfish, a pot of maggots and a tub of hand cream separated her visit and mine.

I stuffed the notes back in the envelope and went systematically through the other drawers. I had to really look this time, but it was worth the effort. At the back of the top one, wrapped in a couple of pairs of M & S bikini knickers, I found another free gift: a small tin bottle of Nitromorse. I undid the top and the concentrated smell that leapt out triggered an instant home movie: me in my newly acquired flat, slapping coats of the stuff on to a Victorian fireplace, waiting while it burned and blistered its way through a dozen layers of paint. Rather like it had burnt its way into the skin of Carol Waverley's hand. I thought of smelling the underwear for any lingering aroma of maggots but it seemed too crude even for me.

I looked up at the window with its drawn curtains. Maybe Jennifer Pincton was worried that someone might peep in and catch her counting her money. I put my eye to the gap in between. At the end of the garden a woman stood staring in my direction. My instant thought was Jennifer Pincton. Equally instantly dismissed. She looked nothing like her. And, anyway, I already knew this woman. Although I was too far away to properly see her face, the body spoke for itself: long legs, small waist, good breasts. Not to mention a fabulous breaststroke. I twitched the curtains closed, then peeked again. She was still there, looking straight at my window.

I slid the Nitromorse back where I had found it and was out of the door, down the corridor and into the spring sunshine before you could say collagen implant. The garden was empty. Just like the atrium after the midnight swim. I was doing so well that I decided not to be bothered by the problems I couldn't solve. I had a kind of feeling that this one would give itself up before too long, anyway.

I spent the afternoon in the beauty salon, just in case. By 5 o'clock my hair was revitalized, my feet soaked and polished and the hands that wash dishes were as soft as my face. I was Julie's fifth manicure and she was already well into the new tub of cream. Loyal to the last she didn't say a thing, just gave me a number of helpful product hints on how to reconstruct my cuticles. The whole pleasure-dome experience added another seventy quid to my bill.

If I had been Jennifer Pincton, by this time I would have been seriously wondering what had happened. Question is, would it be serious enough to come back and check? I was torn between watching now and watching later. It struck me that in her shoes I'd be getting pretty tired of all this middle-of-the-night lark, with no time to catch up on my kip. So I took a chance and slipped back at 7 p.m. after the cleaners had finished and while the rest of the world was busy eating their greens. It was hardly a great sacrifice, despite what my stomach was telling me.

I settled myself at the manicure table in the massage room with a good book, or at least it thought it was. It was one of those clever-clever modern thrillers about a serial killer in drag who only attacked women with the same names as Joan Crawford characters. The cover called it post-modern and witty. They weren't quite the adjectives I would have used. The killer was just about to start dismembering number three with an axe (homage to *Baby Jane*?) when the light began to fade.

I put the book aside. About half an hour later I heard a click and a scrape a little way off. I got up from the table and moved silently round to behind the door. The footsteps were soft, but easy to follow. She had come through the back from the poolside entrance and was evidently feeling her way along the corridor.

The door-handle shook, then opened. In the gloom a smallish figure worked its way across the room towards the manicure trolley and leant over to the lamp.

Its beam lit up the surface and bounced back on to her face. At the same moment I called out her name.

Unfortunately it wasn't the right one.

Chapter Five

There's a theory, of course, popular among devotees of whodunits that it's the person you least suspect who is the most guilty. And, on a scale of one to ten, I suppose it would be true to say that Lola Marsh – her of the warm flannels and bad skin – had not been a chief suspect. Except, of course, for one blatantly obvious fact. The money had been found in her room too, even if the chest of drawers hadn't been by the right bed.

Once I clocked that, it didn't take much to put the rest together, though I didn't get much help from her. Underneath that quiet exterior, it turned out, beat a heart of granite. You might have expected just a touch of shame, or at the least a frisson of terror, as I burst upon her like an avenging angel out of the darkness. But no, not her. She didn't even bother to deny it. She just stood her ground, hands bunched into little fists by her side, and refused to say anything about anything, even after I'd done my bit about the legal definitions of malicious damage and intent to maim.

In the end I just made it up as I went along and waited for her to betray the odd flicker of indignation when I strayed too far from the truth. At least it gave me a chance to look at her properly.

If she hadn't been so small, she probably wouldn't have looked so lumpy. And to be fair, in any other working environment you might even have found that pixie little face in its halo of bushy red hair quite attractive. But here all you could see were the spots. And the scowl. Put her against all the other eager little beavers with their perfect makeup and finely tuned bodies and you could see how she might become the kind to hold a grudge against the beauty industry in general. And Castle Dean in particular. But enough to sabotage the place? Well, money can make monsters of us all. Even the innocent ones.

Since Jennifer had been richer by at least fifty quid the night after her peat bath shift, it seemed logical to assume that she must have done someone a favour. A last-minute swap with her room mate, perhaps? So last minute, in fact, that neither of them had managed to tell the office about it. Which meant that when the sabotage occurred on that shift and Mrs Waverley started to ask questions, it would have been easier to keep on pretending than expose themselves, particularly as Jennifer would have had to take the stick and she'd already had a run-in over trying to change her weekend breaks. And her room mate, Lola, of course, would have known all about that. She would also have known how important the job was to Jennifer, even if it didn't pay quite enough money. So how better to say thank-you than with a little monetary gift.

'What I don't understand is how you explained the money? And what about the new trainers? Was that another "gift" from you or part of the same windfall?' I waited, but nothing came. 'Of course by then Jennifer must have been pretty compromised, anyway. I mean if you wanted to be mean about it, you might say she was acting like an accomplice. Unless of course she was one all along.'

'No.' At last a response. The word came out like a bullet crack. 'Jennifer had nothing to do with it.'

'Good. So now we're getting somewhere. Let's move on to the money itself. And who sent it. Got anything to say about that? No? Seven hundred pounds in two weeks. Was that decided in advance, or did you get a bonus if you showed special imagination?'

No speech this time, just a flash of a look and a twitch of the left hand. But I'm no good at sign language. 'Oh, come on, Lola,' I said, losing my patience. 'I've found the Nitromorse. I know about the maggots and the fish, the whole damn thing. You're well and truly screwed. And if you don't tell me, then you're sure as hell going to have to tell the police. You might find it easier to get some practice.'

I must have touched something in her, because now she talked. It still wasn't a lot, but from the way she said it you sort of knew it was the truth.

'I'm not sorry.' And for such a small frame it was a big voice. 'This place is a shit heap. The business stinks, all of it. But I didn't start it. I just did what I was told.'

'By whom?'

'I dunno. They didn't give me a name.'

'Just an envelope full of money?'

She grunted. I took it as a yes.

'Any instructions with it or did you use your own initiative?'

'The notes just said to stop the place working.'

'Handwritten or printed?'

'Printed.'

'Well you did a good job. Have you still got them?'

She shook her head. 'I burnt them. Like they told me to.'

'And you've no idea who sent them?'

But this time she didn't even bother to answer. I tried a few more questions but she wasn't listening any more, just disappearing into that round little body, closing up and closing down. In the end I let her be. After all, technically speaking, my job was done. The fact that solving one mystery had opened up another was for my employer to deal with, not me.

I got Carol Waverley out of the shower. She didn't seem to mind. We agreed to meet in her office in ten minutes. Which gave Lola and me just enough time to pick up the Nitromorse and the rest of the money (Jennifer was already asleep, her face turned to the photos on the wall). By the time we got to the office Lola was trailing behind me like some unrepentant school girl on her way to see the headmistress. And not just the headmistress, as it turned out. Also the head of the governors.

＊　　　　＊　　　　＊　　　　＊

She eclipsed Waverley as the sun doth eclipse the moon. And she didn't leave much light around Lola and me, either. Of course I knew who she was the instant I walked in and saw her sitting there, all long Lycra legs and casually expensive sweater. She sat in a way that made you think she must practise it daily – an exquisite precision to every part of the body right up to the tilt of her head and the way her hair gathered around her face, with just the right amount of natural bounce. The lamp beside her cast a soft glow, carving the cheekbones Nefertiti-high and the skin even smoother. She was probably the only woman in the building who could put a finger up to the promises of the beauty salon. You could see how even looking at her might have driven Lola Marsh to violence.

'Olivia Marchant, I presume,' I said, ignoring the Waverley, who looked justly uncomfortable beside her.

She inclined her head and gave a little smile, though not enough to alter the landscape of that seriously sleek face. 'It seems I have a lot to thank you for, Miss Wolfe,' she said quietly.

I gave her one of my 'Oh, think nothing of it' nods. The praise could wait. First the end of the story. She turned her attention to her offending little employee.

'Well, Lola Marsh. I didn't expect to see you here. Why don't you sit down? Don't be frightened. No one's going to hurt you. We just need to hear what you have to say.'

But Lola didn't sit. And she didn't say either. Not anything. She simply stared at Olivia Marchant. We all waited. A heavy silence settled on the room. She was the only one it didn't seem to bother. For the guilty party she certainly had a monstrous confidence about her.

'I just don't understand how you could do it, Lola' – Carol, squeaky with incandescent rage, or maybe it was relief. 'We always treated you well. You were lucky to get the job in the first place.' Given what you look like, she added without saying. It hardly mattered. We were all adept at reading the subtitles.

'That's enough, Carol.' Olivia's voice was quiet but with steel in it. 'There's nothing to be gained from that now. Well, Lola?'

But Lola still wasn't talking. Unless the quick look of venom directed at the Waverley could be called talking. Finally Mrs Marchant gave up and turned to me. As I retold the story – or as much of it as I knew – she kept her eyes fixed on Lola, with a face as impassive as her employee's. When I had finished, she sat back in her chair and continued to stare at the girl, while Carol and I sat holding our breath, waiting to see who would break first.

It was hard to work out just what Olivia Marchant was feeling. There was such a still, silent quality to her. I found myself distracted by the perfection of her appearance. How old are you? I wondered. If I were to take one of those lovely firm thighs and saw it in half, how would you ring-date? The body said my age, but the face, despite its sleekness, suggested older. Something about the taut smoothness of those cheekbones tugged at a loose end of my memory. But whatever it was, I couldn't get to it. Maybe I was just wrong-footed by such glaring good looks. With the exception of Kate (who had weathered somewhat under the pressures of child care), my experience has always been that seriously beautiful women are more trouble than they're worth.

She caught my eyes upon her and gave me a small sharp look, then went back to Lola. The silence grew more insistent.

'Oh, Lola,' she said at last. 'What was it we did to offend you so much? It can't have been the job, surely? You weren't qualified. I explained that to you myself.' Lola was certainly listening now – you could see it in the way she held herself. I got the feeling something was building up inside her. Seismic

54

activity at the core. Stand well back. Mrs Marchant felt it too. She waited. But nothing came.

'Well, whatever it was, you're on your own now. I can't help you any more.' And the way she said the words made it feel like a casting-off. Then she turned to me. 'You say she destroyed all the instructions?'

'Yep.'

'How about the envelopes?'

I shook my head slightly.

'Not even a postmark?'

I was about to shake my head again when Lola spoke. 'London,' she said clearly. 'They came from London.'

Mrs Marchant focused on her again, not quite sure which way to step. 'London? It's a big place, Lola,' she said gently. 'You didn't notice what district?'

But the oracle had spoken. And that was all we were going to get. The night grew longer as she made that clear. 'How long has Lola been with us, Carol?' she said after a while.

'Three months. You employed her at the beginning of the year.' From the way Carol put it, it was clear that Lola had never been her first choice. I thought back to her own skilful makeup, hiding the hint of angry skin. Lola's fresh little spots must have been a cruel reminder of the continual battle between beauty and nature. Nasty business, selling perfection. And from where I was standing it was getting nastier all the time. Only Olivia seemed untouched by it. But then she would, wouldn't she?

'Three months. All right, now you listen to what I'm going to say, Lola. When I'm finished, you go straight back to your room and you pack your bags. In half an hour there'll be a taxi outside the front door waiting to take you wherever you want to go. There'll also be a letter of reference. It will say nothing about why you left. If another employer gets in touch with me, I will keep up that silence. You, in turn, will do exactly the same for me. It goes without saying that I could just as easily pick up the phone now and call the police. However, I promise you that if I ever hear the merest whiff of gossip as to what has happened here at Castle Dean, I'll have you out of whatever job you're in so fast it'll make your eyes water. Is that clear?'

Lola, who despite herself was aware of the remarkable generosity of what had just been offered, nodded and opened her mouth.

'Don't you dare,' Olivia Marchant cut in and, finally, the voice was angry.

Lola moved her eyes from Olivia to me. Maybe she hadn't been going to thank her after all. There was, it seems, still one unfinished piece of business. It was lying half in, half out of, a brown envelope on the desk between them. She glanced down at it. And I must say the chutzpah of that glance was astonishing. Olivia Marchant saw it too. She gave the smallest of laughs, then leant over and picked the envelope up. She kept her eye on the girl while she pulled out the notes. She counted out four of them and threw them back across the desk.

'A week's salary. Now get up and get out of here before I change my mind. Carol, go with her, please. Type out a letter and check that she doesn't leave any last-minute souvenirs behind.'

This time Lola went, turning on her heel like some eager cadet and walking straight out of the room, taking her powerful little force field of malevolence with her.

As Carol got up to follow, you could see that this was not quite what she'd had in mind for herself, that she had been more looking forward to a celebratory glass of champagne and a pat on the back. But it was clear that people generally did what Olivia Marchant asked, and so she went too.

Which left me and her, alone at last. She sat for a moment looking at the desk, then leant back in her chair and let out a long breath. 'Well, I think I need a drink. How about you?'

'Sorry,' I said. 'But I've had it with rose-hip tea.'

She smiled. 'That's not what I'm offering.'

She got up from the desk and went over to a cabinet under the window. She took out a full bottle of single malt and poured two generous hits into a couple of mugs usually reserved for herb infusions. You could almost feel the porcelain shudder at the violation.

We sat for a moment in silence, then she said, 'You know, it wasn't Carol's fault. I told her to tell you I was still in London.'

I nodded. 'I assumed so. Why?'

'Because I wanted to see how good you were.'

'And?'

'I'm impressed.'

'I wouldn't be,' I said. 'I couldn't even get her to tell me why she did it.'

'You mean the job she didn't get?' She shrugged. 'To be honest I'm not sure it was the right reason, anyway. Lola came to me about eight weeks ago. She told me that she wanted to leave the health business to get a position in London, working with my husband. There were no vacancies available, and even if there had been she wasn't qualified. So I refused. She was upset. But it hardly seems enough to warrant her trying to wreck the place.'

'Maybe she just got fed up with not being a size 10.' She looked at me, but let it pass. 'What was the job, anyway?'

'Nurse/receptionist.'

'Nurse?' I frowned a question mark. She took a slug of her drink and put it down slowly in front of her, moving her tongue around the top of her lovely lips. What had Carol called him? A consultant? How come I had assumed business rather than medicine? 'Your husband's a doctor?'

'Yes,' she said, looking me straight in the face. 'I thought Carol told you? He's an aesthetic surgeon.'

'Excuse me?'

'Aesthetic. You know – as in cosmetic and plastic.'

'Ah.'

And, ah, ha. The night silence was temporarily disturbed by

the sound of a satisfying number of pieces falling into place: the posters in the beauty salon, the emphasis on reconstruction, young Julie's born-again enthusiasm. And something else. That uncomfortable fact I'd been trying so hard to remember as I studied those fabulous cheekbones. The answer was Marlene Dietrich. It must have been in the same magazine as Barbara Hershey's lips – an exquisitely gruesome story of how later in life on the cabaret circuit Dietrich had taken to gluing up bits of her cheeks to her ears in a primitive attempt at a face-lift. I remember thinking at the time how it explained why she never seemed to open her mouth wide enough to get the words out properly. But times and technologies have changed. And now there are women who have face-lifts in the family.

So – was I looking at the results of one of Julie's beloved chemical peels or something more drastic? Whichever it was, I found myself a little disappointed. Not to mention embarrassed. Olivia Marchant watched me thinking it through. Presumably people always wondered at this point. I have to say it didn't particularly faze her. Maybe I was wrong. Maybe he'd picked her rather than made her.

When you can't ask one question, try another. 'I'm interested to know why you didn't call the police?'

She shrugged. 'The police would mean charges, and charges would mean publicity. These are difficult enough times for the health business without making it worse with rumours of sabotage. I couldn't risk it.'

'You could just have let her go. You didn't need to be so generous.'

She sighed. 'I suppose I felt a little sorry for her. And a week's salary is hardly generous. Anyway, I could say the same about you,' she said with a slight lift of the eyebrow.

I was absurdly grateful for the show of facial mobility. I frowned.

'Martha,' she continued softly. 'You could easily have got her the sack. Carol's terribly cross you wouldn't tell her who it was.'

I shook my head. 'If I'd given Carol Martha, then I wouldn't have had any leverage to get her to talk to me. It was Martha who led me to Jennifer and from there to Lola. And, I presume, led you too,' I said, thinking back to the figure on the lawn.

She shook her head. 'No. Martha didn't tell me anything. I just happened to see you go into the girls' block. I never saw which room.'

I wasn't entirely sure I believed her but I decided to let it go. 'So how do *you* know about Martha?'

'Aah.' She paused and smiled. 'I've known about Martha for some time.' I waited. 'Well, I'd hardly be a good owner if I didn't, wouldn't you say?'

And then I remembered the little note on her file in that delicate italic hand. What was the gist of it? Good rapport with the clients? 'But you turn a blind eye because she's good for business?'

She gave it some thought. 'Something like that. Besides, Martha's destined for higher things. She was up for Carol's job, you know. In the circumstances I couldn't really give it her. But she's almost certainly got an assistant manager's post in one of the London salons. I wrote her a reference the other day.'

'Which means that when she goes you've got a way of keeping her quiet too.'

'Yes . . . yes, you're right, though I hadn't thought of it until now. Thank you.'

I stifled a yawn. Not so much boredom as the lack of food beginning to bite. Much longer on this calorie intake and I'd be dead before I got thin. I looked at my watch. It was after midnight. Time for her to change into a mermaid and me from a wealthy health guest back into a regular private eye. Shame. I'd rather been hoping to see her in the daylight. See if I could spot the joins.

'Well, if that's everything, I think I'll be getting a little sleep and be on my way in the morning.'

'What about payment?' she said, not moving.

'Oh, the office will invoice you later.'

For 'the office' read me struggling over a VAT form. She looked mildly surprised. They all do. Funny how people still think it ought to be cash in a plain envelope, just like in the movies. I tell you it's hard for this profession to shake off its sleazy reputation.

'Perhaps I could give you a bonus.'

She picked up the envelope and tossed it across to me. I turned to greet it and in the glow of the desk lamp there was something so exquisitely old-fashioned about the whole scene: a beautiful dame, a wad of notes and a definite sense of unfinished business. At that moment I didn't even mind about the face-lift, or whatever it was. Truth is I must like the sleaze after all.

A couple of fifties fell out as the envelope landed in front of me. Eight more inside. That made five hundred – a bonus more than the job was worth. Must be nice to have the money to be so flamboyant. But then of course it wasn't hers.

'Well, what am *I* going to do with it?' she said as if in answer to my silent question. 'Put an ad in the paper and try to give it back to them?' I smiled. 'Unless, of course, you'd like to do that for me.'

'Mrs Marchant,' I said. 'Are you trying to make me an offer I can't refuse?'

Chapter Six

We got through most of the bottle of malt that night. Which surprised me – partly because I didn't think that I could handle so much booze on an empty stomach and stay upright; and partly because Olivia Marchant didn't give the impression of being a drinker. But she was. She told a good story too: a family saga about the Marchant couple and the possible enemies they might have made during their rise and rise to wealth and success.

At fifty-three Maurice Marchant was, apparently, one of the country's leading aesthetic surgeons, working out of a private clinic in Harley Street and catering to large numbers of the rich, famous and physically imperfect. I resisted the temptation to ask for names, and she was too discreet to offer them. I think she already knew I found the whole idea a little less than kosher. But then as of midnight I was either working for her or unemployed. Fortunately she needed me as much as I needed her. Because though the massage nails and the Nitromorse may have been the most dramatic statement of malice, they had not been the only one.

Mr Marchant, it turned out, had also been having trouble; in the last few months he had been receiving some anonymous notes, calling him all manner of nasty names and even threatening violence. Nothing else had happened but it was only a few days after the last one that the sauna door had stuck and the Marks & Sparks lady had turned blue.

'How did they come?'

'Brown envelopes. Various postmarks, mostly central London.'

'Exactly like Lola's.'

'Exactly like Lola's. Except the notes inside weren't printed. They were handwritten, but with the words all chopped about.'

'What did they say?'

'Oh, stuff about how if he hurt people he deserved to be hurt back, that kind of thing.' She gave a little shudder.

'Have you still got them?'

'Only one.' She shrugged. 'I'm afraid I threw the others away. They were so unpleasant and I was sure they were written by a crank.'

'Can I see it?'

She dug something out of a desk drawer. She'd obviously been pretty sure I'd take the job.

It was a standard brown office envelope, badly crumpled at the edges. Inside was a folded sheet of regular A4 with nine little words glued on to it separately.

'You have damaged me so I will damage you,' it read. Hmmm. To the point and with a neat sense of chill. Quite an art, anonymous letters. Often the drama can overload the style. But not here, though it was a bit of a give-away to use handwriting. Unless of course, it wasn't their own.

'What did you think?'

'Well, I thought it might be an ex-patient.'

'And now?'

'Now I don't know. I mean it wouldn't take much to find out about the health farm. In the business our partnership is quite well known. But it seems a bit extreme – to go for both of us.'

'Does your husband treat the kind of person who might resort to terrorism?'

She shrugged. 'It's a private practice. Maurice treats anyone he thinks he can help, as long as they have the money. I doubt he checks their police records first.'

I had an instant vision of an East End villain, whose wife now had one tit bigger than the other, offering to rearrange the surgeon's face for him. Or worse – a Mafia informer waking up after the operation to find that he still looked like himself. The kind of case to die for. Literally.

'So, does he have any idea who it might be?'

There was a pause. 'He doesn't actually know about it.'

'Doesn't know?'

She sighed. 'The first one came while he was away at a conference and I was in the office. I asked his secretary to check for more and when she found the second she called me rather than him. Maurice works incredibly hard. He's under a lot of stress. I thought – well, I didn't want him disturbed unnecessarily by some lunatic.'

Absolutely. Making that much money a day must put one hell of a strain on a guy. And he had to keep that knife hand steady. Unlike me who was fast finding both of mine tied behind my back.

'In which case I presume you haven't told the police about this, either?'

She shook her head. 'As I say, I thought it was a crank. We do get them sometimes.'

I took a slug of scotch. Sometimes it helps. Sometimes it doesn't. Back to the coal face.

'So tell me what happens when a patient's not satisfied.'

She sighed. 'It all depends. How much do you know about aesthetic surgery?'

I made a face. 'I thought it was still called cosmetic.'

'That's what the cowboys do.'

'What's the difference?'

'They're the ones who work out of the clinics you see advertised at the back of women's magazines. Most of them haven't even finished their basic surgical training. Someone like Maurice is not only fully trained, but has got ten years of complex reconstructive surgical experience behind him.'

She made him sound like God's gift to a Bosnian relief mission. Shame they wouldn't be able to afford him.

'At his level the work is incredibly skilled. Aesthetic is the right word to describe it. There are acceptable standards, of course, as for any kind of surgery, but in the aesthetic area there's a much larger margin for personal taste. And that means, sometimes, over-expectation.'

'Sows' ears into silk purses, you mean?' Not like you, I thought, but didn't say.

'Most respectable surgeons will only operate if they think they can make a reasonable difference, and if they're sure that the client understands what that difference will be.'

'But sometimes the patient still gets a shock when they look in the mirror?'

'Yes.'

'So then what?'

'Then they come back and complain about it. And you do what you can. No one wants a malpractice suit on their hands. So you try and placate them. And if you can't do that and you think it'll help, you try another operation or procedure.'

Maybe she wrote her husband's lines for him. She'd certainly had her hands on some kind of script. 'For free?'

'It depends. Sometimes. Although even if the surgeon doesn't charge, there'll still be hospital costs, and the anaesthetist's fees. But if you really think there's nothing you can do, you stand firm, suggest they get a second opinion and hope that will back you up.'

'You know a lot about it,' I said evenly.

'Yes,' she said, 'I do.'

Mr and Mrs Health and Beauty. Partners in profit. Now. But what about then? Receptionist? Nurse? It seemed a little unfeminist to suggest such a Mills and Boon type of courtship. But what the hell. We were hardly sailing in ideologically sound waters anyway. So I did.

'What do you think?' she replied quietly.

The water beneath the boat got shallower. We could be running aground. Drunk in charge. I let the scotch do the talking. 'Well, a bit of me wondered if you might have been a patient?'

She left a hint of a pause. 'Which bit in particular?'

It was my turn to be embarrassed. 'You could always take it as a compliment,' I said, rather feebly.

She thought about it, and it was impossible to know just how much I had offended her. 'You know,' she said after a while, 'I've learnt over the years that the secret is not minding whether people know or not. It's a very British disease, anyway, being so shocked. Not like America. I once went to a convention with Maurice in San Diego. California's the home of the profession, of course. It's perfectly culturally acceptable there. Almost compulsory in some circles. They do a lot of body work, breast augmentation, liposuction, that kind of thing. But the real business is in faces. Sun damage. There must be a million women out there who spent the first forty years of their life trying to get tanned and the second forty trying to get rid of the wrinkles. The best advert a surgeon can have there is his wife. There were almost as many face-lifts at that conference as there were women. I counted them. They didn't have any trouble with it. They were proud to be there. Thought of themselves as a walking advertisement for their husbands' skill.' She paused. 'Of course some of them were wrong, some of them looked dreadful. Do you know how you can spot them?'

I shook my head – my eyes must have been on stalks I was so interested. She pulled back her hair from the side of her face to expose a rather handsome little ear with a small, but perfect pearl stud in it. 'They tend to wear clip-on earrings. To hide the point where the tuck meets the bottom of the ear. The bigger the earring, the bigger the tuck.'

Stud earring, no tuck. But whether that made her natural or him just bloody good I wasn't sure. She let her hair drop and poured herself another drink. I pushed my glass in her direction. Maybe it would help to get more drunk. It couldn't make the story any weirder.

'You don't like the idea, do you?'

I shrugged. 'I think I'm just squeamish about somebody

cutting up my flesh.' Maybe because someone once did it without my permission.

'You believe women should just accept their lot and grow old gracefully, is that it?'

What did I believe? I suppose that depended on how much I wanted the job. I thought about how best to put it. 'I suppose I think if God had meant us to stay young, he wouldn't have invented gravity.'

She didn't laugh. But then I suppose she didn't find it funny. 'How old are you, Hannah? Thirty-six, thirty-seven?'

Not bad. But then she was a pro. Do I get to ask the same question back? I thought. What would I guess? I thought about that gorgeous swimsuit body, every single muscle in tone. A mixture of his work and hers. Forty plus? But how many? I nodded. 'More or less.'

'Then let's have this conversation again when you're fifty-five.' She paused. 'Or maybe you could ask your mother how she feels about ageing?'

Don't be ridiculous, I thought. My mother's perfectly happy about it. But then, of course, she's never really been young. Or not that I've noticed. I picked myself up from the heffa-lump trap I'd fallen into and saw Olivia waiting at the top of the hole. She looked so good, I got grumpy. 'I think if the world weren't so obsessed with what women looked like, we wouldn't have to worry about it so much,' I said, falling back on to ideology.

'Absolutely,' she said firmly. 'I couldn't agree with you more.' And I couldn't tell if she was taking the piss or not. 'I mean we women are just victims of male stereotyping. Left to ourselves we'd never want to be slimmer or more attractive or even a bit younger, would we? We don't care about how we look. Ugly, beautiful – makes no difference to us. The whole thing is their fault. We all know that.'

Fuck you, I thought. I don't need to take this from a woman who's been reconstructed. Single malt. It always brings out the Glaswegian in me.

'And you know the other thing, Hannah? In my experience, it's always the women who don't need it who think like you do. The ones who've never felt crippled by their appearance, or who are still young enough to think that age is something that happens to everyone else.' My turn to feel the backhand in the compliment. 'Good-looking women can afford to be above it all. But would you feel the same if nature hadn't been so generous? If at puberty your breasts had sagged like a couple of pancakes, or if whoever gave you that fine little scar above your right eye had hit an inch lower and taken the whole thing out instead. How much confidence would you have then about flirting with some man at a party, or even standing in a queue outside a cinema with a bunch of prettier girlfriends.'

Well, not a lot I could say to that really. Except who wants to work for someone you can knock out in the first round? On the other hand Glaswegians in their cups traditionally don't have much truck with intelligent women. I'm ashamed to say I behaved rather brutally.

'And is that who you were, then, Mrs Marchant? Somebody who was crippled by it?'

'Who I was is my own business.' She said it like a slap across the cheek. I could almost feel the sting. 'Who I am now is what counts. And how much I have to lose. My husband and I have worked long and hard for what we have. Now we're being targeted by some loony. And I'm scared to death about what they might do next. But you're clearly not interested in helping us stop them.'

She was angry, but she was also great. Oh dear, here was a sticky one: was I really going to let myself be more influenced by a woman's body than her mind?

I wonder how much I'm going to regret this, I thought as I lifted my glass and drained the rest. Frank says it's my down-fall – always wanting the women clients to be feistier than the men. 'On the contrary,' I said. 'I've already taken the job.'

*   *   *   *

I left the next afternoon. I would have gone earlier, only I couldn't be sure that my blood levels would have made it through a breathalyser. I had slept till 11 a.m. and woken with a mother of a hangover and no clear memory of how I'd actually got to bed. I had a swim, force-fed myself a bowl of bran and three pint glasses of water, then sweated out most of it in the steam room alongside my Cezanne bathers and the museum curator.

It was her final day as well, so after the heat I treated her to a caffeine-free cup of coffee by the pool to say goodbye. I felt fabulously light-headed sitting there, a mixture of oxygen and my own sense of success. Her stay had left her looking healthy but no younger. It was a glorious day, the sun pouring in through the roof of the atrium, lighting up her face with its elaborate network of wrinkles and frown lines. Edith Sitwell once wrote how as Elizabeth I aged the wrinkles fell like snow upon her face. I've always remembered that. Such a gentle image, with its echoes of transformation and silence. It's sort of what I hope for myself – although with my luck I'll probably be more like Auden's wedding cake left out in the rain. Unless, of course, I succumbed to Maurice's superior cuts.

I wondered if it had ever been an option for her. Or if this obsession with image was more the preserve of the babyboom generation for whom youth had been such a definition of life that they didn't know how to leave it behind. I wanted to ask her how she felt about growing old, if she embraced or railed against it, but she was deeply preoccupied by government cutbacks in the museum world and I couldn't see a way to tease the conversation in the right direction.

As we were sitting there, Martha came out from the massage room in search of her next lucky customer. She saw me across the poolside and nodded, a hint of a question in her eyes. Being Martha she would already have made it her business to know that it was Lola and not Jennifer who had packed bags and fled like a thief in the night. In which case that wouldn't be the question she was asking.

It wasn't that I hadn't thought about it. Somewhere on the edges of my drunken sleep I'd had an extraordinary dream about women's bodies being moulded by sets of hands dangling on puppet strings. It had not been without a certain erotic charge, but the message was by no means clear, and if I was going to lie down on Martha's couch without my clothes on again, I would need to be a little more certain of any impending change in my sexual orientation. Anyway, I was still working for her boss.

Officially I didn't start work until after the weekend. It would take her till then to duplicate the list of files that I needed from her husband's office, a record of all Maurice Marchant's patients over the last ten years who'd been back to complain.

It would, of course, have been a hell of a lot easier if I could have talked to the man himself, but Olivia remained adamant: Maurice was not to be disturbed. In the end I stopped arguing the point and decided to use a bit of initiative. I'm a great believer in what the client doesn't know they can't grieve about. Maurice Marchant probably saw dozens of women every day. I would just be one more eager for a little advice on a body curve that wasn't going my way. At least that way I'd get some sense of who he was.

I was also going to have to track down wherever it was that Lola Marsh had fled to last night, just to see if I could winkle any more out of her bruised, sealed little soul. No doubt that too would send my client into paroxysms of paranoia about unwelcome publicity. Ah well, it wouldn't be the first time the client found the investigation as painful as the crime. Maybe I'd get the sack. I could always apply to go on *Mastermind* afterwards. Special subject: cosmetic – oops, sorry, aesthetic surgery. Maybe when I knew enough, I could offer my mother a cheekbone augmentation for her golden wedding anniversary. If we all lived that long.

*   *   *   *

My flat seemed altogether dull after the drama of Castle Dean. Usually I like to come home. Find it relaxing being in my own company, pottering about trying to resuscitate the window boxes or cleaning out the bath. But not this time. This time there was a restlessness, almost a dissatisfaction.

Suspecting the sudden reintroduction of caffeine, I threw my coffee down the sink and made myself an omelette, which I ate with half a loaf of bread. My stomach was so surprised at what felt like the weight of a dead sheep arriving on top of it that it took a while to get digesting. Gradually though the carbohydrates started to kick in and by mid-afternoon I felt almost normal enough to work. Although Castle Dean might now be a safer place for its health guests, the job wasn't over until Frank had the report on his desk ready for his stamp of approval. But try as I might I couldn't get into it. I looked at my watch. It was after six. I decided to take the rest of the day off. It was then I remembered Kate and Amy.

I dug out the envelope of vouchers that Olivia Marchant had left for me at main reception (I think she'd been rather amused that a feminist ideologue like myself had been so keen to give to others what she disapproved of for herself) and wrote Kate's name on the front. Then I went via the local supermarket and bought a clutch of whatever looked most interesting from the children's bookshelf. Not forgetting one for Ben, of course, just to avoid the threat of a third world war.

It was nearly 7 o'clock by the time I got there. Since Colin hardly ever got home before then I don't think I even registered his car parked on the other side of the road. In fact the first realization I had that he was back was the sound of him shouting from inside as I stood with my finger poised over the doorbell.

I couldn't hear any words but it was clear he was pretty upset about something. In general Colin's not an angry kind of man (might be more exciting if he were), although I have been known to get his blood pressure up on occasions. But this time he was definitely enraged. So, from the sound of it, was Kate. Her voice rose up and clashed in reply, loud, almost shaky. I found myself rather disturbed – like being a child again sitting on the stairs listening to my parents rowing when they thought we were asleep in bed.

I rang the doorbell firmly. The shouting stopped. I heard someone fling something down and a door slam. Then watched a figure coming up the hall. The front door opened.

'Hello, Colin,' I said. 'Pleased to be home?'

I swear I didn't mean to. It was more of a knee jerk reaction really, habit getting the better of me. I regretted it immediately. He looked terrible. Very drawn, and almost out of control.

'Hannah,' he said, as if he couldn't quite remember who I was. 'Er . . . We're . . . we're a bit busy at the moment.'

'Hannah!' From the top of the stairs a little figure appeared, one arm stuck half out in a white-plaster Nazi salute, anxious and pleased all at the same time. 'Hannah, Hannah,' cried Amy. 'Look, I've broken my arm. Come see.'

Colin gave a little moan and turned to face her. 'Amy, you're supposed to be asleep.'

'Well, how can I sleep with you guys screaming?' she said, and there was a rather chilling adult tone to the rebuke. By then she was halfway down the stairs and almost into my arms. From the kitchen below the door opened and Kate appeared. She had been crying.

'I'm sorry,' I said. 'I just got back and I had something to give you.'

She nodded. 'You always were great on timing. Well, you'd better come in.'

I wouldn't call it the most relaxed of visits. Colin's middle-class manners prevailed enough for him to make polite conversation in the kitchen as we sipped at our glasses of wine. But I couldn't help thinking that if Amy and I hadn't been there he'd probably have been throwing the bottle rather than drinking it. Kate for her part sat unusually silent, her fingers playing fretful jazz piano round the stem of her glass. It was clear that she was worried about Amy, kept asking if she wanted to sit with her. But Amy was busy exploiting her own power base, choosing me as the favoured one, oohing and aahing over the books and egging me on while I carved elaborate felt-tip designs on her virgin-white plaster.

It didn't seem quite the moment to give Kate her present. I tried to relieve the mood with tales of health-farm pain and pleasure, but whatever I had stumbled into was too serious for my clowning to lighten. So I gulped down the wine and said I had an appointment for the night. Amy yelled, but she was already up well past her sell-by date and when Kate offered her a last bedtime story she didn't push her luck. She thumped her way upstairs to choose the book while Kate saw me out. Colin stayed in the kitchen.

There was a nasty silence on the doorstep. From the way her jaw was clenched I got the impression Kate was trying not to cry. It made me anxious just to look at her.

'Are you guys OK?' I said. Stupid question.

She frowned. 'That's where Amy gets the word from.'

'What?'

'Guys. She keeps calling us guys.'

'Kate!'

'Hannah, listen, will you just go away. I . . . I can't talk to you now.'

'OK. I'm out of here. But I'm at home all weekend. If you need me.'

I walked down the steps. But when I turned she was still there. And she looked so awful, so bereft, that I decided to give it to her, anyway. 'Here,' I said digging it out of my pocket, 'this is for you.'

She took it frowning. 'What is it?'

'It's a holiday,' I said, but somehow I knew she wouldn't take it.

Chapter Seven

I took the next day quietly – watered the window boxes, scoured the ring off the bathtub and caught up with a couple of movies which weren't cartoons – or at least not intentionally. I made sure the answering machine was on, but Kate still didn't call. Families. Who needs them? Not me.

Sunday morning I stayed in bed. Why not? Outside winter was making an unexpected comeback, the wind hurling the rain horizontally against the windows. At 1 p.m. the doorbell rang. I had to open it in my bathrobe. Not the way to impress a client. Special delivery from the lady herself, the lovely Olivia dapper in full-length black PVC mac and hat to match. She looked like a designer fisherman. She was bowed down under a box of files. Such manual labour seemed rather out of place, but then we were talking sensitive material here, not the kind of thing you could leave to a courier service. Given the humbleness of my abode, I didn't invite her in. She didn't seem to mind. Presumably she must have given her husband some kind of excuse as to what she was doing with her Sunday afternoon. Her business, not mine.

I humped the box upstairs and unpacked it on the kitchen table. It contained a set of maybe fifty big brown envelopes. Not a lot if you consider it was a trawl through over a thousand operations, but still enough to reintroduce me to caffeine.

Inside each file there were four or five pages of notes and the odd set of pictures, all photocopied from the originals. I settled myself down and spent the rest of the day working.

By late afternoon I had been through the lot and had three stacks arranged on the table with a list of names Blu-Tacked to the wall. It's called strategy. One pile contained the discards – the people who'd come, complained and left apparently reassured; next came the ones who had been mollified by further treatment (some at Marchant's expense, some at their own); and finally those who were either still unhappy or appeared to have gone elsewhere.

I can't tell you how much fun it had been. Like having your own proof copy of *Hello!* before they cut out all the nasty bits. Those who had returned for further treatment included a very minor member of royalty needing a nip and tuck after too many big babies in quick succession, a rock star who had trouble losing weight, a politician who'd spent a number of years telling us how safe the health service was in his party's hands but obviously couldn't get his eyebags removed on the NHS, and two TV personalities, one of whom had been growing noticeably younger over the years. Her complaint was that her mouth was now too tight and she had trouble talking. Maybe somebody had paid Marchant to get it wrong.

Sadly for me only one of the seriously famous had continued whinging. And the final pile of those who were still dissatisfied wasn't that big at all. It seemed that Maurice Marchant was indeed good at his job. There were some fairly amazing body photographs to prove it. The most extraordinary were those of fat and its deadly enemy – liposuction.

Liposuction – it's one of those terms, such as collateral damage, that has wheedled its way into the language, like a confident gate-crasher at a party, so confident that it takes a while to realize who they really are and how much you don't want them in your house.

The pictures showed 'before' and 'after'. Or rather stuffed and sucked. Like porn they were deliberately not glamorous, but then also like porn this was flesh without personality. For lipo read hippo. The most common view was of the buttocks and the upper thighs, circus-lady rolls of flesh above or below the hips. Of course I'm a child of my ideological age. I know fat is a feminist issue and diets only cause you to put on more weight, but whatever the orthodoxy it seemed to me that walking around with that much extra weight could hardly be perceived as a liberating experience. On the other hand, I wasn't that crazy about the 'after' photos, either. There was less fat, certainly, but the bodies just looked as if they had lost something rather than gained any natural shape of their own.

Marchant's notes carefully recorded his conversations with the owners of the excess fat (did it still belong to them after it was out, or did it become the property of the extractor?). He was scrupulous in pointing out the limitations. Although liposuction could drastically reduce the amounts of fat, what it could not do was to totally reshape your physique. In other words, once a pear still a pear, or at least not quite the hourglass you had hoped to become. Two ladies, and one man, had found this a considerable problem.

I was most interested in the man, not least because he was the rock 'n' roll star. Well, sort of. He'd been fairly big in the early eighties and had recently tried to make a comeback. I vaguely remembered seeing him on a retro music show a couple of months before. I tried desperately to remember how much of him there had been inside his trousers. Ugh. Interesting how something that was becoming almost acceptable for women spelt instant death to masculinity. On second thoughts maybe I could actually wait to meet him.

Of the two women, one was definitely more promising than the other. Her notes read like the denouement to a slasher movie. According to Marchant by the time she had arrived on his doorstep there wasn't much of her left that hadn't been under the knife already, and Marchant was careful to stress the limits of what was possible. Even from his notes she sounded sad, and he believed in this stuff.

The next complaint was noses; and most interestingly the one that had started off as West Indian and ended up, well, not as near to Anglo-Saxon Britain as its owner, a young model, would clearly have liked. Marchant's observations were mainly technical – a lot of stuff about the difficulty of rebuilding sufficient height structure and cartilage. I got the impression that he had treated it more as an architectural than a cultural challenge and for that reason had no way of understanding why she was still dissatisfied.

Other complaints involved droopy eyelids that had closed rather than opened and several pairs of breasts. The most promising of these, as far as I was concerned, was a suspected silicone-implant leak, but Marchant's notes showed that the removal operation had been immediate and without charge, and that the implant had been found intact. The client (did she now have one tit bigger than the other or had she gone for double deflation in the interests of symmetry?) had gone away apparently content.

In another case the complaint was less from the owner of the breasts than from her boyfriend. They might look great (he'd been the one to suggest the operation in the first place), but he didn't like the feel of them – like trying to knead an overfilled water-bed. This comment was in inverted commas to show it was reported speech and not Marchant's own assessment. Nice boyfriend. I could think of at least one operation that he would benefit from.

The last mammary problem was to do with size and shape. The lady in question had been hoping for something more substantial. And her disappointment had made her pretty angry, to judge from the notes. I looked at the pictures and thought back to Olivia and her spirited attack on my sense of physical adequacy. The 'before' photos were definitely on the pancakey size, but otherwise she seemed to have a rather beautiful body. Whether it had been enough to blight her life – well, presumably I would find out.

One disgruntled client stood out above and beyond the rest. Marcella Gavarona had come all the way from Milan last summer to have a face tuck and was not at all happy with the result. She had made two subsequent visits and four months ago was still whinging loudly. She was also still living in Milan. It was only an act of unbridled self-denial that prevented me from putting her top of the list. Instead she ended up about halfway down a group of ten.

Now I had a shortlist I thought about how I might reduce it further. The most obvious way would have been to compare the handwriting of the patients with that of the anonymous note. But in this computer age no one does with a pen what can be done with a keystroke, and, although presumably they must have signed a consent form, or at least a cheque, there was no record of such anywhere in the files. No matter. I could always ask them to write something down when I saw them.

After a Chinese takeaway and two lagers I had such an obvious idea that I was almost too embarrassed to ring the client in case she realized that I had failed to notice earlier. Blame it on the alcohol. The number she'd left for emergencies was a London one. She answered, then took the call in another room.

'I'm not sure what you mean . . .'

'Well, whoever sent the notes to Lola obviously knew the health farm well enough to target it pretty precisely.'

'Yes.'

'So it's likely that at some point this person might have stayed there, even perhaps talked to Lola, got a sense of how unhappy she was?'

'It's possible, though they could probably have got all the information they needed from the brochure.'

'But you do do referrals from the health farm to your husband's clinic? Or vice versa?'

There was a slight pause. Maybe it wasn't allowed. I thought of all that free advertising on the walls of the beauty salon. Olivia Marchant was nothing if not a business woman. 'We don't directly refer, but we can recommend, yes.'

There's a difference? 'So there's a chance that the person we're looking for might also be on your files?'

'Yes. I see what you mean.'

'How soon can you get me a list of those names?'

'Well, we make a note on their files on the computer, but we don't keep them separately so it'll mean going through them all. I have to go up there tomorrow, anyway. I could fax it to you around lunchtime or drop it off later.'

I was tempted to ask her to deliver it in person to the office. Since Frank recarpeted the stairs, he's always whining about how he'd like more clients to see the place. And Mrs Marchant was just the kind of client he was talking about. But what the hell. There may be a new carpet, but I'm still getting backache from the same second-hand chair. Let him find his own long-legged beauties. This one was mine, bonus and all.

Chapter Eight

Next morning I took a long, hard look at my body and called my aesthetic surgeon.

The receptionist at his Harley Street office was awfully nice, and devastated that she couldn't get me an appointment any earlier than the seventeenth of next month, only he was so frightfully busy and away at conferences in Amsterdam and Chicago from Wednesday. But when I mentioned that Castle Dean had referred me, hey presto, she managed to find me a last-minute cancellation for tomorrow afternoon during his Embankment Hospital clinic. She gave me the address. 'Looking forward to seeing you, Miss Lansdowne.'

My body, but somebody else's name. Well, it wouldn't do to have my own coming up on the computer screen when Olivia Marchant looked for more Castle Dean referrals to Harley Street. I had thought my way around my table at the lettuce banquet a few nights before and alighted on the television producer. She was younger and cuter than me, but she had left the same day and her bill (which I had caught sight of in the register) betrayed a fairly intense relationship with the beauty salon. Who knows what sweet word poisons Julie had poured into her ears?

There was still no sign of Olivia's fax, so I used the wait to check out a few names on my list. Since I was into media territory I decided to stay there, using the old journalist's approach: I was doing a story on problems with the cosmetic surgery industry and I had heard from a friend of a friend that they might like to contribute.

The model with the faulty nose job, otherwise known as Natalie West, was no longer at the same address – her old flatmate told me that she now lived in Bermuda with a record producer. I pretended to be a friend who'd been away and she happily filled me in on the bits of her life that I'd missed. Natalie, it turned out, had given up modelling just under a year ago, and was now helping to run a recording studio with some guy she had met on a shoot there. When I asked her how about the trouble with the cosmetic surgery, she was surprised I knew about it, but told me Natalie had had another operation done with someone else that hadn't been that much better. On the other hand, you know Natalie. Most girls who looked like her would have been thanking the gods for their looks, rather than trying to stretch the envelope of perfection. I agreed and took down a Bermuda address, anyway, like a good pal should.

Then came Elvis thighs. His answering machine referred me to a manager. When I spoke to him, I pretended to be a music journalist and put in a request for an interview. He said he'd let me know.

So to the breasts. The woman with the implant problem had emigrated to Australia with a new husband who presumably had no trouble with the size of her de-siliconed tits. The lady with the dissatisfied boyfriend was happy to talk, but no longer complaining. She'd kept the breasts but dumped the man, which I suppose in the circumstances qualified as a small triumph for feminism. She certainly seemed content with the arrangement.

The last and most dissatisfied breast customer, one Belinda Balliol, turned out to be a message on an answering machine. Still, she had a nice voice – young and energetic, as if life was holding on the other line and she had to get back to it quickly. If I wanted to join in, I could leave my name and number after the beep. I did so. Then, just in case, I went back to her notes. There was a second number jotted down in brackets with a little w by the side. It turned out to be a recorded message for a casino near the Strand. Opening hours 2 p.m. to 4 a.m. Exciting. This was going to be a job with some night life at least.

Egged on by images of glamour, I called Milan only to get another answering machine, this time in glorious, speedy Italian. I left a message in dull, slow English. Let's just hope she'd remembered to tell her husband about the face-lift.

I was about to try Mrs Muriel Rankin, the walking case of scar tissue with serious liposuction trouble, when the fax activated. Hold the front page. And the next call. When I'm rich and successful, I'm going to have a separate line for the fax, so I can talk and read at the same time.

I lay and watched it chuntering its way over the machine and on to the floor. The minute it stopped the phone rang.

'You haven't broken the portable already, have you?'

'No. It's on charge.'

'Good. Cos I'll want it back when you leave. I presume you've written your letter of resignation?'

'What?'

'Well, you're no longer at Castle Dean and you're not at the office. And this is 11.33 a.m. on a working day. Do you want me to send on your P45?'

'Sod off, Frank. I worked all weekend. And how the hell do you know I'm not at Castle Dean any more?'

'Because I've just spoken to them, that's how. If you remember, Hannah, employees are supposed to call in every two to three days with a progress report. That is what we decided.'

For 'we' read Frank. And for 'employees' read me. He has these brainstorms sometimes. They usually don't last long. Truth was I was going to leave a message on the office answering machine yesterday, but then I'd got my head caught between a couple of overweight thighs and everything else had been wiped from the back memory. 'What's your problem, Frank? You got nothing better to do on a Monday morning than whinge?'

'*Au contraire*, my little frog bait. As of 9.30 I've got a

custody snatch case in Madrid and a tasty computer fraud job in Newcastle both jumping up and down on my desk calling for volunteers.'

Madrid versus Newcastle. No prizes for which one I was being offered. Computer fraud in Geordie country, eh? More macho than tracking down women whose fat has been sucked out from the wrong bit of them, certainly, but in my experience regional detecting is like local radio – it's a liability having a London accent. 'Sorry, Frank. I'm afraid I've already got a job.'

'Oh. Have you formed your own company, or is this strictly moonlighting?'

'Frank! It would bloody well serve you right if I had. I haven't noticed my name going up on the door yet, despite all those promises.'

Comfort and Wolfe: there was a time when I used to play with the sound of the words, like a teenager testing out rock stars' surnames in place of their own. Fantasy. Good fun as long as you know that's all it is. Of course it'll never happen. I know Frank. He doesn't want to lose the pleasure of bossing me around. And if I'm honest with myself, I'm not that keen on becoming the kind of person who runs the business rather than just does it.

To placate him I told him a bit about the job and asked his advice. He was sulky but not unhelpful. He pointed out the obvious connection of the handwriting, though said in his experience anonymous-letter writers could go to untold lengths to disguise themselves, using left hands instead of right, or even holding the pen with their toes. He also found the fact that Olivia Marchant had kept everything from her husband a bit odd. But then that's Frank for you. As he never fails to mention, he probably wouldn't have employed me in the first place if he could have got a man cheaper. It is, of course, bluster. I tell you for nothing if I were in a tight spot and was offered a choice between Cat Woman and Frank Comfort I'd ditch my feminism any day.

I went back to the fax and all the little Castle Deanies who'd plumped for surgical self-improvement as a way of spending even more money. It wasn't that long a list and second page in I found her – Muriel Rankin, or Mrs Pear Shape with the slasher past. Forty-eight last year, she had spent ten days at Castle Dean in a super de luxe room with all the trimmings. Ten days – she wouldn't have come away with much change out of two grand. I checked out her occupation. She didn't have one. Her husband did, though. He was the owner of a fleet of garages. No encouragement to walk, I suppose. Which is why she had such trouble with her thighs. And still did, despite her appointments with Maurice Marchant. I went back to his notes on her case. In the margin, by her return visit (to which she'd brought her husband) there was a little scrawl, made even scrawlier by the photocopier. I had noticed it yesterday afternoon but couldn't be bothered to try and decipher it. Now I tried harder. 'Unstable personality?' I think it read. Her or the garage owner?

It was all so easy I was almost ashamed.

Chapter Nine

I won't bore you with the journey. One trip round the North Circular is much like another and although the A10 may end up in the romantic fens of Cambridgeshire, it passes through a lot of crap on the way.

Not her address, though. It was on the outskirts of a sleepy little town called Hoddesdon, and although the house may have been built on axle grease it was sound-enough property. Neo-Georgian I think the term is — all new brick, fake cornices and carriage lamps, the kind of thing that makes brave young architects want to throw themselves from the Lloyd's Building lifts to draw attention to the alternative. It had probably always had a queasy relationship to kitsch, but the dozen or so brightly coloured garden gnomes scattered liberally around the front garden had definitely pushed it over the edge. Weird.

It was mid-afternoon by the time I had parked the car and walked up the front drive. The weather had reinvented itself in the way that only English weather can, and after the rain of the day before, there was now warmth and stillness, summer already kicking at the heels of spring. I rang the doorbell. No one answered. I wasn't surprised. They probably couldn't hear it over the sound of Roy Orbison blasting out from the back. 'Pretty Woman'. In this case not so much a song as an attempted way of life. I peered through the front windows into a large dining-room, empty save for a handsome table and a set of removal boxes stacked at the sides.

I went round the side to the back garden. It was what estate agents call 'well established', mature fruit trees and flower beds framing a cricket-pitch lawn. There's a limit to what a girl can learn from tending a window box, but it so happened I had just been listening to *Gardeners' Question Time* on the car radio, and they'd been getting so excited about bedding plants that even I noticed the gap at the front of the beds where this year's petunias should have been. Put that together with the packing cases and you might be forgiven for thinking that someone was leaving. I tell you, people pay me money for this kind of thing.

They hadn't taken everything, though. The art remained. The French windows were flung open and on the lawn were a number of large paintings, some propped up against boxes, some just lying on the ground. On closer inspection they were all by the same artist.

There was one straight in front of me as I turned. Large, maybe ten by twelve, it was a family portrait: a blond man and a red-headed woman sat on a sofa with two little girls around Amy's age in front of them, all staring directly out of the canvas. I'm not a great one for art appreciation, more of a 'I know what I like' kind of girl, but even I can read crude homage when I see it. The artist didn't have anywhere near the subtlety or talent of Lucian Freud but did share some of his obsessions – most notably nakedness and a Leigh Bowery size of body.

It wasn't quite what you expected in your average happy family. The word 'dysfunctional' crept into mind (another gatecrasher or a helpful social addition?) and I found myself checking out the man's penis for signs of unacceptable life. But when I managed to find it, a curled slug on a bed of crispy kale, it seemed remarkably benign, not to mention almost forgotten. I thought back to the before and after pictures of Mrs Rankin's bottom and thighs. And I must say I was rather disturbed.

The other pictures were more of the same. In some of them the background was different – for sofa read a kitchen table (the chairs looking dangerously uncomfortable and spindly under the weight of their occupant) or a garden rug – but the nudity and the bulk of the family remained the same. And so did the gaze. Look at us, the figures seemed to say, aren't we challenging?

'What do you want?'

I turned to see her standing in the frame of the French windows, the sun straight on her. My first thought was how small she was, lost in a pair of baggy men's overalls, untidy long fair hair caught up in a dirty band. My second, how young.

'Hello. Are these yours?'

'You're on private property. You'd better leave.'

'Actually I was looking for Mrs Rankin. Muriel Rankin?'

'She's gone. She doesn't live here any more.'

'Oh.' I glanced down at the paintings. 'Did you –'

But she just wasn't the chatty type. 'This is my house now.'

'Fine. Well, if you could just tell me where I can find her?'

She stared at me, eyes squinting into the sun, then she sniffed loudly and rubbed her hands down on the side of her overalls. 'Sure. It's not far. If you go back out of here and take the first turning on the left. Follow that road for about three, four hundred yards and the entrance is on your right, just after the traffic lights. You can't miss it. Hers is one of the new ones.'

'Thanks,' I said, feeling her eyes on me as I walked away.

*   *   *   *

She was right. It wasn't hard to find. And hers was one of the new ones. Four months to be exact.

In terms of size Muriel Rankin had definitely traded down. The stone tried hard to make up for that. Pink marble, veined and carved. Fancy. Worth a few bob. The writing was fake gothic script. The kind that they used to put on the tombs of Dracula's victims so the master would know where to find his loved one again.

Muriel Rankin
Beloved Wife of Tom
And Mother of Sarah and Cilla
Into The Shades
February 28th 1995

That was it. No words of comfort, no hope for the future. Dust to dust. I wondered how far the worms had got with their alternative method of flesh reduction. Not the world's most comforting thought. Maybe I should have accepted Frank's offer of the computer fraud after all. The only thing overweight there would have been the numbers.

I stood for a while working out how much petrol I had wasted on the journey. But those naked bodies kept coming back into my mind – mother, father and little Sarah and Cilla, and I knew I wasn't finished with the Rankins yet. Not least because Big Daddy was still alive.

I drove back and parked outside the house. Roy Orbison had given way to Bonnie Tyler's 'It's a Heart Ache'. She was singing her lungs out. Good tragic stuff. For a young girl she had old tastes. Maybe it was her mother's collection.

She was standing in the lawn with a brush in her hand, staring at one of the canvases. It was the portrait of the family around the kitchen table. The sun had been chased away by some showery clouds and the garden looked a little less vibrant. The paintings, though, were still striking. 'Well,' she said, her eyes on the figures. 'Did you find her?'

Good hearing, I thought. 'Yes, thanks, I did.'

She didn't say anything for a while, just kept on looking. Not so much emotional as professional. And the animosity from before seemed to have faded away. Sarah or Cilla? Not Cilla, surely?

'I'm sorry.' But she didn't say anything, just gave a little shrug. 'I . . . wonder if I could ask you some questions, Sarah?'

'Farah.'

'I'm sorry?'

'The name is Farah. F not S.'

Gothic script. It plays havoc with the curly ones. Farah and Cilla. God save the children of mothers who watched too much television.

'Farah, then. I'm Hannah Wolfe. I'm a private investigator.'

'Really,' she said with a twang of bad American in her voice. 'I thought they only existed in books. Or else they were greasy little men snooping round hotel rooms.'

I have to admit that my mouth dropped open with surprise. I mean for me Raymond Chandler is just part of the myth, the kind of thing PIs read instead of fairy-tales, but I don't expect others to be so well versed. Or so interested. But was it the book or the movie? 'How do you know that?'

'Muriel had this video of a film –'

'*The Big Sleep*?'

'Yeah. She used to play it all the time when we were growing up. She was in love with the woman in it.'

'Lauren Bacall.'

'Yeah, that's her.'

In love with Lauren Bacall, eh? She wasn't the only one. I shot a glance at the big woman in the painting. They didn't look like they had a lot in common.

'In the same way she loved Farah Fawcett Major?'

The young woman laughed. 'No, that was more of a crush. The kind of thing you get when you're pregnant. Poor me, eh? At least Cilla's famous again.'

Sixteen weeks on and she was coping very well. Now I could see her better I realized she was indeed as young as her name suggested. Seventeen, maybe eighteen. Cilla presumably would be older. 'Can I ask how your mother died?'

And now she turned towards me. 'Why? What makes you want to know?'

I gave her a massaged version of the truth.

'Marchant? Yeah, I remember him. I didn't think he was that bad. She'd been to others who'd done worse.'

'Really?'

'Oh yes. She was quite an expert on cosmetic surgery, was my mother. Before the guy in Harley Street she'd had her nose and tits done at some clinic, and then her face lifted somewhere up north.'

Cowboys, that's what Olivia Marchant would have said if she'd been here. 'Had they been successful?'

She laughed. 'I've no idea. She looked a bit smiley, though.' She put up her hands and pulled her cheeks tight back against her ears. Her face took on a definite death-skull look. She released the skin. Boy, the young. They sure know how to bounce back. 'It never made her look like Lauren Bacall, though, that's for sure.'

'And she minded that?'

'Listen ... My mother minded everything. She spent her entire life wanting to be someone else. Having her hair done to look like a magazine picture, her teeth fixed so she smiled better, her thighs sucked to make her legs look longer. And the more she did the worse she felt.'

'Did she see anyone about it?'

'You mean a real doctor, as opposed to a flesh man?'

'Yeah.'

'I think my dad took her somewhere once. But it didn't help.'

My, I thought. Some people. All I had were parents who aspired too high and set a teenage curfew an hour earlier than any of my pals. And for that I went ballistic. How about you? I wanted to ask. How did you cope? Maybe being sisters helped. Someone to talk to when the going got rough. But I got the impression the question wouldn't be welcome. 'I see. So the operation with Maurice Marchant –'

'Was just like all the others. She got excited before and then depressed when she saw the result. I think she might even have threatened malpractice. She often did.'

'What about your dad?'

'Oh, he just went to work a lot. The weird thing is he really did love her. Or at least what he could remember of her.'

I looked at the pictures scattered over the lawn. How much was caricature? When you really looked, there was quite a sweet face inside all that chubbiness. And that big body would have offered its own expansive comfort to a couple of little girls. Except for the fact that in none of the pictures was anybody touching each other.

She saw me looking. 'They're not meant to be realistic,' she said tartly.

'No,' I said. 'I didn't suppose they were. According to my client files your father went back with Muriel to see Maurice Marchant after the operation. Would he have been angry?'

She shrugged. 'Well, he's a businessman, Dad. Likes to get value for money. So he might have been a bit uppity. But he wouldn't have done anything. I mean he knew her. That one was the last straw for him. It was only a couple of months later that he moved out.'

'And what happened to your mum?'

'She went into a decline. I think that's the phrase. She killed herself three months later. Swallowed a bottle of sleeping pills.'

'Where were you two?'

'I was at art college in Manchester and Cilla was working in Scotland.' She shook her head. 'And in answer to the next question. No. I don't feel guilty at all. She didn't really bring me up, anyway. Cill and me spent more time with my gran than we did with her. If you ask me, I think she probably did exactly the right thing. Growing older would have killed her, anyway.'

'How about Cilla? How did she feel?'

'Pretty much the same, I think. She's not a great one for feelings, is Cilla. She came back for the funeral and we haven't seen her since.'

'And your dad?'

'I think he was more relieved. He stayed to sort stuff out, then packed his bags and moved to Majorca. He's started a new garage business there with a couple of his pals.'

'Leaving you two the house.'

'As you see.'

I wanted to ask her how it was for her now. I had a suspicion that the big overall might be hiding a too skinny body, over-compensation for all that fat. But I could have been wrong. Some people survive the most amazing things, probably do better than if they'd had it easier. On the other hand in my job you have to believe that.

I took an address for Cilla and her dad, just in case (her handwriting was long and fluid, a real artist's flourish, not at all anonymous), and left her to the touching-up. When I looked back at the paintings again, I found they didn't freak me so much. She was busy applying a little extra beige to the line of her mother's thigh. Oh, Lauren. You and your sort have got a lot to answer for. But I still love ya.

Time to go home. In the front the gnomes were even more vibrant. And very new. It passed through my mind that they might have been a deliberate satirical commentary on the notion of a happy home. These post-modern days you never can tell.

*   *   *   *

It was dark by the time I got to London and I was hungry. The evening stretched out before me like an empty formica tabletop and at home there was bound to be nothing to put on mine. So I stopped at the Malaysian in the Kentish Town Road, where I ate some slices of an indeterminate animal larded with peanut butter and accompanied by some very strange beer.

The place was half empty. Near the window a group of young men in suits were strutting their professional stuff, waving their forks in the air as they waxed technical about new computer support systems. The rest, a smattering of couples, sat silently, apparently more interested in the food than each other. Sometimes there's a lot to be said for eating alone.

I borrowed an *Evening Standard* from the bar. The front page was a report on the latest serial killer scare: some man who was going round London opening up women with a switchblade. I thought about Muriel Rankin and the box of files on my kitchen table. Women under men's knives. The ones that carve you into femininity and the others that slash it out of you. I wondered if Maurice Marchant had ever thought about the connection.

By the time I paid the bill it was after ten. Too early for bed, too late for work. Or most work, that is. Had the day been more successful, I might have been tempted to quit while I was ahead. As it was, I didn't feel tired enough – or maybe I just worried about the idea of sleep and the fat families and open wounds that might muscle their way into my dreams. I went back to the list in my little black book. And there was one name that stood out in the night silence. A working girl who only came out when the sun went down.

I decided to take a gamble.

Chapter Ten

Rumour has it London is one of those cities where foreigners come to have a good time when the sun goes down, frequenting the sort of places you find in tourist guides under the heading Night Life. In retrospect I should have read the chapter on casinos. It would have saved me a good deal of time and aggro.

According to the address it was attached to one of the big hotels near to the Aldwych. It didn't exactly call attention to itself. But then presumably most of its clients knew it was there. I turned off the main road and followed the parking arrows down below.

There was a time when I loved underground car parks, saw them all as homage to Deep Throat and the fall of the Nixon government (now there's a man who managed serious reconstruction of his image as he grew older). But a million bad movies and conspiracy documentaries have devalued their sense of urban paranoia. Even my local supermarket has one now. Now, alas, the only thrill they offer is death by shopping.

I stashed the car radio under the seat and straightened my skirt. I had had a little trouble deciding what to wear. Since my only experience of casinos was a James Bond movie so old that Sean Connery still had hair, I was somewhat ignorant of the prevailing dress codes. There are, however, advantages in having my limited size of wardrobe. I went for smart over shiny, but broke out a new pair of Lycra tights for the occasion. In homage to Pussy Galore I used a lot of eyeliner.

The entrance was modest. A thick pile carpet, a set of racing prints and a security camera blinking quietly on the wall. I was feeling almost at home. Trouble was I couldn't get in.

'I'm sorry, Madam,' said the man at the reception desk. 'That's the law.'

'What is?'

'That after joining you must wait forty-eight hours before you can gamble.'

'Why?'

'I'm afraid I don't know the reason. Only the law.' He was about my age, with chiselled good looks and a jaw that looked as if it had come off a Thunderbird puppet. He had a similarly natural way with dialogue.

'If it's a question of checking out my credit ratings?' I said, confident of Olivia Marchant's crisp fifty-quid notes in the bottom of my handbag.

'No, Madam, it's not to do with credit. It's simply the law. First you must join. Then you must wait.'

'I see.' I bet he wouldn't treat Lady Penelope like this. If only I'd come in the pink car. 'So how much does it cost to join?'

'Twenty-five pounds.'

I considered asking if I could just slip in and have a look around, check out whether it was worth the money, but you could see how from his point of view anyone who thought twenty-five quid that important wasn't the right kind of customer, anyway.

Behind me a small queue was forming. 'Well, I suppose I'd better join, then,' I said, though not with quite the grace I would have liked.

In a perfect world I would have preferred to be somebody else on this form too, but there's a limit to how many pseudonyms a girl can handle in any one case. As I fished out my money, I watched the queue growing smaller. They were an interesting bunch of folks, not quite what one would have expected at all. A middle-aged couple, probably Greek or Cypriot, two sharply dressed, tough-looking American

95

women and a group of what looked like average British businessmen, bored with the idea of going home.

I took my new membership card and hovered by the reception desk. Across the foyer an elderly man in a classy suit was handing his coat to the check-out girl. He nodded at me. I returned it. Then I went back to trying to charm the puppet.

'I don't suppose now that I've joined I could just slip in to look around? I mean I wouldn't gamble or anything.'

'Madam –'

'It's all right,' I said, gaily. 'I know, I know. It's the law. Don't worry about me. I'll just go and distribute my hundred thousand pounds' inheritance on the homeless instead.'

I moved out of the way, as the old man moved past me and up to the desk.

'Evening, Mr Aziakis. How are you tonight?' said the receptionist, his head nodding up and down frantically.

'I am well, thank you, Peter,' he replied, and the accent was definitely east of Suez. 'But I have a guest with me.' He turned to me and smiled. 'I'm sorry, but I didn't catch your second name?'

Well, well. Don't you just love men with manners? 'Wolfe. Hannah Wolfe.'

The Thunderbird puppet's jaw went suddenly slack. Who knows, maybe this was against the law too. If so, then whoever Mr Aziakis was clearly was more important that the law. The receptionist gave a 'well, what's a guy to do if he wants to keep his job' type of gesture and waved us through.

Lycra. It does it for a girl every time.

Mr Aziakis motioned me to walk ahead of him and we went down a flight of stairs past a small dining area and into a bar. Through a set of arches to the left the gambling floor beckoned. I was so excited I had to stop to look.

Alas, James Bond it wasn't.

First impressions presented a ballroom that had fallen on hard times, a big windowless space with a chandelier in the middle and two rows of roulette tables in the centre, each lit by its own hanging lamp. I had a sudden flash of those Second World War films, in which fancy London buildings were requisitioned by the government and young women push models of ships and aeroplanes around a pretend battlefield while retired generals sat refusing to contemplate defeat. My companion would have been a young man then. Although I'm not sure whose side he would have been on.

'Well, there it is. What do you think? Worth the membership fee?'

I turned to face him and saw an old man more amused than attracted. Which, of course, is attractive in itself. 'I think that depends on how much I lose,' I said smiling.

He made a tut-tutting sound with his lips. 'You shouldn't think of it in such terms. Gambling is like life. If you expect to be treated badly, that is how it will be. Assume you are going to win, play it to the end, but never risk more than you are able to bear losing. Am I right in thinking you no longer need my company?'

Hmm. Confucius, he say the wise old bird has no need of the morning worms. The night grubs will give themselves up to him instead. 'No. Thank you. Thank you very much indeed.'

He nodded (did I imagine the click of the heels?) and turned towards the bar. I watched him till he was out of sight, then got down to business on the floor.

The background noise was less people than machines; the one-armed bandits along the back wall whirling like the beginning of a Pink Floyd track that had got stuck in the groove. In the middle I counted twelve roulette tables and four semi-circular ones at each end, where people were playing a card game that looked like blackjack. There must have been forty, maybe fifty people in there. They came in all shapes, races and sizes, but the mean age was near to fifty and none of them looked anything like Pussy Galore. Not even the croupiers.

In fact they were the worst disappointment. I suppose I had been expecting something more outrageously glamorous, a set of siren-like beauties arranged over the gaming tables with exposed breasts like ripe pomegranates drawing your eyes down to the lucky numbers beneath. Not these girls. They were all dressed exactly the same: a purple chiffon uniform that made British Airways stewardesses look well designed. A dozen of them were at the tables, with the rest perched on high stools overlooking two or three games at a time. They looked, with the odd exception, like the tellers at a local building society waiting for their morning coffee break. There wasn't a Belinda Balliol among them. Of course I was at something of a disadvantage, since all I had to go on was a grainy photo of her naked upper torso – 'before', rather than 'after'. But even so, I just sort of knew she wasn't there.

A woman in a maroon velvet cocktail dress, circa 1966, came past me with a pad and pencil in her hand. 'Can I get you something to drink?'

I ordered a mineral water and when she came back gave her a big tip. She grinned and stuck it in her pouch. That much at least was like the movies.

'I wonder if you can help me. I'm looking for a friend. A girl I met on holiday once. She said she worked here, and that I should drop in to say hello if I was in London. But I can't see her anywhere.'

'What's her name?'

'Belinda Balliol.'

She nodded and looked up. 'She's over there. You probably didn't recognize her. She's changed her hair. Do you want me to tell her you're here?

'No. No, thanks. I'll surprise her.'

I gulped down the mineral water and followed the waitress's finger. Belinda was standing to one side of the tables. And I was right, she hadn't been there before. She was tall with curly fair hair, and on her the dress looked pretty good.

More than that – in terms of the success or failure of the surgery underneath – it was hard to tell. The closer I came the better she got. If her breasts were still giving her trouble, you wouldn't know it from her face, which was smooth and pretty with a sweet little nose and full mouth. Nice job. Nature or whoever. God, I was even beginning to think like them. 'Belinda Balliol?'

She frowned at me. 'Yes?'

'I wonder if I could have a word with you?'

'I . . . I'm about to start work. Who are you?'

'The name's Hannah Wolfe. I left a message on your answering machine. I'm a journalist, doing a piece on aesthetic surgery. I gather you had some problem with a breast operation some time ago?'

'*What?*' It came out like a long hiss, as if someone had punched her in the solar plexus. 'How do you know about it?' she whispered, the horror obvious in her face. 'Who gave you my name?'

'Er . . . a friend of a friend mentioned you. Listen, I just need to ask a few questions, that's all. You'll be anonymous – and it'll be totally confidential. I guarantee that.'

'I've nothing to say.'

'I can wait.'

She shook her head as if she still couldn't quite believe it. One of the male croupiers overseeing the tables was staring at us. Obviously it wasn't done for the gamblers to fraternize with the croupiers. She saw him and turned quickly back to me, pointing her hand in the direction of the bar, as if offering directions. Under her breath she said angrily, 'I've told you, I've nothing to say. And if you don't get out of here, I'll call the manager.'

She turned on her heel, gave a quick nod and a shrug to the man, then moved into place behind table 7, as the girl there picked up her handbag and slid away.

I thought strategy. Of course, I could see it from her point of view. A quick chat about the failure of your breast implants was not what you'd want when you were on duty looking poised and lovely. But then if she didn't answer her phone messages, she had to expect people to come looking for her. And given her embarrassment, the last thing she was going to do was draw attention to it further by having me put out.

My sixties cocktail waitress came by and brought me another mineral water. I asked her how long the shifts were. She told me they worked till 4, with a half-hour break in the middle. Well, what better did I have to do with my time?

Belinda was getting into her stride now. She stood straight, with better posture than the rest, manicured hands resting lightly on the baize. That she was the best-looking girl on the floor was beyond dispute. Which might account for the hum of activity building up around her table. But she certainly wasn't giving anything away. I placed myself on the edge of the crowd. She saw me coming and flashed up a look. I deliberately didn't catch it.

'Place your bets, ladies and gentlemen, place your bets.'

The six or seven players did as they were told, a flurry of hands sprinkling brightly coloured chips all over the board, some single, some in Tower of Pisa little stacks. With her right hand she started the wheel spinning, then with her left deftly slid the ball into the groove. It raced off like a hare on a dog track, a dozen pairs of eyes mesmerized by the race. Its escape set off another little flutter of activity round the table – last-minute inspiration, news from beyond the wheel.

'No more bets, no more bets, please.'

The wheel was slowing, the ball chattering and clunking its way off the top and into the middle. It jumped a couple of times and came to rest.

'Thirty-two black. Thirty-two black.'

The number went up on the small neon board above. I looked down at the table. There was nothing at all on thirty-two. She leant across and with a wonderful swoop gathered unto herself most of the hopeful chips and swept them into a hole at the end of the table. The noise of them clattering into the profit box below sent the smallest of shudders round the players. A few chips remained placed at the edges of the board. To them she dealt out neat little piles of winnings. Then she turned her attention back to the wheel. 'Place your bets, ladies and gentlemen, place your bets.' And off they went again.

Every two or three spins she glanced up to check I was still there. It was time to tell her I wasn't planning on leaving. Maybe I should have sat down. But the people who sat were the people who played and, shameful though it is for someone in my position to admit it, I didn't really know the rules.

On a coffee table near by there was a helpful stash of leaflets. I pretended to be doing something else while I read it. When I got back, I could, in theory at least, have broken the bank at Monte Carlo. I stationed myself behind an elderly lady with purple fingernails like talons and a frail frame weighed down by the family jewels. She was pushing her last few chips to a point where four numbers met. I knew now, of course, that her pay-back should any one of those four come up would be ten times her stake. The wheel spun, the wheel stopped, the ball landed. But not on any of hers. Belinda scooped up her chips. The woman's face remained utterly impassive. Whatever pain or pleasure there was to be had in this game, it was a seriously private affair. She gave a little flutter with her hand which might or might not have been a substitute for emotion, and got off the chair. I slid on.

Great moments in a private eye's life. Here we were at one of them. I pulled two fifty-pound notes from my bag and slid them across the table. Belinda looked up at me and there was a moment of panic in her eyes. I tried not to look at her breasts. I smiled brightly and pushed the notes a little further. Her hand reached out for them. She held them briefly up to the light then laid them on the table in front of her. 'One hundred pounds,' she said flatly, just in case neither of us had noticed. 'Fives, tens?'

'Fine,' I said.

She had clear eyes. Less blank than the other girls. She counted the chips deftly off from the bank and pushed them towards me without making further eye contact.

'Place your bets, ladies and gentlemen, place your bets.'

My fingers tingled as I slid three five-pound chips on to the 'odd' box. Any odd number and the bank matches your stack. The ball whizzed and spun. 'No more bets, no more bets.'

I watched it fall. 'Number five.' They don't come any odder than that. She pushed three chips my way, again without looking at me.

I took all six of them and moved them to the 'even' box. And waited. The ball did its thing and came up red 22. And now there were twelve.

I looked up at her, but she was keeping her eyes firmly on the table, as if I was just another punter. I had made near on fifty pounds in five minutes. My palms were getting clammy. To move or not to move? I didn't have time for a soliloquy. I moved and briefly shut my eyes. Number nine. 'Number nine,' she said in a monotone. The old tracks are the greatest. Thank you, John Lennon.

The subplot was fast becoming more exciting than the main story. At this rate I wouldn't need to wait for Frank to make me a partner, I could buy him out. The four sets of chips nestled side by side. I left them there. But they were still lonely. They wanted others to join them. Number twenty-one. They got it.

I was staring at winnings of over two hundred quid. I moved my little army over the border on to the red square. Same odds. 'If I win again,' I said to myself, 'I'll take it all off and give half to the guy who cleans windscreens on the Holloway Road, honest I will.' The ball had a social conscience. It went red.

It took her a while to count the chips out. When she pushed them my way, this time she shot me a venomous little look. Behind her the guy who had seen us talking was watching carefully. Four hundred and eighty quid. Not exactly breaking the bank. But then big problems start small, especially if you've reason to suspect something. It gave me an idea. 'Place your bets.' I apologized to the windscreen man and moved the stack, this time on to 'even'. Never more than you can bear to lose, wasn't that the advice? We weren't even close. I stared at the chips. I knew I was going to win again. I just knew it. Is this what they mean by a streak? 'No more bets. No more bets.'

Then suddenly I was just as appallingly certain I was going to lose. So much for instinct. My fingers itched to get at the chips, pull them back over the safety of the line. I was so scared they might do something without my approval that I had to entrap them tight between my legs.

The ball jumped and shimmied and flung itself into number thirty-five, then on a dying gasp back into thirty-four.

My heart was beating so fast I had to put a hand on my chest to stop anyone else from hearing it. No one cheered. No one said anything. Possibly there was a communal intake of breath. The only thing I could say for sure was that people were concentrating. Not least the man on the pedestal. To give her her due, Belinda didn't blink. 'Thirty-four,' she said quietly, as she went about her business, scooping it up and giving it out.

I had to trade some in for higher denomination chips and even then I needed two hands to pick up my pile. My legs weren't all that steady, either. As I walked away, I saw the guy lean over and say something to Belinda. She turned and talked to him for a moment. Whatever she told him seemed to do the trick. He turned his attention to the next table.

I cashed in my winnings. My wallet was positively embarrassed. What with Olivia Marchant's bonus and now this it had never seen so many fifty-pound notes together. I looked at my watch. It was after 1 a.m. Add gambling to the list of occupations that make time fly. I went into the bar and bought myself a drink. I had rather hoped my wise old bird would be there to share in my bounty, but there was no sign of him. I settled down and waited.

Belinda came off the table at 2.30. I watched her pick up her bag and make her way to a sign that read: STAFF ONLY. I checked that no one was looking and followed her in. There was a corridor and two doors marked MEN and WOMEN. I went into the right one.

She came out of the cubicle to find me studying my frown lines in the mirror. I didn't let her get a word in.

'OK. Here's what we do,' I said without turning. 'You agree to talk to me about your cosmetic surgery problems or I go out of here right now and tell the guy on the big stool that we're good friends and that you just let me win.'

Two blackmails in the same plot. There had been a time when I wouldn't stoop this low. Fact is my career's gone much better since then.

'I don't believe this. You wouldn't dare.' I didn't say anything. 'You little shit.'

Disbelief, denial, anger. Classic journey. All that was missing was resignation. Just a matter of time. 'You're absolutely right,' I said. 'I am.'

She stared at me. If only I had been Superman, I could have looked right through her. What would I have seen? Two little bags of silicone behind each tit, heavy and squishy like those plastic ice packs before they go into the fridge. Unless, of course, they'd already started to freeze. Or leak. Jesus ... What price a bigger pair of melons?

'So, do we have a deal?'

She squirmed. But it's like fishing. If you hook 'em right they just can't get off the line. She swallowed. 'Listen,' she said, and it was clear I had made her very angry indeed. 'I've told you once, I'll tell you again. There's nothing to say. I had an operation done. It didn't quite work out. I went back. They did it again. The second one went fine and now I've got nothing to complain about. Which is more than can be said for some women I know,' she added waspishly. 'Now, will you just get the hell out of here, before somebody sees you?'

Chapter Eleven

Because I wasn't quite sure how much I believed her I stayed around for a couple more hours, just to see if my presence made her any more nervous, but once back on the floor she studiously ignored me. I dabbled with the fruit machines and lost a couple of tenners at the blackjack tables. When I started to feel my wallet itching to go back to the numbers, I made a break for home. As I turned at the door, I saw she was watching me go. I cupped my hands under my breasts and gave her a cheeky little uplift salute. Mean, but fun.

It was just me and the milk float along the Tufnell Park Road. Rather romantic. I bought myself a couple of pintas and watched the dawn come in. By the time I got home it hardly seemed worth going to bed. On the other hand if I was going to be showing my flesh to an expert at midday, I needed my skin to look its best. I was asleep before you could say rhinoplasty.

The phone woke me just after 8. If things continued at this rate, I was going to need major eyebag surgery by the end of the week. There was no one at the other end. Bastards. I was about to hang up when someone said my name very quietly. 'Amy? Amy, is that you?'

'Hello, Hannah.'

'Hi, darlin'.' I pulled myself up through layers of fog. 'How's the arm?'

'Stiff. I drawed a picture of a dog on it. Hannah, will you take me to the cinema again?'

'Sure I will. This weekend, maybe.'

'Yes.'

There was a pause. 'Amy, does Mum know you're calling?'

'No. She's in the kitchen.'

'Is everything all right?'

'Yeah, I just want to go out with you.'

'OK. Well, listen, maybe I'll try and pop in tonight too. See you then.'

'Yes. But don't tell Mummy I called you, all right?'

'No. No, of course not. It'll be our secret.'

Another silence. Kids always worry that if they can't hear you, you're not there.

'I'm still here, Amy. How about you?'

'Hannah?'

'Yes?'

'When you come, will you bring a bunch of flowers? I made her a card, and she liked that, but I think flowers would be good.'

'Amy, have Mum and Dad had another row?'

'Umm. Not really. He went out early this morning and Mum started to cry. She said she's got a toothache. So I think she'd like flowers better than chocolate.'

'OK. OK. I'll see what I can do. Now you look after that arm, all right. And make sure your brother doesn't get on her nerves.'

'Oh him,' she said, sounding more like her own self immediately. 'He's just a baby.'

'Yeah, well, so were you once.'

The phone beeped in my ear. Another call was coming in. I disentangled myself gently from Amy and put my finger down on the button. It rang straight away. Olivia Marchant looking for a progress report. Christ, not a woman to let the dust settle. My first day had been so busy it took me a while to get through the list of failures. She listened carefully, but didn't seem too disillusioned with me.

'Well, I'm sure you know what you're doing. You'll let me know if you find anything?'

'Mrs Marchant, you'll be the first. By the way, have you had any luck tracking down Lola Marsh?'

'I got back to the taxi company as you suggested. They said she asked to be taken to Reading Station. They don't know where she went from there.'

Reading Station just before midnight. We weren't talking a lot of choice apart from London. Unless of course she just got out of one cab and into another. Which didn't seem likely. To be honest lumpy little Lola wasn't high on my list of suspects, anyway. In memory she'd become more of a victim than an aggressor, but then the client always likes to feel you're leaving no stone unturned. Gives them a sense of confidence. 'If she did try to get another job, would the employers contact you to check the reference?'

'Not necessarily. We don't always bother.'

And, thanks to Olivia's generosity, Lola's reference had, of course, been just fine. I made a note to myself to dig out her file sometime, just for interest's sake. But not now. Now I needed a cup of coffee. I was still making it when the phone rang again. My, my, aren't I the world's most popular private eye?

'Did Amy just call you?' And her voice was flat, small, like a steamroller had just run over it.

'Yes, she did.'

'What did she say?'

I sighed. 'Let me see . . . She said she wanted to go to the pictures, that you had a toothache, that you needed some flowers. Oh, and that Colin went out early and you'd been crying.'

'Oh God.'

'But of course I'm just your sister, so I couldn't really help her with what was going on.'

On the other end of the line there was a long silence. Then she said, 'I think I'd better see you, Hannah.'

And the way she said it nearly broke my heart. 'Any time, Kate, any time.'

'How about this morning?'

'What about the kids?'

'Millie's next door. I can leave them with her for an hour.'

I drank two cups of coffee fast, then tidied the flat. You'll probably find that pathetic, but even with kids Kate lives in less chaos than I do and I wanted her to feel at home.

I looked around. I know that some people (my mother for one) wouldn't think it much to shout about after thirty years as a potential consumer. Kate had done much better there. But I like to see it as my contribution to eco-consciousness: if I don't consume, maybe someone in Vladivostock can. I also think it'll be easier when I die. I still remember my grandmother sliding off into that last goodnight, leaving behind her a council flat in Hammersmith stacked floor to ceiling with bits of collected detritus that nobody could possibly want; my mother had to spend six painful weeks sorting it out. I was twelve at the time and I still recall how oppressed I felt, sitting in the spare bedroom with the smell of decaying memories all around. At least my descendants will be grateful – if I ever get around to having any.

The doorbell rang. I buzzed her up. She looked like shit. But maybe it was too little sleep rather than too much life. God, she used to be so lovely. That's my first real memory of her, really: sitting on my father's lap with those great dark blue eyes, a mane of black hair cascading down her back and dinky little white ankle socks with a frilly trim. She must have been what – four, four and a half? Which would have made me around three. I remember she looked so proud and possessive up there that I tried to push her off. She yelled, but in the end made room for me. Which is what she's always done, really. I've heard enough stories of sibling rivalry since to know how lucky I was. Maybe being pretty made her more secure. No doubt Olivia Marchant would have had something to say about that. Whatever it was, we just became friends. Even the age gap didn't seem to matter. Eighteen months. For the longest time I simply assumed I would catch up. Thought it was only a matter of time till I became as old as her. I realize now that I probably never will. Although sometimes I think she feels the same about me. Today was definitely one of those times.

She asked for coffee, then sat for the longest time stirring it, even though she doesn't take sugar.

'Thanks for the vouchers,' she said at last. 'I was going to call earlier, but . . . I didn't get a chance. You didn't have to pay for them, did you?'

I shook my head. 'Perk of the job.'

'It looks wonderful.'

'Only if you go,' I replied.

'And what would I do with the kids?'

A week ago I would have told her to give them to Colin, let him take some time off for once. But today I said nothing. She was busy with the spoon again. We sat and listened to the sound of it scraping its way round the bottom of the mug. I know better than to push Kate.

'We're in trouble,' she said at last. 'Colin and me. It's been going on for a while.' Another long pause. 'And now I think he's having an affair.' And although my imagination had been working overtime, it had still not got to within a million miles of the right answer.

'Colin?'

My manifest astonishment made her laugh despite herself. 'Oh, Hannah. I know you don't like him, but . . .' She bit at her lip. 'I didn't mean to tell you. Not that bit.'

'Sounds to me like you have to tell someone. Better me than the milkman.' And I realized I was just a little offended. 'Was that what the row was about?'

She shook her head fiercely. 'No. He doesn't know I know.'

'Know what exactly?'

But she was having trouble with her spoon again. I thought if I talked for a bit it might help. 'I . . . I didn't realize things were so bad. I mean . . .' What did I mean? I thought about it. 'I mean you guys always seem so . . . so involved with it all – the babies, the house, family life. As if it may be hard work, but it's exactly what you decided, what you wanted. Both of you.'

'Yes, well, I thought it was.' She put her hand up to her face and rubbed her forehead. 'Hannah, I don't know how to talk about this with you. You don't have kids . . .'

'That doesn't make me emotionally illiterate,' I said firmly. 'And I'm not so prejudiced against Colin that I can't take him seriously.' Though that may not have been entirely true.

She nodded and swallowed, then closed her eyes tight. 'I don't know where to begin. I can't even remember when it started . . . Maybe when Ben was little. He was such hard work, always crying, needing attention. And Amy was jealous. I just didn't have any energy left for anyone else. They were both so demanding. And Colin was busy. The company was expanding. He and John had just borrowed that money from the bank and then the interest rates went sky-high, and they had to make sure they could make it work. I hardly ever saw him. I suppose I thought it'd get better of its own accord. That there'd be more time – the kids would get easier, we'd be together more and we'd sort it out then . . .' She stopped.

'But you haven't?'

'No.' And she gave the longest sigh. 'No, we haven't.'

'Exactly how bad is bad, Kate?' I said, desperately trying to think of myself as someone more qualified.

She shook her head. 'We don't really communicate any more. The only thing we ever talk about is the kids. We don't . . . Oh, I don't know.' And she made an angry little gesture, as if even thinking about it was too painful.

'Is this about sex?' I ventured, but only when it was clear she wouldn't.

She was staring at her spoon as if it contained the meaning of life. Her face was so rigid I thought it was going to crack under the strain. Then she said carefully, 'I didn't think it was sex at the time, but I suppose it is really. Some of it.' She paused. 'Christ, Hannah, this must be like me talking Russian to you.'

'Oh, I don't know,' I said, thinking of Nick and what I had finally felt to be his unbearable compassion and tenderness. 'You'd be surprised.' Do you need my confession, I thought, to make it easier to go on with yours? 'Why do you think I stopped seeing Nick?' I said at last.

'Oh, Hannah, I'm sorry,' she replied, realizing the implication of what I'd just told her. Smart lady, Kate. And not the only one who kept things to herself. Must run in the family.

'It's no big deal. In my case I think I just haven't found the right way back into it.' And despite myself I thought of Martha's hands and that look on her face. 'Maybe it's the same for you?'

She shook her head. 'I don't know ... I'm really not interested.'

'You're tired.'

'No. Not that tired,' she said quietly. 'Although I've spent rather a lot of time pretending I am. Sometimes I think I've just given it all to the kids.'

'So maybe that's how it is for a while. What does Jessie say about it?'

Jessie was Kate's closest friend. So close that for a while I had had trouble not feeling jealous. She shook her head. 'I don't see Jessie much since she and Peter moved away. Anyway, she's pregnant again. This wouldn't mean anything to her.'

Yet, I thought. Not that it meant that much to me. Across the great divide. What did I know of the sensuality of child-rearing? Sure, I had done my share of cuddling Amy and Ben, had even had Amy to stay for the odd night or two, curled up next to me, nest ripe and clinging. But she had never felt like a substitute for sex. On the other hand I hadn't been getting into bed with Colin for the best part of eight years.

Time to talk about the man. 'How about him?' I asked. And as I did so, I remembered a conversation that Kate and I had once had, sitting on the staircase of her house while a party went on down beneath us, a conversation about how she'd married Colin partly because he was more a father and a husband than a lover. Because in the end lovers only bring you grief. It was the nearest we'd ever come to talking sex. Apart, that is, from the teenage fantasies. And we were a long way from the Bay City Rollers now.

'I can't say. For a while I thought it might have been the same for him. I thought that he might have been using work as a substitute. But not recently.'

Oh, Kate. I'd been bound up in my own traumas for so long now that I hadn't noticed, had misread signs of tension as just the chaos of normal family life. 'So what makes you think he's sleeping with someone else?'

She gave another big sigh. 'He's taken to going out early, three times a week. Gets up around 7 and goes to the local gym for a work-out, and from there straight into the office. It's been going on for almost two months now. He says he doesn't get any exercise and it makes him feel better.'

Colin exercising. I had to beat down a certain aesthetic gag reflex. Bastard. As if he didn't spend enough time out of the house leaving Kate to look after the kids. Just as well nobody told me about this earlier. I could have got a couple of good shots in over the dinner table.

'And?'

'And last week he was going on to a conference afterwards. Some really important thing that he was delivering a paper for. And when I went upstairs after breakfast I found the paper he was supposed to be giving lying on the bed. He'd left it. So I piled the kids into the car and drove to the gym to give it to him. Imagine. I'm feeling so guilty about not sleeping with him that I have to act as his secretary. Anyway. He wasn't there.'

'You're sure?'

'Absolutely. Not a sign.'

'Did you tell him?'

'I was going to, but then I thought I'd let him mention it. So when he got back that night, I asked him how the conference had gone and if the work-out beforehand had helped. And he said yes, it had.'

'Umm. What about his paper?'

'Oh, he had another copy in his case all along. I needn't have bothered.'

'Kate, you know this is all just circumstantial. It doesn't need to be a woman.'

'No. I know. But there's something else.'

'What?'

'He's been spending extra money on something.'

Hmmm. Not just an affair, but a mistress. Oh, Colin, have I been guilty of seriously under-estimating you! 'How much?'

'About three hundred pounds every month. I wouldn't have noticed it, only we suddenly went seriously overdrawn while he was away this week. The bank bounced a couple of cheques and I had to go back to the statements to check them. I spotted it then. It's been going on for at least two months.'

The same length of time as the early exercise. 'Cash or cheque?' I said, and there was no doubt the professional in me was muscling in on the sister.

'Cash. Some here, some there, but it adds up.'

'And that's what the row was about on Saturday?' I said.

She nodded.

'What did he say?'

'He completely over-reacted. That's what made me so certain it was something else. He told me to mind my own business. He said he had expenses through work and that I had no right to go snooping into his personal finances. God, Hannah, we have a joint account. What did he expect me to do?'

'What else did he say?' I said, thinking of his face in the doorway. But she shook her head. Obviously there are some things between a husband and wife that a sister can't share. I was relieved, really. 'And since then?'

'We haven't discussed it.' She paused. 'We haven't discussed anything.'

I looked at her. And I think I knew then that we were talking domestic apocalypse here. And I tell you I was scared. Dear Kate. For so long it's been easy. For so long I've been able to be the footloose, 'don't give a damn' one, because she's always been there, grabbing at all the security, doing all the things I was supposed to do but couldn't face. The idea of all that changing brought a tremor to my soul. Maybe the fact was I needed her to be stable so that I could be crazy.

'Do you have any idea who she might be?' I said after a while.

'No,' she said softly. Then she looked up at me. 'Though he's had a new assistant at work for a while. He talked about her quite a bit when she first arrived. But not so much now.'

'What's her name?'

'Gillian somebody . . . Peters, I think.'

'You could always ask him, you know,' I said gently.

She shook her head. 'Not now. Not yet.'

'But it would help to know?'

'Well . . .' And the shudder changed to an earthquake, opening up a great hole in the middle of my stomach. 'Well, I thought perhaps –'

'Oh, Kate,' I said quietly. 'Please, don't even ask . . .'

Chapter Twelve

By the time she left, I was seriously late. I flung myself into the car and dodged traffic jams all the way to Chelsea. But it didn't stop me thinking. As I sat waiting for the traffic lights to change, I was imagining myself in surveillance outside some basement flat in Notting Hill Gate, Polaroid at the ready waiting for Colin and a bit of fluff to come out of the front door. Snap, snap, snap. Pictures in a brown envelope on the client's desk first thing next morning.

I'd done it before. Cleaning round the U-bend. That's what Frank calls it. In the old days most agencies couldn't do without it. There was a lot of money in those old divorce laws. By the time I joined, it was already more the exception than the rule. But Frank gave me a few cases, anyway. I think he was trying to test how serious I was. I didn't mind as much as I had expected. I didn't know who they were, and from what I saw their husbands or wives were probably well shot of them. Looking back on it now, I think I was so phlegmatic because I'd somehow always regarded adultery as unavoidable, a kind of inbuilt structural defect of marriage – like a need to eat out after too much home cooking. And nothing to do with me. But it didn't feel quite like that when it came to Colin.

The guy behind me hooted. The lights had changed and I was still in la-la land. I hit the accelerator. In fact, my outburst had been premature. Kate hadn't come to ask me to spy on him. She'd laughed at the very suggestion of it. Said that she just wanted my advice on the problem, my 'expert detective mind'. Maybe that was the truth, maybe it wasn't. But even turning it into a joke had cost her, and I could hardly bear to watch her trying to make light of it. She had left swearing me to secrecy and she promised to think about the health farm if only just to get away for a few days. What she would do about Colin she didn't say.

I drove in a growing frenzy around the Chelsea Embankment looking for a legal parking space, my mind still raking over it all. I kept thinking of Colin, humping it in some young woman's bachelor flat every morning before work. Trouble was, it was as incongruous as it was distasteful. I just couldn't see it. I mean there was something so . . . well, steady about Colin. So I didn't like him. That was only because I thought that she could have done better for herself. But even if she had sold herself short, there had never been any question in my mind that Colin loved her. So maybe I didn't like the way he showed it: the house, the kids, her becoming the traditional wife and mother, at home all day and at night turning into the business hostess when he needed her. But that was the whole point. A guy like Colin was traditional. Boring. He didn't have the imagination to go elsewhere. Or did he? Oh, Hannah. The trouble with men is women like you just don't understand them.

Given that I was about to spend the next half-hour in the company of one, it wasn't the most helpful of feelings. I stuffed Kate and Colin into a box marked 'not to be opened during working hours', spotted a meter that wasn't working and parked, badly. I ripped off the official 'Out of Order' sticker and left a lying little note on the windscreen to the parking warden, about how I'd put the money in but it hadn't registered.

The hospital was tucked away around the back of the Embankment not far from the Tate Gallery. I ran all the way. The health farm had done me more good than I realized. I could still breathe when I arrived.

You knew it was private from the minute you got in the door. Not so much a case of looking for what was different as finding anything the same. The entrance and lobby were newly designed, with fresh paint and corporate landscape paintings placed at strategic points to soothe the eye. In the reception area there was a glass table with a stack of glossy magazines (this month's) and a very arranged bunch of flowers. It looked more like the headquarters of a multinational than a hospital. But then for all I knew about private medicine it probably was.

The lady at the desk was different, too. More spit and polish than your average health worker. Especially the polish. She looked a bit like a débutante who'd gone through the season without catching anything, and was now reduced to earning a living. She had a gold brooch holding up her scarf at a cheeky angle and pearl studs in her ears. Studs, mind you. Maurice Marchant had not found her. Yet.

She knew where to find him, though. Fourth floor, right at the swing doors and down the corridor. I went up in a nicely decorated lift. The swing doors were nice too, and the corridor. At the end of it there were two nice comfy sofas, another glass table and yes, you guessed it, more of this month's magazines. There was also a good-looking gal in a white coat. I was so late that the next client had gone in before me. Breathlessly I explained about the road works and the ghastly traffic accident in Parliament Square. She listened sympathetically and offered me a cup of coffee while I was waiting. Mr Marchant would, of course, do his best to fit me in. There's a lot to be said for money, I thought. Shame everyone can't have it.

I settled myself down. To guard against another tidal wave of family feeling I applied myself to the magazines. They turned out to be quite an education. When you really look, it's amazing how many references you can find to cosmetic surgery these days, and how enough column inches can make anything seem respectable.

For instance there was a 'How to Remake Yourself in Time for Summer' article, which included suggestions from face packs to face peels, and from daily push-ups to a little lipo; a consumer guide to simple surgery entitled 'The First Cuts Are the Cheapest' with a price list for the varying ways you could rearrange yourself and the pros and cons of silicone implants after their withdrawal in America; and an article about how London was becoming a holiday centre for wealthy women who arrived with one shape and left with another. Then came the ads for the clinics: little boxes full of hope and phone numbers for those with hippo hips and eagles' noses, made user-friendly by glowing testaments from Mrs A of Brighton and Carol Smith from Middlesex. If Olivia Marchant was to be believed, they were probably the cowboys' wives, sacrificing their flesh for their husbands' good name.

The only dissenting voice was an opinion piece by a woman journalist on how age was still the greatest ism of the twentieth century, for which the answer was surely to stop trying to make ourselves continually younger. Compared to the other articles, it seemed almost as brave as a Vaclav Havel play in 1970s Czechoslovakia. I was surprised Marchant's assistant hadn't acted as official censor and cut it out.

I stopped reading and went instead for the pictures. No words needed here to get the message across. Maybe cosmetic surgery was like a visit to the hairdresser's. You sat browsing until you found something that you liked, then took it in and asked them to do the same for you. I came across a particularly striking spread of a barely pubescent Chinese girl in varying designer dungarees. The waif as fashion accessory. Now she would be a challenge.

The oak-veneered door to my right opened and a well-groomed woman of about fifty came out. 'Before' or 'after' I thought, desperately checking the ears, but she was off down the corridor before I could get a proper look. Now, Hannah, give the guy a break. If you couldn't bring yourself to hate his wife, you might even be surprised by him.

The door opened again and a man in a suit appeared.

'Miss Lansdowne?' he said, holding out a hand. 'I thought you might not be coming.'

'Yes, well, I'm already half an hour older than I intended to be,' I said, then felt something kick me in my mental shin. I was obviously going to have a little trouble with my subconscious on this one. I gave him a big smile to compensate.

First impressions? Well, even without the white coat he looked like a doctor. To begin with he had that 'Trust me, I've been trained for years' smile. You know the kind of thing – not too insistent or pushy, just radiating quiet confidence. We pumped hands. Nice grip. Not too hard, not too weak. By the time we got into the room I already felt like a supplicant.

He beckoned me to sit down and arranged himself behind the desk. We looked at each other. Even sitting he was a big man, a touch of the Paddy Ashdowns to his rather broad face. His hair was already grey around the ears and the forehead furrowed by some fairly prominent frown lines. Evidently not a man interested in tasting his own medicine. But then why should he? In place of the word ageing, read distinguished. Let us count the ways in which life is not fair.

He let the silence run, then sat a little forward in his chair. 'Well, Miss Lansdowne. I gather you come to us through Castle Dean. I hope you had a pleasant stay. You certainly look well enough on it.'

'Pure relaxation,' I said. 'I'm grateful you could fit me in so quickly.'

He made a 'think nothing of it' gesture. He took down a few details, just so we could get used to each other's voices and then he sat back and smiled. 'Right, so what can I do for you?'

'Well, I've heard some things about liposuction. That it's good for taking excess fat off certain places.'

'Yes, it is.'

'How does it work exactly?' I asked, playing dumber than his waiting-room's magazines allowed.

'Well, basically you make a small incision through the skin into the subcutaneous layer of fat and suction out the excess. It's quite a simple procedure.'

'And is the result immediate?'

'Pretty nearly. You usually get some bruising around the area. But that passes within a couple of days.'

'What do you do with the fat?' I said, because this might be my only chance to find out, and it's the kind of thing we women need to know.

'Er . . . Well, we can freeze it and keep it for use on other parts of the body – around the face, maybe under the eyes, to give a fuller shape. What we don't need we discard.'

Ooh. Remind me not to go through your rubbish bins for clues. How would you feel, I thought, walking round with bits of your bottom under your eyes? I suppose it isn't any weirder then having someone else's heart beating inside your breast. Life versus vanity. Maybe there's no difference any more.

'So which part of the body were you thinking of?'

'Oh, er, the bit around my waist and thighs,' I said, and behind me I saw the Castle Dean nurse waving her Slender tone leaflets about like a cheerleader's pompoms.

He looked at me for a moment without speaking, then nodded slowly. 'Right. Well, I think probably the thing to do is for me to have a look at you and then we'll talk about it. If you'd like to get yourself undressed and slip on to the couch.'

I was mildly surprised that he didn't get the nurse in at this point. Instead he just drew the curtains around me and waited. The etiquette of undressing was a little beyond me. How much did I have to take off? I settled for the trousers but left on the pants. After all, this guy was my client's husband. You couldn't be too careful. I looked down at my legs. And I can't tell you how glad I was about Julie's waxing. I bet he doesn't get to see much new forest growth on this couch.

His chair scraped and the curtains opened. He came and stood beside me. We nodded at each other, just to make it feel more normal. He put his hands on my stomach then ran them down on to my upper thighs. He poked around a bit. I watched his face. He caught me looking at him and smiled slightly, then went back to my flesh. He said to turn over. I did. He prodded a bit more, then said, 'OK. If you'd like to pop your clothes on, Miss Lansdowne, we'll have a talk.'

Back at the desk he was busy making a few notes. He was using a sleek black fountain pen. Expensive by the look of it. You could tell that from the flow of the marks on the paper. I had, of course, seen those marks before – little amendments on the files. He and his wife. No doubt both of them Mont Blanc people. He looked up. 'So, would you like the good news or the bad?'

'Both.'

'Miss Lansdowne, there's nothing I can do about your thighs. Because, quite frankly, there's nothing that needs doing. You have a perfectly acceptable shape already, and the amount of extra fat you're carrying is really minimal. You could probably shift it better by cutting down on carbohydrates and taking a little more exercise.'

He paused. Oh, give me a break, I thought. An honest cosmetic surgeon. What's a girl got left if you strip away all her prejudices? 'I see. Well . . . I had hoped . . . I mean I don't mind if the result isn't that dramatic.'

He sighed. 'What I could do would make so little difference that you'd probably be banging on my door next day asking for your money back.'

'Does that happen often?' I asked lightly.

He stared at me for a moment. 'No, not often.'

I paused. 'I . . . I've also been thinking about maybe having some work done on my breasts.' He dropped his eyes quickly to my chest and then back up to me. And was it my imagination or did he not look quite so benign any more?

'What exactly did you have in mind?'

'Enlargement . . .? You still use silicone, I gather?'

'Yes.'

'Is that OK? I mean I've heard it's had some problems in America.'

'Yes. It's still OK. But the FDA – the American drug agency – has always been a very conservative body. Here we have a very high success and safety rate with silicone.'

Just so long as you don't overfill the water-bed, I thought. I was on my way to the next question when he said suddenly, 'You work in television, Miss Lansdowne?'

'Yes.'

'Does that put you under a lot of pressure to look a certain way?'

God, what do I know? A bevy of weather girls rushed across my screen, each one cuter than the last. And then I remembered his angry star patient, the TV presenter of the diminishing age and rictus lips. 'Er. No, I work behind the camera.'

'Uh-huh. What kind of programmes do you make?'

'Oh . . . documentaries, that kind of thing.'

'Would I have seen any?'

'No, I doubt it.'

'Tell me about a few.'

Hey. What's going on here? In order to think, I had to make the answer easy. I plundered my CV for something that might fit the bill. 'Well, I made a film about factory farming. Animal rights, that kind of thing. And before that one on surrogacy.'

'Investigative journalism,' he said quietly. And not quite as politely as before.

'Yes.' And there was a small but nevertheless potent silence in the room. Oh dear. A little late I arrived at the same place as he was. 'But my being here has nothing to do with that,' I said firmly.

'No, of course not,' he said, still looking. He made another little note. Then: 'Do you mind if I ask you a question?'

'Go ahead.'

'How did you get the scar above your right eye?'

Of course. How did I ever think I'd get away with it. 'Er . . . I was in a car accident.'

'You hit the windscreen?'

'Yeah.'

'You were lucky. I've seen a great deal worse. You must have been wearing your seat-belt.'

'I was.'

Obviously that's what he'd been expecting – a woman who couldn't bear to look into her makeup mirror. With this little beauty on show, my thighs must have insulted his professional intelligence. Me and my scar. Seems like recently I'm the only one who doesn't mind it being there. But then there are some things you have to learn to feel OK about.

'Why? Could you do anything about it?' Now excuse me, I thought, who gave you permission to say that? Well, why not? You know you've thought about it, you just won't admit it. Oh, my God, at this rate something ugly and vicious would start exploding out of my stomach.

'Yes, I should think so. Do you want me to look at it?'

He got up and came over to where I was sitting, pulling the desk lamp with him so it threw more light on my face. 'Close your eyelid for a moment.'

He ran his fingertip along the line. I swear I hadn't thought about it till the touch connected – about what had happened to the last man who'd fingered me there. But then he'd been one of the bad guys. And as of now I had nothing on Maurice but a few dodgy alterations.

'Is that painful?'

'No. I'm just a little sensitive.'

'I'm not surprised. Nasty thing to have happen. Was anyone else hurt?'

'Yes, the man who caused the accident.'

'What happened to him?'

'He's dead.'

And there was something in the way I said it that made him pause. He removed his finger and sat back against the desk.

'Well, a small skin graft would improve it no end. You'd hardly notice it.'

'I see. And how much would that cost?'

He pursed his lips. 'Oooh, at a rough estimate somewhere I would say in the region of a thousand pounds.'

Oh fine, I thought. I'll just slip back to the Majestic and he'll have it on his desk at sundown. Listen, said someone else. You should think about this. Add the bonus to the winnings and you've got it. Hey, sleaze bag, that's the wind-screen cleaner's money you're talking about.

Aloud I said, 'Thank you. I'll give it some thought.'

'Why don't you do that?' he said, and this time his tone definitely wasn't that friendly.

I got up and held out my hand. The goodbyes were short. I got as far as the door when he said, 'By the way. Did you meet my wife at Castle Dean?'

I turned. 'Your wife?'

'Yes. Olivia Marchant. Tall, good-looking woman. I think she mentioned you.'

And I think she didn't. 'No. No, I'm afraid not.'

'Ah, well, good luck with your films, Miss Lansdowne. And let me know about that eye.'

Chapter Thirteen

As double whammies go it was a good one. The consultation fee came to one hundred and twenty pounds. The extra thirty was the time I had been late. When I queried it, the girl at the desk downstairs said she'd only just been told about it. Which meant that he'd only just decided. But then why not? He knew I wasn't coming back and presumably he still thought I was on expenses.

Which of course I would have been if I hadn't been disobeying orders. I plucked three fifties from my wallet. 'No, don't go,' shouted the others. 'We're getting to like how snug it is in here.' Christ, I thought. Three hours' sleep and I'm disintegrating.

I walked back to the car trying to make sense of it all. Either Mr Marchant had good reason to fear what a journalist might discover (in which case the chances were that I was on the right track), or he knew something about me that he shouldn't. Maybe he had found the Castle Dean notes on Miss Lansdowne glaringly inaccurate. Certainly there would have been no mention of the scar. And when you think about it, of course, who in that profession would have dared to omit it?

Oh well, so my cover was blown. Just as long as he didn't make it part of his dinner conversation with his wife tonight. Had I been a real professional, the danger would have been an incentive to wrap up the case that afternoon. But no private eye can work without wheels and, although technically I still had mine, they had someone else's bloody great yellow clamp on them. Fantastic. I ripped the letter off the windscreen. Not even so much as a reply. Some people are so unfeeling.

By the time I was mobile again there was nothing left of the day and whatever my id was saying to my ego (or was it the other way round?) I could have barely afforded the eye operation any more, anyway. I was even going to be hard-pushed to fulfil my promise to the Holloway Road windscreen washer.

I drove home via his set of traffic lights, but I was too late. He'd already gone. Shame. Given my present state of schizo-phrenia, I might well have given the money to someone else by tomorrow morning.

I got back to four messages. The first two were from Amy. 'Hi, Hannah . . . Hannah . . .?'

Then the second, slow, very deliberate: 'Hello. This is Amy. Mum says you can take me to the cinema on Saturday, but tonight I have to go to bed early. What?' A mumble in the background. 'And she says thank you. She'll call you soon.' More mumbling, a small 'bye', then finally a click.

The third message was even less intelligible, the accent thick as olive paste. 'Missa Woolf, diz is Marcella Gavarona, you call me about dat little shit Marchant. Yesa, I can tell you. You call, I tell you all.'

Well, at last. Someone who had something to say. It was 7 o'clock in Milan. I opened a bottle of wine – Italian, of course – and dialled her number.

The woman who answered couldn't speak any English at all. But eventually she worked out what I wanted. She put down the receiver and I heard her yell 'Signora Gava-rona' a number of times. I got the impression it was a big place.

The tap of the heels on the tiles gave her away. I almost didn't need to go to Milan to meet this one. She would be size 12, nipped at the waist, have black stockings, black hair, shiny shoes and some serious eye makeup. The apartment would be originally sixteenth century, one of those gorgeous urban numbers that went on for miles, and it would be lovingly and expensively restored. She'd probably be getting ready to go out to dinner with her businessman husband, unless of course he was already in jail for offering bribes. Almost made me wish I had studied Italian instead of French.

'Ah yes, Miss Wolfe. You want to know about Maurice Marchant? I come to him last year, in May it was, because I hear that he is very good at the faces. So I ask him to do a little lift. You know, not the big cut, just a tuck around the eyes, give it a little more cheekbone. He say yes, he has developed a special new mini-lift, no marks, no problem.

'It is not cheap. Not cheap at all, but is good. Until six months later when my face, he go funny on one side, droppy, pulled. Imagine. I cannot go out of the apartment, I cannot do anything. I am absolutely like a – what do you say? – leeper. So I ring him up. He say he never heard of such a thing. I tell him I have it. He say I must come back. So, I get on a plane with a big bandage on my face and I come to him. He looks, he say no good. He does it again. But it's still not right. Still I have little lumpy bits in the cheek. He say I am imagining them, that it is fine now. I say he is bad doctor. And I want my money back. Or I make big trouble for him, make sure everybody knows what he does.'

Oh . . . Horse's head in the bed, nails in the sponge. All my life I've wanted to be in one of these plots. I could hardly contain my excitement. 'So what happened?'

'What happen? He doesn't give it. He say there's nothing more he can do.'

'And?'

'And so he is a pig. And I tell everybody this, all the best women in Milan. He is finished here. Kaput. Over. And if you want to put this in your newspaper, I say it to you happily. But, please, no real name and no photos, OK?'

Goodbye, Signora Gavarona, and may all of your face-lifts be droppy ones.

Had there not been a last message to follow I might have given way to the slough of despond. As it was I was saved by the beep.

'Hello. Hannah, this is Marty Tranchant, Pete Pantin's manager. I gather you're interested in doing a feature on him? I've faxed you some stuff and arranged some tickets for you to see his gig tonight at the Camden Palace, second set, starts around 10.30. Maybe you could catch a word with him afterwards. Though he might be a little tired. It's great that the *Guardian* sees him as a post-feminist figure. I know that's going to knock him out. He's very into politics and girl talk.'

If my flat had been big enough, I would have run to the fax machine. The photos were wonderful: Pete in a Paul Smith suit with one foot on the body of a half-naked woman who was snarling into the camera. There was also a magnificent piece of PR-speak that called him a poet of the sex war.

I grabbed a couple of hours' sleep, then dressed for the occasion. All this late-night trucking. Just seemed a shame I wasn't having more fun.

Camden Palace on a Tuesday night. For the last couple of years it's made me feel old just driving past the place. I tell you I'd be more tempted to try new music if I didn't feel I could have given birth to most of its fans. Tonight though was different. For once I didn't feel out of place. But then Pete had been around a long time. In the foyer I counted at least a dozen balding pates and donkey jackets that were old with, rather than despite, their owners. Obviously he had taken some of his fans with him.

I sat at the back. The songs were dire – a touch of the Robert Blys over a bed of decidedly old-fashioned rock'n'roll. My favourite was 'Drumming in the Dark': 'You're not the only one who hurts, babe. If you want it equal, you got to take it as well as dish it out.'

Mind you, the old boys seemed to like it. Maybe they were all being pursued by the Child Support Agency. Maybe Pete was too.

The second set ended around midnight. I waited till the crush had gone and then found the stage door. I told the doorman Pete was expecting me, but he turned out to be busy. So I waited. He took his time.

It was getting on for two when the call came. He was sitting in his dressing-room, freshly showered in a clean shirt and new old jeans, with a bottle of Foster's and a Will Self novel on the table. He obviously thought he looked OK. He was wrong. The years had taken their toll on him. The face was puffy round the edges and there was still a definite straining at certain key trouser seams. Either Maurice had really blown it or whatever fat had been sucked out Pete had sucked back in again. Seeing the over-stretched crotch reminded me of that divine moment in *Spinal Tap* when the bass guitarist sets off the security alarm at the airport with a roll of coins stuffed down his inside trouser-leg. Now there's an operation that would make Marchant's fortune. I had trouble not laughing.

He got up to greet me. 'Hi. Sorry for the wait. Business matters. So, d'you enjoy the set?'

I nodded and found myself gushing out an enthusiasm I didn't feel. Rock'n'roll. That's the amazing thing – makes everyone sixteen again.

I asked him for his autograph first. Well, I had this sneaking suspicion that he wouldn't want to give it to me later and I needed to have an example of his handwriting to compare. He signed his name with a flourish. It was of course unreadable. So I asked him to write a little dedication above it.

To Hannah. May she always write the truth. 'Thanks,' I simpered. 'I'll do my best.'

I won't insult you with the interview. Released from the discipline of a song lyric, his views on sexual politics were about as profound as Margaret Thatcher's, although somewhat more muddled, caught as he was between liberal claptrap and male backlash. But then my attempt at impersonating a *Guardian* journalist was hardly more successful. Still, at least we didn't row. Until, that is, we got on to the bit about image, and how much he hated living in a society that emphasized what you looked like rather than what you were.

'You really sympathize with women about that, do you?'

'Sure. That's what the new album's all about. Men and women both being true to themselves and not to some image that others have built up for them.'

'So you don't mind – I mean not being a sex symbol any more?'

And he laughed. 'I think people can be attractive at any age, don't you? As your body gets older, then so does your mind. That's what it's all about.'

'I couldn't agree more,' I said, and we grinned at each other. 'In which case why did you have the liposuction done?'

'What?' You could see he was absolutely stunned.

'The liposuction on your thighs. Was that . . . like . . . your decision? I mean I've heard it said that it was your way of showing solidarity with the pressure that women are under. Except I gather it didn't go too well.'

'Who told you about that? Who told you about that? That fucking greaseball Marchant. Did you get it from him?'

'Who's Marchant?' I asked. 'No, I heard it from another journalist. Sorry, I didn't know it was sensitive. I thought you knew . . . It's all around. It's made you a bit of a hero figure for women, actually. Because you did it, and then when you weren't satisfied you complained. Lots of women don't feel they have the courage to do that. It's like you showed us how to connect our sensitivities to our aggression.'

But he wasn't listening (just as well, given the crap I was talking). He had gone a strange shade of puce, a bit like a frog blowing up with air, and he was on his feet shouting.

'Get the fuck out of here. This is invasion of privacy, that's what this is. I've never had anything done to myself. Nothing at all, you hear. And if you say I did, I'll sue you. It's people like you who ruined my fucking career first time around. You aren't going to do it again. Fucking liberty. Mangy old tart . . .'

I left him exploring the outer reaches of his New Man vocabulary. It was a good deal more vivid than his songs.

I stood out on the pavement enjoying the night silence. Well, there you go – the only chance I ever had of a one-night stand with a rock'n'roll star and I blew it. What the hell. I always liked Jackson Browne more, anyway. Despite the rumour that he beat up Daryl Hannah.

Once again it was the middle of the night and I was wide awake. This case was turning my body clock around. At least no one had nicked the car.

I drove into town and found an all-night café just off Leicester Square which I used to frequent when my nights were about having fun. It was quieter than I remembered. Or maybe I was. And the prices had gone up. I ordered a cappuccino and a toasted sandwich. A guy came out and started to play sub Jools Holland on the piano. It sounded quite nice. I settled myself down, dug out the files and my little black book (PIs don't have lovers, they just have suspects) and did some office work.

First I laid out the anonymous note to Maurice Marchant on the table and put Pete Pantin's vacuous message next to it. They had been written by two different people, although of course that in itself didn't prove anything. I put a pencil cross by his name. I had now followed up on six of the suspects. And none of them, alive, dead or living in Bermuda seemed quite the sort to conduct a sustained campaign of malice against that 'greaseball' Marchant.

Or maybe the reason I wasn't getting anywhere was that I was looking in the wrong place. With no one else clamouring for my attention, my thoughts strayed back to little Lola, and that stubborn silence of hers. But even if I had got her wrong, it still didn't make any sense. She might have been capable of malicious intent, but then why bother to pay herself seven hundred pounds to pretend it wasn't? There was a copy of her application form in her file, but it was typed. The signature was big and rather childish and, anyway, didn't have that many letters in common with the note. There was perhaps a certain similarity between the *s*s, but the *m*s and *a*s looked totally different. But presumably you'd make an effort to disguise yourself. Frank would no doubt be able to dig out a handwriting expert from his old police filofax, but there was no point in calling in precious favours unless I had more than one suspect to show him. In the absence of anyone more interesting I promoted her higher up the list. Her application form included a reference from a salon in West London. I made a note to go there the next day.

I had a second cappuccino and a doughnut. Jools had stopped caressing the ivories and someone had put on a tape. Bryan Ferry's greatest hits. I paid the bill to the strains of 'Let's Stick Together'. And here's one for a certain family in Islington. Hey, hey, Colin, the message is in the words.

It was already light outside as I shovelled all the stuff in the car. And later than I thought. Detecting can be engrossing business. Already after 5. Well, tomorrow was going to be a full day.

On the road up past St Pancras, a works lorry was unloading a whole set of orange bollards. Just what the new British Library needed. More pneumatic drills. I turned east to avoid it, round the back of King's Cross, then out up by the Caledonian Road. I wasn't that far from Kate's house. Well, well. Funny the way your wheels turn when you're not thinking about it. I crossed into the Liverpool Road and let the car do the driving.

Their street was awash with bird noise. A bloody great dawn chorus scattered over a line of elder trees, with a couple of fat blackbirds like conductors in evening dress leading the throng. Surprised anyone was still asleep, really. I parked a few yards down from the house and waited. I still wasn't thinking. If you'd asked me, I probably would have said that no private eye likes to waste a good night's work. And one suspect is much like another. I wouldn't have believed it of course, but then that's hardly the point. When I got tired of the birds, I played with the radio, bouncing my way up and down the dial. Lots of people wished me good morning. I had no reason to believe them. They also gave me time checks. The hour between 6 and 7 positively sped by.

Three times a week, Kate had said. Not necessarily today, so it was up to fate and the calendar. At 7.04 a light went on in one of the upstairs windows. The bathroom. I knew it well; many a time I had sat on the edge of the bath while children water-bombed me or checked out the medicine cupboard on the nights I baby-sat, just in case. The light snapped off again. I counted the steps down from the first floor. The front door opened and Colin came out wearing a grey tracksuit. He was carrying a suit on a hanger and a plastic bag and briefcase. He trotted down the street away from me to his car. I watched him go.

I tried to look at him as someone else would, someone more neutral than I. He must be – what? – forty-one, forty-two now. Not a bad figure, spreading just a little (the imaginary gym wasn't doing much to help that) and the hair style a little too seventies for my taste. But at least he still had some hair, and a reasonable face underneath it. Mr Average, really. Middle-class, middle-aged and middle-browed (and none the worse for that, my girl, I heard my mother say, for all that you sneer at it).

He bleeped his key at the car, which lit up in anticipation. That's another thing I hate about him. Him and his gadgets. He carefully hung up the suit in the back, slid in the front, checked himself (rather than the road) in the mirror, and drove off. I waited fifteen seconds then did the same.

I played coy. Well, you have to be a little cautious when yours are the only two cars on the road. At Highbury Corner the pace quickened and others joined the dance. I let him keep one car ahead until he turned left halfway down Holloway Road. He was, as far as I could tell, heading straight for the Caledonian Road pool and gym, or the Cally as it's known locally. I couldn't decide whether I was pleased or disappointed.

But we never got to the Cally. Instead he took a right off Camden Road and then did a square dance of one-ways until we landed up in a tree-lined street at the back of Kentish Town. He stopped so quickly halfway down that I had no option but to sail right past him and turn the corner. By the time I had done the circuit he was nowhere to be seen. He could have gone into any one of a dozen houses. I parked about fifty yards back in the direction he wouldn't be travelling and waited. How long would it take? How long's a piece of string? Sorry, Colin. Didn't mean it personally.

In the car I listened to *Today*. The same stories were coming around again when he emerged, nearly an hour later, up some stairs from the basement flat across the road. He walked smartly to his car. But then he was smart now, all dressed and ready for work, the tracksuit presumably in the bag by his side. Well, if you're going to take your clothes off, why not change them at the same time? Ready for the office. A new man. Interesting. I've always suspected that really they are just the same as the old ones underneath.

I watched as his car drove past me. I had to resist the urge to jab the horn. A little blast up the backside. So Kate had been right. Colin was on the razzle. A man with a mistress. Oh my, oh my, oh my. Who would have believed it? It was the kind of thing Pete Pantin probably had a song about. Remind me not to buy the album. Question was, what next? I don't exactly remember making the decision to get out of the car and cross the street. But once I was there, I was pleased I had. No. 34. My lucky number from last night. I went down the stairs and rang the doorbell loudly. It took a while, but at last she opened it.

She wasn't exactly Julia Roberts – probably in her late thirties, early forties, dark hair in no particular style, with a slash of lipstick across the mouth and a smattering of mascara. She was already dressed in trousers and a sweater.

Nothing special. I have to say she didn't look much like a woman for whom the earth had just moved. But then that's Colin for you.

'Yes?' She was, however, definitely edgy.

'Good morning. I'm looking for a Miss Peters, Gillian Peters?'

'There's no one here of that name.'

'I see. Is this 34 Stratton Gardens?'

'No, it's Fairwood.'

'Oh, I'm so sorry. I wonder –'

But I didn't get any further. Behind me I heard footsteps on the stairs and I turned to see a man of around fifty carrying a briefcase and an umbrella. When he spotted me, he went decidedly pale and hesitated. Bloody hell.

'Excuse me,' she said to me sharply.

'What? Oh yes, of course. Sorry to have disturbed you.'

He kept his eyes well down as I moved past him and clattered up the stairs. Behind me I heard the door shut.

I stood in the street feeling like someone had just smashed me in the ribs. It did, of course, all make an appalling kind of sense suddenly: the regular timing, her less than glamorous appearance, the cash going out every month. Gentlemen callers. Christ, I thought they went out with the ark. Mind you, our Colin has always been a traditionalist at heart.

The humour didn't get me far. Back in the car I began to get an idea of what Pandora must have suffered – the way in which the minute she'd opened the box the very air was thick with the malevolence of what had been released. But at least in her case everybody knew about it. Mine was still a secret until I chose to share it. And who exactly was I going to tell? 'Hi, Kate, you'll be relieved to know it's not anyone special, just some professional in Camden Town.'

What would Kate do? Change the locks? Burn his under-clothes in the front garden and pour the ashes into his petrol tank? Or maybe swallow her pride and ring up marriage guidance. I suppose that would depend on how much she wanted to hold her family together. And at what price? Not something Colin had given much thought to obviously. He'd just followed his prick and now couldn't get out of the hole he'd fallen into. The image was not an enticing one. Maybe I should just drive straight to Colin's office, lift him out of his seat by the lapels and batter his head on the inkwell for a while till he saw things from my point of view.

I tell you, there are some moments in your life when you realize you are neither as wise nor as brave as you hoped you were. This was one of those. Finally I decided to go for a second opinion.

Unfortunately Frank had made it one of his late mornings. Or maybe he was already in Madrid. I was still trying to open the triple office locks when I heard the phone go and the machine click in. I almost didn't make it in time. Although the way her voice was shaking certainly gave me an added incentive.

'Hello. Hello. This is a message for Hannah Wolfe. I've been trying to call her at home, but there's no answer. Mrs Marchant needs to talk to you urgently, Hannah, there's been –'

'Hi. Hi. Mrs Waverley? It's me, Hannah. Sorry, I was just coming in the door. What's the problem?'

'Oh, you're there. Thank God. The police are here. They're with Olivia now.'

'Why? What's happened?'

And she took a big gulp before she told me. 'Maurice Marchant's dead. They found him this morning in his consulting room.'

And cruel though it is, I have to tell you that for that brief moment I was relieved to have something else to think about.

Chapter Fourteen

For this journey I put on the blue flashing light inside my skull. It was so bright, it wiped out most of the other activity in there. I would have exceeded the speed limit if I could, but then central London during rush hour has no speed to exceed.

The address Carol Waverley had given me was a posh one, an apartment just off Wigmore Street. Olivia Marchant had been picked up by the police from Castle Dean just after 7 a.m. and driven to London to make a formal identification of her husband's body in the morgue at Westminster. The list of what I didn't know was so long there seemed no point in trying to invent things. No doubt the police would tell me as little as they could get away with, and I would find out as much as I dared.

I played safe with the parking. The police, of course, just flaunted it, their go-faster stripes sitting proud on a double yellow outside the apartment block. I resisted the temptation to break in and use their car radio.

It was the kind of place that had its own full-time reception-ist. I didn't need him. Carol Waverley was waiting for me in the entrance hall. She greeted me in a way that made me feel we'd been best friends for years and hurried me up in the lift. As we rose, I got what I could. Apparently he'd been found by a cleaner in the early hours of the morning in the Harley Street consulting room. The weapon had been a knife. More than that she didn't know.

They lived on the fourth floor. Big, very nice. But no one was talking interior design right now. The sitting-room door was closed. In the kitchen a uniformed policewoman was on the phone. I nodded to her and moved towards the door.

'Hang on a minute, Alan.' She put her hand over the receiver. 'Hey, you can't go in there.'

But I already had. Start as you mean to go on, that was today's motto.

The room was in semi-gloom, a set of fabulous French windows partially obscured by curtains drawn against the sun. She was sitting on the sofa, in a pair of jeans and a soft white polo-neck T-shirt, her legs tucked up under her, her body still and taut, the half-light falling softly on that designer face. But this time she didn't so much look beautiful as unreal. You see more than your fair share of distress in this job – well, people don't usually come to private eyes when they've got something to celebrate – but in my experience you can always tell the grief that comes with death. There's a particular quality of blankness to the eyes, as if they have emptied in sympathy with the dead. It might also explain the sense of rigor mortis in her face. Though in this case that might have had more to do with Maurice Marchant alive than dead.

She looked up and saw me just as the two plain-clothes officers in the room turned to give me trouble.

'Hannah Wolfe,' I said, as I passed them. 'Private detective. Mrs Marchant's my client.'

The older one nodded. 'Yes, she told us. Well, Mrs Marchant, thank you for your time. We'll be back in touch in a while. And please accept our condolences.'

I looked at them. They didn't seem particularly sorry. But then, of course, they had no reason to be. They didn't know him. He was just today's unfinished business. And the other bad news was that I was part of it. 'We'd appreciate a word, Miss Wolfe, after you've finished,' the older of the two said, waving a card in my face.

I waved mine back. 'As many as you like, officer,' I said with all the grace and civility that three years working with Frank has bestowed upon me. The younger officer raised an eyebrow. It takes one to know one.

They closed the door. Her eyes followed them out, then came back to me. I moved into the room and sat where they had sat, the sofa still warm from their bodies. Grief. You ought to be able to earn a proficiency diploma. Not quite the same as life-saving. In the end I resorted to cliché. 'I'm so sorry,' I said softly.

She nodded. The face remained the same: serene, as if it had been finished in marble. But behind the face there was a pain, trapped, welling up in the eyes, desperate to get out. The tears broke free and started rolling slowly down her cheeks. She did nothing to stop them. The effect was mesmeric, like watching some venerated statue of the Madonna cry, or worse, one of Amy's ghastly dolls that weeps when you press the right part of its anatomy. Look at you, I thought, he's sewn you up so tight you can't even grieve for him properly.

I sat and watched her cry. I wanted to offer her a tissue, but it didn't seem right. After a while she gave a couple of large sniffs, not Madonna-like at all, and ran her fingertips across her cheekbones, brushing aside the tears.

'I saw him, you know,' she said in a matter of fact kind of voice. Then she made a funny sharp noise in her throat. 'Yesterday afternoon. He was due to go to Amsterdam today, then on to a conference in Chicago. I went to say goodbye. We had a row. He accused me of trying to wreck the business. Said that if what you were doing got out, the publicity would ruin us. I told him I was just trying to protect him. That he could be in danger. But he wouldn't listen. We left shouting at each other. I drove back to Castle Dean and went to bed. The next thing I knew the police were on the phone. I didn't even get a chance to tell him I was sorry.'

She stopped and I felt a cold hand squeeze my heart. 'How did he know about me?'

'How do you think?' she said, staring at me.

'I didn't tell –'

She shook her head. 'You didn't need to. He's sharp about such things. I tried to pretend, but he always knows – always knew – when I was lying.'

'I have to ask you this,' I said quietly. 'Was there any note, any communication at all?'

She looked up at me. 'Nothing. But I don't think there's any doubt, do you?'

'What do you mean?'

'Didn't they tell you?'

'Olivia, I haven't spoken to the police yet.'

She made a little sound, then said: 'They say it was a knife. There were wounds in the neck and the chest. All over the chest. So many of them.' She swallowed. 'And then, after he was dead, they . . . someone stabbed him in the eyes.'

Ah . . . Beauty no longer in the eye of the beholder. I suppose you could say that whoever it was had left a calling card. And Olivia was the one who'd had to identify the body. For once in my life I didn't know what to say.

Against the odds, she recovered herself quicker than I did. She got up and walked over to a small bureau near the door. When she came back, she had an envelope in her hand. She held it out to me.

'What is it?' I said, though I sort of knew.

'Six hundred pounds. Cash.'

'Olivia, this is far too –'

'My lawyer says they have to freeze the bank account. But this should see you through for a while.'

'I'm sorry,' I said, 'but –'

'I want you to find who killed him,' she interrupted curtly. 'You owe me at least that much.'

Her face was rigid again now, the jaw clamped tight, skin taut over the bones. Standing there with the envelope thrust out in front of her like a drawn sword, she reminded me of an illustration from a childhood fantasy novel. The immortally beautiful Aeysha, She Who Must Be Obeyed. For a girl brought up on stories of doe-like princesses, she had been a fabulous heresy, a woman so consumed by love that it had made her cruel. There had been no happy ending for that beauty, either. Ah, Olivia don't go into the flame again. This time it could turn you into a shrivelled monkey.

I don't need all this, I thought – the pain, the fury, the hassles of negotiating my way around bloody-minded police-men. You're out of my league, lady. Look at you, you may be desperate now, but you're rich and beautiful. You'll get over it. Give it a while and the world will be queuing up to be nice to you. You don't need me either. Sometimes it's important to know when you've failed.

'I'm sorry, Olivia,' I said quietly. 'But I can't work for you any more. We have to leave it to the police now.'

She stared at me for a while, then slowly brought her hand down. The docility of her surrender surprised me. The Olivia of a few days ago would have pushed harder, gone deeper into the jugular of my guilt about disobeying her orders. But not this one. This Olivia just nodded her head and said, 'I see. Well, thank you, anyway. I know you did your best.'

And that, of course, made me feel worse.

Carol was waiting for me outside the door, all het up and fluttery. For a manager she really didn't respond well to stress. The plain-clothes hunks had gone, leaving instructions for me to join them at the station at my earliest convenience. Which meant now. They'd already had a little chat with her. She obviously hadn't enjoyed it. Kept asking me why they should have wanted to talk to her at all, what on earth could she tell them? She was so agitated about it that I wondered for a moment if she could have done it. But it seemed such a negative move given her proposed career path. I told her it was just routine and she shouldn't worry.

I asked how long she'd be staying in London. She said she wasn't sure. Olivia didn't have any family or relatives. Her parents were both dead and there was no one else. That was the point. Maurice had been everything. Husband, father, friend. It made you want to weep, she said. Which of course, it did.

But whatever the crisis, Castle Dean couldn't get by without her. At Olivia's suggestion she'd left Martha in charge (well, at least grief hadn't completely overwhelmed their business sense), but she had to get back as soon as she could. But what about Olivia? Who would look after her? It was then that she grabbed hold of my arm.

'You won't abandon her now, will you?' she said with a passion that I hadn't thought her capable of. Abandon. Emotive word. How come Olivia was suddenly turning into everyone's favourite victim? Maybe people knew something I didn't. Curiosity. In my line of work it's more fatal than compassion. I opened my mouth to tell her there was nothing more I could do. But it didn't come out quite like that. Oh God, Hannah, when will you ever learn?

* * * *

According to his card, Detective Inspector Meredith Rawlings belonged to the Tottenham Court Road police sation, near Goodge Street on the West Way.

I left the car where it was and walked. I was beginning to feel the effects of a second night with only two hours' sleep. Of all the things I didn't want to do right now, talking to policemen came high on the list. They apparently felt the same way about me. I had been sitting in reception for so long that I began to wonder if this was deliberate company policy, or if someone else might have died in the meantime, when eventually the call came. Third floor. I'd be met by the lift.

They didn't even apologize. Bad start. I tried not to let it affect my sense of prejudice. In their little interrogation cubby-hole off the open-plan office I got my first good look at them both. *El Jefe*, Meredith (I wonder what his nickname is?), was very much of a type. A big man in a suit which would have fitted him well three years ago, and a face on which the late nights and the pints had started to show, almost to the point of distracting you from the intelligence in his eyes. The first time I had met Frank I had felt something similar – and as a result done myself no good at all by seriously underestimating him. But then Frank was one of the ones that got away. And according to him the longer you stayed the greater the brain damage.

Meredith's sidekick, Detective Sergeant Grant, still had a way to go. He was younger, probably about forty and vain enough still to be trying. The result could have been worse. No stomach to speak of and a chin that was still at right angles to his neck. More than that was hard to judge. They offered me coffee and put an ashtray on the table in front of me. Big boys don't care about cancer. I felt a bit of a wimp not lighting up.

Meredith had evidently been reading my card. 'Comfort and Security, eh?' he said, twirling it round his fingers like a preliminary to a Paul Daniels trick. 'Well, well. So you're Frank Comfort's girl.'

Fame at last. 'That's me. Why? Whose boy are you?'

He gave a little smile, as if he couldn't be bothered to rise to it. 'Good man, Frank. Left in '88 after the first Stannish inquiry,' he said, but certainly not to me. The younger one nodded, but he kept his eye on me. I rewarded him with my special smile. He managed to withstand its radiance.

'I knew your boss,' said Rawlings.

'I'll tell him. So, is that the small talk over?'

'You even talk like him, you know.'

'Yeah, well, I'm just the dummy,' I said. 'If you look out the window, you'll see Frank down on the pavement saying the words.'

He looked at me for a moment, then rubbed his chin. 'Do you want to have a go at this, Michael?' he said good-naturedly.

Michael made a slight face and then wetted his lips. Collagen, I thought. Keeps 'em plump and moist.

'Thanks for coming, Miss Wolfe,' he said with hardly a trace of irony. 'We'd appreciate it if you could tell us a bit about how you got involved with Mrs Marchant and exactly what you were doing for her.'

'I'd be delighted.' I paused. 'As soon as you've told me a few things first.' He shot a glance at Rawlings who just sat and looked. 'Frank likes a clean report. You know, dotting the *t*s and crossing the *i*s,' I said, abasing myself before the god of police procedure.

Rawlings gave a little sneer. Or it may have been a smile. He hadn't got the two quite sorted out. 'Yeah, well in that respect he hasn't changed.'

I took it as a yes and turned my attention to the more tender mercies of Grant. 'How was he killed?'

'We haven't got the PM report yet, but it was almost certainly one of two knife wounds to the back of the neck, with more on the shoulders and the chest.'

'Weapon?'

'We won't know until the PM, but apparently he kept a surgical knife on his desk as a kind of gimmick letter opener. It isn't there now.'

'What about the eyes?'

'First thoughts are that the mutilation took place after death.'

'She didn't see them?'

He shook his head. 'We covered them up for the ID.'

Mind you, I thought, you're talking about a lady who's probably no stranger to a bit of slicing around the peepers. Though, as I could tell you, one cut is not quite the same as another. I wondered if they'd noticed. It was something of a relief to have gone through this many hours with no one bringing it up.

'Time of death?'

He humphed a bit, just to let me know he was getting impatient. 'Somewhere between 11 and 2.30.'

'What was he doing there so late? I thought he was due to fly to Amsterdam first thing in the morning.'

'He was. We found the ticket in his wallet. A reservation on the 6.30 a.m. flight. Presumably he had work to finish before he went.'

Or someone to see. Hmmm. 'Any sign of a struggle?'

'No. But then that first blow would have incapacitated him.'

I wanted to ask a little more about that, but I didn't want them to know I was interested. My hesitation lost me the initiative.

'So,' said Rawlings, slipping in right on cue. 'How about we swap roles now? You know, have us play the policemen, just for a few minutes.'

I looked at him. God, I thought, you're like dinosaurs, you lot, brains too small to realize you're already half extinct. Now, now, Hannah, remember Frank. 'Of course,' I said smiling. 'Whatever you want to know, officer.'

They did it between them, nice and smooth, so as you could tell they were used to hunting in pairs. First they asked about the stuff they already knew just to make sure I was playing ball, then went on to what really interested them.

'So you've got one of the anonymous notes he received?' It was Meredith's turn and he was cooking.

I nodded. He held out his hand. I smiled. 'Not here,' I said. 'I don't keep it on my person. It's in the files.' See. Five minutes in and already I'm lying to them. Policemen and private eyes: well, we have a traditional antipathy to keep up.

He scowled. 'So do you want to tell us about it?'

'What's to tell? It came in a plain brown envelope, postmarked central London with a note made up of cut-out written words.'

'Any thoughts about the handwriting?'

'Yeah,' I said. 'It looked like Camus.'

'What?'

'Nothing. Slip of the tongue. No, I didn't recognize it.'

'And the communications to the health farm?'

'Well I didn't see any of them, but from what the girl said it was more or less the same pattern. Although they were printed notes.'

'So you thought the two were connected?'

I paused. Was this a trick question? 'I . . . I did stumble my way to that conclusion, yes.'

'What about the girl who did the sabotage?'

'Lola Marsh? Well, I didn't have her down as a killer, but I suppose this puts her back on the list.'

'Olivia Marchant says you don't know where she is?'

I shook my head. 'Not a clue. Taxi dropped her at Reading Station and she disappeared into the night. But a trawl of all the major beauty salons in the country might find her. I didn't have quite the resources.'

The younger one smiled. 'So tell us about the files on Marchant's patients?'

'What about them?'

'Did you find anything?'

'Yes and no. There were about thirty possible suspects. I narrowed them down to ten and saw or contacted most of those.'

'And?'

'I didn't come across anyone using a cardboard cut-out of Maurice Marchant as target practice.'

'How about the others?' Rawlings prowled in now, smelling pastures new.

'They're all yours,' I said sweetly. 'One liposuction, a pair of hooded eyelids and a jaw reduction with rhinoplasty.'

'A what?'

'It's when your chin's too big,' I said. 'They cut a bit out and add it to your nose.' I didn't really mean him to take it personally, but then you never know what someone's weak spot is. He scowled. It struck me that this probably wasn't

Rawlings' kind of case. No doubt he'd seen his fair share of the damage that knives can do to women's bodies, but they were usually the corpses in the plot. Like a lot of coppers he felt like a man's man and I couldn't see him at ease interviewing rich, reconstructed ladies about their favourite ways of spending money. Not butch enough for him. Not the right kind of glory.

'Right,' said Grant, slipping in to help his partner out. 'So we can pick them up from you, can we?'

'Be my guest. I've only ever seen myself as a guardian until someone more worthy comes along,' I said, in a blatant attempt to get further up their noses.

'When did you last see her?' And I must say with Rawlings, I was certainly succeeding.

'Who?'

'The Queen of Sheba. Your client, Mrs Marchant.'

'Er . . . Sunday morning. She dropped the files off to me at my home.'

'And that was the last communication?'

'No, she called me Tuesday morning to ask how it was going.'

'Where was she then?'

'I have no idea, I didn't inquire.'

'What about her husband?'

'What about him?'

'Did you meet him?'

'Yes. I saw him yesterday lunchtime.'

'Did you indeed? Did you ask him about the threats?'

'No. No, I . . . er . . . went as a patient.'

And of course he couldn't resist it. 'What was your problem?'

'I was working undercover,' I said patiently. 'You must have heard of it. You go in and pretend to be someone else, take the drugs, break the law and then bust the others for doing it.'

'God, I don't know how Frank stands it,' he said under his

breath to Grant. Then to me: 'Listen, lady, any trouble you give me, I'll triple it back, understand?'

'Understood,' I answered meekly. Come off it, Meredith, don't you know girls just want to have fun?

'What did you make of Marchant, Miss Wolfe?' The nice guy again.

'Confident, successful. Your average cosmetic surgeon, I presume.'

'Attractive?'

I shrugged. 'Not like his wife, if that's what you mean.'

'Did he strike you as at all nervous or frightened?' Rawlings in there with his fists up.

'No. On the contrary. But then he wouldn't be, would he, not if he didn't know he was being targeted?'

'Was he the kind of man that a woman might take a violent dislike to, would you say?'

God, Rawlings, it's called fishing. You use a little hook because the fish can recognize a club. 'I suppose it depends what he'd done to her,' I said. 'Women can be very picky about their appearance.'

The phone rang. Grant picked it up, grunted into it a couple of times, then handed it over to his partner.

'Rawlings,' he said, just in case they didn't know. He kept looking at me while he listened. And then he said, 'Is he sure?' He kept on looking.

Oh, God. I thought. This is just like *NYPD Blue*. I was so excited I could hardly breathe. Somehow I managed to contain myself.

'I'll be there,' he said tersely, then put down the receiver and leant over to say something to Grant. They both looked very pleased with themselves. He got up.

'Well, thanks for your er . . . help, Miss Wolfe. And give my regards to Frank. Sergeant Grant will accompany you back to your office to get the files. I'll see you there, Michael.'

I waited till the door closed. Then I said, 'He's marvellous, isn't he? It must be a privilege to work with him. Is that an arrest, then?'

And I could tell from the way his mouth quivered that he thought it funny, he just didn't have the balls to laugh.

Chapter Fifteen

Still, he liked my company so much he wouldn't leave me alone. In fact when he discovered that the files were at my flat rather than my office, he insisted on accompanying me all the way home. Even took me in the squad car. I must say, it was a blow realizing they didn't trust me to deliver them myself, but then in my line of work you get used to being disappointed in people.

The traffic was terrible. If I hadn't been there, he probably would have put on the siren. I told him it was all right with me, but he just smiled. In the end I had to talk to make sure I didn't fall asleep.

'So Rawlings is your partner?'

'I work with him, yes.'

'How long?'

'Just under a year.'

'How's it going?'

He pursed his lips. Funny gesture, almost like a girl's. In profile the face looked better. On a desert island would I sleep with him? Or would I, given the recent revelations about myself, prefer Sue Lawley? Give it a break, Hannah. Do try and keep your mind on the job. He still hadn't answered, but then I hadn't expected him to.

'How about you?' he said instead. 'How long you been with Frank Comfort?'

'Three and a half years.' And I only came for a temp job, I thought.

'You like it?'

Do I like it? 'I can't do anything else,' I said.

'Why don't you join the police?' and once again the line

between irony and ignorance was too slender for me to be sure.

I shrugged. 'It used to be the uniform. Now I think I've got an attitude problem. I'm surprised you haven't spotted it by now.'

'Inspector Rawlings tells me you were the woman who was with that kid when she was blown up by the Animal Rights nutter last year.'

Rawlings certainly knew his stuff. Yes, I was that woman. But she was much more than just 'that kid'. She was Mattie, fabulous, fierce Mattie, so gloriously alive that there are times when I think she still is — just hasn't chosen to be in touch for a while. Hmm. Not the time to dwell on failures.

Instead I thought of all the places I could be but there. 'If you're going to be going through my list again,' I said, 'you might get yourself a trip to Milan.'

'Milan?'

'Yes, some Italian woman had a face-lift that slipped. Was very upset about it.'

'But you crossed her off?'

'Just a feeling. She didn't seem like the one,' I said keeping her alibi to myself.

'Well, I don't think we'll be doing much travelling on this one.'

'Really?' I let the pause run. 'I could always ask Frank, you know. They tell him everything, anyway. The old boys' network.' He looked at me. 'Go on. If it's a male thing, you could tell Rawlings I tortured you.' And this time he actually cracked a smile. Not bad. Almost human. 'Well?'

'What do you think of her?'

'My ex-client, Mrs Marchant, you mean?' I said, to make it easier. 'I don't know. I was still making up my mind.'

He grunted. 'She's fifty, you know. Amazing. She looks at least ten years younger. How much work do you think he did on her?'

'A lot,' I said. 'Why? Does that make her a suspect? I thought she was one of the happy ones.'

He smiled. 'Apparently she saw him yesterday late afternoon.'

'Yes, I know. She told me.'

'They had a row. Did she tell you that?'

'Um ... no, not really,' I said, putting down my two of clubs when I could have played the ace.

'The receptionist had stayed on to do some extra filing. She overheard bits of it.'

The receptionist, of course. That's what they'd be doing while I was twiddling my thumbs in the police waiting-room. I was lucky they bothered to come back before solving the crime. 'And?'

'It was about some other woman he'd been seeing.'

'Oh,' I said, trying to sound suitably impressed. 'Really?'

'It turned into quite a shouting match. Each accusing the other of ruining the business. She stormed out crying, very upset.'

I left a pause. 'Did the receptionist hear a name?'

'No, but when Marchant realized she was still there he got very rattled. Told her his wife wasn't well, and asked her to forget everything she'd heard.'

He paused. And it struck me that Rawlings wouldn't be too pleased to hear him giving away trade secrets. Or maybe he was trying to solve the plot on his own. Earn a few brownie points. 'What do you think?' he said. 'Was he the kind of man to play around?'

'I don't know.' I shrugged. 'He spent most of his waking moments with his hands on other women's bodies. But he seemed pretty straight to me.'

'Hmm.'

'What did Olivia Marchant say about it?'

'Nothing. She told us it was nothing, just a tiff about business.'

Oh, dear. Co-operating with the police. It clearly wasn't

Olivia's strong point, either. I was going to have to have a word with her about it. Still, it was hardly what you'd call conclusive evidence. 'So they had a row. On the strength of that you're throwing up a trip to Milan?' I said after a while.

The way he didn't answer told me there was more, but that this time I wasn't getting it. I glanced at him. He noticed me looking. 'Rawlings said that after the Animal Rights girl died you didn't tell the police everything you knew.'

'Did he?' I said in mock horror. 'Well, I must say that one really hurts. And here I am about to hand over all my files to you without a murmur.'

'Yeah,' he said. 'I've been wondering about that.'

After such an unwarranted attack on my ethics I didn't, of course, invite him upstairs with me. Well, we'd only just been introduced and it's a lady's prerogative not to go any further on a first date. Even the police would agree with that. Also, I couldn't be entirely certain where I'd left my dope stash.

It was a drag not to be able to duplicate everything, but I managed to get the most relevant stuff through the fax copier and back into the files before he had time to get suspicious. The anonymous note was so crumpled that the copy came out looking like a Jocasta Innes idea for wallpaper design, but at least I could still make out the writing. I was packing the files into a box, good as gold, when I did something so evil that I could hardly believe it myself. At the last moment I took one of them back out again. To make myself feel better about it I let it slide down behind the kitchen table, as if it could all have been some terrible accident. Withholding evidence. Immoral and illegal. Even the police only do it sometimes.

*   *   *   *

'Is this it, then?'

'You've got it,' I said, smiling, as I leant over the passenger window to wave him off. He had offered me a lift back into town, but I refused because I didn't really want him to know where I was going. He opened the box and thumbed through a few of the files. 'I think you'll like the photos,' I said as a particularly gross back view fell into his lap. He gave a little grunt. 'Men do it too, you know. It's supposed to make them more attractive to the opposite sex.'

He looked up at me. And it was clear he didn't know what to make of the comment. See, I told you. I'm useless at courtship rituals. Just as well I wasn't trying. 'It's a shame he's dead, actually,' I said brightly. 'He did a great line in tummy tucks. Maybe Detective Inspector Rawlings should ask Mrs Marchant to recommend someone else. She could probably get him a discount.'

He shook his head. 'You know, I don't mean to be rude, but why don't you give yourself a break. Stop trying to live up to the image. It's a waste of energy, and it just puts everyone's back up.'

'Does it, really?' I said, but not quite jauntily enough. 'And I thought it was amusing.'

'Yeah, well it may be, but it's also stupid, because at some point or other you're going to need us, and we're going to give you hell back.'

I laughed. He was right, of course. Shame I wasn't humble enough to admit it. 'Sorry. Old habits die hard,' I said. 'I'll give it some thought.'

He nodded, neither of us much convinced. 'Well, I'd better be going.'

'Yep. Back to the scene of the crime?'

He didn't answer, of course. I lifted my hand off the window just as it began to slide up. When it was almost to the top, he took pity on me. 'Listen,' he said through the two-inch gap. 'If we find out anything, I'll let you know, all right?'

And it was so straight that I almost believed him.

The car drove away and I walked upstairs. I felt bereft. With him gone, my mind had the space to move from murder back to adultery. It was hard to know which hurt more. As I got to the door, someone was talking to my answering machine: 'Hannah, this is Kate. I was ringing to –'

'Hi, Kate. Kate. It's me. I'm here. Let me turn off the machine.'

I hit the stop button. Well, here we were, then – the wronged wife and the private detective. Maybe I should have seen it as fate telling me what to do, but it didn't quite work out that way.

'Listen, I'm ringing to let you know that I'm taking the kids away for a couple of days.'

'Away?'

'Yes. We're going to Mum's.'

'To Mum's?' I echoed again stupidly. 'Does she –'

'No, no. She doesn't know anything.'

'I see. And Colin?'

'He just –' She broke off, and I heard a little voice in the background, a recognizable whining catch to it. Then Kate, exasperation colliding with sudden anger: 'No, Amy, I said no, OK? Now will you go downstairs and give it back to him. No, I'll be there in a minute. Go.' Then to me: 'Sorry.'

'It's OK. Listen, is this –?'

'It's nothing. It's just a visit. To give us both a bit of space.'

'Right. I see.' Of course I didn't. 'Well, can I do anything while you're gone?'

'No. Everything'll be fine. Hannah, I wanted to say I'm sorry about yesterday. I mean I don't want you –'

'Kate, it's all right. Really.'

'No, it isn't all right, that's the point. I don't want you to feel responsible for anything. I shouldn't have told you. This thing is – well, it's between Colin and me. No one else. We'll work it out somehow.'

'Yeah, sure,' I said.

'I don't want you to feel –'

'Compromised? No, I don't.'

'Good.'

I waited, but that was it. 'Anyway, I'm a busy little bee now. Up to my eyes in crime. Give me a call when you get back. And give Mum my love. Tell her I'm using the new saucepans.'

'She won't believe you.'

'No, but maybe if neither of us is telling her the truth she won't notice quite so much,' I said, even though I knew it was mean. There was a pause. 'Kate, I'm sorry –' I said. Then: 'Listen, there's something I have to tell you . . .'

'Yes?'

In the background I heard Benjamin let out a huge yowl of fury from downstairs. Whatever Amy had given him back, she had evidently taken away again. I could feel Kate's attention distracted. Tell her what exactly? That I followed her husband to a basement flat in Camden Town. Forget it, Hannah. Neither the time nor the place. 'Er . . . nothing. Nothing. I'll see you when you get back. Have a good time.'

I slammed down the phone. Great. First the police give me the brush off, then my own sister. So now I wasn't even supposed to be involved. Leave it to the grown-ups. They'll sort it out. Yeah, well, it was a shame she hadn't told me that earlier, before I went off doing her dirty work. Christ, what would happen if she and Colin made it up now? I'd never be able to look him in the face again. On the other hand what would I do if they didn't?

In the circumstances it seemed easier to concentrate on solving murder. I made myself a viciously strong cup of coffee and fought off a sudden, overwhelming desire to sleep. There'd be time enough for that later. I went over to the kitchen table and tried to look surprised as I noticed a single grey file on the floor underneath – well, you never know where there may be hidden cameras these days. I slipped the file into my bag and hit the streets.

The Northern Line was having a good day. You could

almost believe it was public transport. I sat opposite a young couple who couldn't keep their hands off each other, giggling and touching and murmuring sweet nothings into each other's ears. They made me feel about eighty years old.

I got out at Warren Street and walked. The sun was out and the day had definitely warmed up. I took off my jacket. London was almost tasty – all shimmering pavements, green leaves and blue sky. Harley Street looked particularly trim and wealthy.

There were two police cars outside. I recognized one of them as Grant's. Got your number, I thought as I walked into reception. Marchant's consulting rooms on the third floor were, of course, out of bounds to a humble private eye. It gave Rawlings and Grant a completely unacceptable advantage, being the only ones who'd been at the scene of the crime. Time for a little infiltration.

The uniformed officer in reception was a young wee thing, barely out of watching *The Bill*. I gave him my card, told him who I was and that Detective Sergeant Grant had asked me to meet him here at 3 p.m. Could I go up?

'No, I'm sorry. No one's allowed in.'

'But he is here, isn't he?' I said cheerfully. 'I mean that's his car outside and he told me he was meeting Rawlings as soon as he could get back.'

'Er ... yes ... They're both upstairs.' You could tell he was impressed with how much I already knew. So was I. 'But they're interviewing someone and are not to be disturbed.'

'That's OK,' I said. 'I'll go up and wait.' And I started to walk towards the stairs.

He put out a hand to stop me, but wasn't exactly masterful. 'Constable,' I said, 'I don't mean to be rude. But I have with me important information about the murder and mutilation of Maurice Marchant, directly relevant to the interview they are conducting, and I think you might find yourself in some trouble if you stopped me from delivering it. Now if you'll excuse me.'

And so falleth the first hurdle.

The door into Marchant's suite of offices was open. The lock, I noticed, had not been forced. I slipped carefully under the yellow tape which had been drawn across the entrance. The door to one of the rooms off the hall was partly open, and through the narrow gap I could see Rawlings and Grant talking to an elderly man. They all looked grave. Far too grave to notice me. I tiptoed past and glanced into the consulting room itself. No sign of forced entry there, either.

PVC sheeting covered the floor and a plain-clothes man was busy methodically painting off the desk and the chair. The place where the body had been found near to the desk was marked by a big white outline, just like in the movies. There were blood stains on the carpet and the furniture, but all in the same area. Marchant must have died where he had fallen, and whoever had stabbed him must have been already well into the room. I chanced a step, but the PVC gave me away.

'Hey. Get off that. You're not allowed in here. This is a police area.' The plain-clothes man waved his paintbrush in the air.

'Sorry. I've come to see Sergeant Grant. He's expecting me.'

'Is he?' I turned to see the man himself standing in the outer office, Rawlings and the elderly fellow beside him.

'Hello, Michael,' I said without a trace of sarcasm. 'I'm sorry to disturb you, but just after you left I found this had fallen behind my desk. I thought I'd better get it to you straight away in case it was important.' And I held out the grey file.

To his credit he didn't let his disbelief show, simply nodded and took the file. 'Hello,' I said to the old man next to him. 'I'm Hannah Wolfe, and you are . . .?'

Rawlings growled. 'Get her out of here,' he said as he pulled at the old man's sleeve. 'Come on, Mr Mather. We'll find a car to take you home.'

Mr Mather, who looked as if he'd been up all night, gave me a tired little smile and shuffled off obediently. Grant and I watched them go.

'Do you think he was standing by the desk or the window when he was struck?' I said, as soon as they were out of earshot. He didn't reply. 'The desk,' I said. 'Yes, I'm sure you're right.'

'Hannah –'

'Was that the cleaner who found him? No, bit too old. How about the janitor? Did he see something? He looked as if he saw something.'

'Hannah, if you don't get out of here –'

I turned. 'I'm going. I'm going.' He came with me as far as the stairs. Down below we both heard the lift door opening. The old man would soon be gone and Rawlings would make sure that I couldn't get within a hundred miles of him, at least for now. I gave Grant the evil eye. 'You said you'd tell me, you know. I didn't need to bust a gut getting that file to you.'

'No,' he murmured quietly. 'You didn't.'

Rawlings' voice wafted up our way, as he indulged his temper tearing strips off the young constable. He would be back soon, bad, mad and no fun to talk to. It was now or never. 'Well?' I said. 'I'd hate to think I'd forgotten anything else that might be of help.'

'Don't push your luck, Hannah,' Grant replied, then made his little gesture with the lips again, pursing them in and out. My, I thought, aren't we getting intimate? I even recognize your mannerisms. This was the one he used when he was deciding what to say. 'It was the janitor. He told us he thought he heard someone coming down the back stairs at around 12.30.'

'And?'

'So now we know more about the exact time of death.'

Well, whoopee, hold the front page. 'But he didn't see anyone?'

'A figure, leaving by the back door, that's all. Couldn't describe it. His eyesight's poor.'

I looked at him for a moment. Sometimes it's hard to tell. Policemen are a lot like politicians. They manage to look shifty even when they're telling the truth. 'How about earlier? Did he see anyone coming in then?'

'No, but he was off making a cup of tea around 11.30. So if Marchant had buzzed his visitor in from upstairs, he could easily not have heard.'

'Well,' I said at last, 'the world's perfect witness. Blind and deaf. What a shame.'

'Certainly is. Though, who knows, maybe you just brought me something better.' He tapped the file against his other hand. Yeah, yeah, don't patronize me, you schmuck. 'Thanks for coming, Hannah,' he said, holding out his hand. I left it where it was just in case he hadn't got the message.

I passed Rawlings at the bottom of the stairs. He was looking so pleased with himself he almost forgot to scowl. It was not a good sign.

The day had turned from warm to hot – the kind of temperature that would soon have the weathermen talking. I took off my jacket again and strolled to the car park. Although I was probably naïve, I didn't take Grant's lying personally. If Mather really had seen something, Grant would hardly have told me before they had had time to check it out. Still if I leant on Olivia, she would probably be able to dig up the janitor's contact address.

I so much hate people who use portable phones on the street that I waited until I got to the car to call her. But the Wigmore Street apartment had an answering machine on with an old tape taking messages for both of them. I told it who I was and waited, but she still didn't pick up the phone.

I closed my eyes. The lack of sleep was beginning to bite again. Boy, some case this was turning out to be. I had spent the first three days starving in a health farm, the next three up all night in casinos, concerts and police stations. No wonder it was all beginning to feel unreal. I dug my suspect list out of my bag and used it to kick-start my brain again. With no sign of forced entry we were looking for someone who knew Marchant well enough to be invited in. Unless he or she had a key. Since everybody else seemed so keen on her, I decided to give Olivia some serious thought. The fact that I liked her was neither here nor there. It is, of course, only traditional for the client to have done it, especially a good-looking one. What's the old cliché? The more beautiful the more deadly? And by now Marchant would have been worth a few bob. So there was an obvious motive. On the other hand money can't buy you youth. And for once this was a marriage where the husband was clearly more use to his wife alive than dead. I thought back to that tear-stained face. Hard to know whom she was crying hardest for – him or herself? I decided to keep an open mind on Olivia – in contrast to the police, who, it seemed, had already closed theirs. Which brought me to the alternatives.

Sadly I had to discard Mr Rock 'n' Roll (even a man of his prodigious talents couldn't be slaughtering an audience and a doctor at the same time). The main contender after him was probably Daddy Rankin of the overweight family portraits. But Majorca was a long way away, and it would take some checking to find out if he was still there. Signora Gavarona, on the other hand, had most definitely been in Milan last night. Which left Belinda Balliol and Lola Marsh. But as far as I knew, Lola had never even met Maurice Marchant, so would hardly have been able to walk straight in after office hours, unless she'd made a secret appointment, while Belinda, despite her bad temper, seemed altogether too cute to be indulging in something as nasty as a form of Oedipal revenge. However, since she'd complained and since being a feminist these days means having to accept that women can be as angry as men (there's your next failed hit, Pete), I had no option but to keep her on the list.

The digital clock on the dashboard said it was 4.80 p.m. I

rubbed my eyes and looked a little harder. It became 4.50. Clearly the night watchman wasn't the only one with sight problems. I put my head back on the seat and watched the world go by. My eyes were hot and prickly and the images started to spin.

I made a last stab at solving the plot before the police did and drove home via the Majestic Casino. But even alert I wasn't that good at maths. The man at the desk (luckily not the Thunderbird puppet) kindly pointed out that since the forty-eight hours' membership period had not elapsed my card was not yet valid, although if I was really desperate I could always come back at 10.38 that evening. I would have argued, but I might very well have fallen asleep mid-sentence.

So I gave up and told the truth. Well, almost. I said I was a close friend of Belinda Balliol's and I needed to see her urgently because I had some very personal news to give her. And when he asked me how urgent it was, I told him it was a death in the family. So he rang someone, talked for a bit and then put the phone down.

'I'm sorry. Belinda's not here. The floor supervisor says she's on two weeks' leave. Left yesterday morning.'

'I see. Does he know where she's gone?'

'Yeah, Mexico.'

Mexico. Now that's what I call an alibi. I decided not to think about what this news would do to the state of my list and went home.

The only message was from Amy. Grandma's house didn't have a video and she wanted to come home, but Mum said she had to stay. So could I go to her house, pick up their video and bring it over? If I hadn't been so tired, I would have been tempted, just to see how Colin was doing on his own. Instead I poured myself a large thick vodka from the freezer and lay down on my bed.

I stayed awake long enough to put a call through to the international operator for Majorca. The address Farah had given me turned out to be some kind of villa. A housekeeper answered and told me in broken English that Rankin was out. I left a message asking for him to call.

The vodka started to work. I lay back and thought about all the women I knew who'd be feeling worse than I was right now. From Olivia I soon moved on to Kate. I thought about her so much that I even considered setting an alarm early enough to catch Colin in his basement seraglio. But luckily for him the vodka did its stuff and I fell asleep before I could reach the switch.

Unluckily for him, I had a nightmare and woke early.

Chapter Sixteen

I was curled in a ditch in a rerun of a certain country lane, his breath already sour on my face. This time I knew it was a dream, only I didn't know how to get out of it. Then, as he leant down to hit me as he always did, I found I had a carving knife in my hand. He pulled me up towards him and in a kind of slow motion I lifted up the blade and scored a long deep cut from his scalp down the edge of his face, opening up a rich seam of red. His hand came up to register the damage, and then, more in surprise than in pain, his fingers grabbed hold of the edges of the skin exposed by the cut and he began to pull slowly. The skin lifted up and off in one long searing tear, ripping up over the cheekbones, the nose and the eyes, as if it were a rubber mask. I caught a flash of pulpy raw flesh below. I closed my eyes and started to scream, but of course there was no sound, only the echo of my fear down the long dream corridor as I struggled to pull myself awake. I was clammy with sweat, caught between my clothes, the duvet and the heavy air of another already scorching day.

I lay for a while, blinking in the light, my body so leaden I felt that I'd just come back from the dead. Coward, I thought. You should have kept your eyes open. Seen whose face it was underneath. For all you know it might have been God's way of solving the crime.

I looked at the clock by my bed. 6.10 a.m. The west London salon where Lola Marsh had worked didn't open till 9.30. Poor Colin.

Outside there was early hazy sunshine. If the world hadn't been such a shitty place, full of sabotage, murder and adultery, it would have been a lovely day. I didn't bother with the bit outside his house, but went straight to hers instead. Of course I might have got it wrong. Thursday might not be his day. Or could be he was so genuinely upset by his wife's absence that he'd given up the other woman as his way of trying to save the marriage. On the other hand while the cat's away . . . It was up to him, really.

At 7.27 his nifty G-reg Rover turned the corner and came cruising in search of a parking place. I ducked my head under the dashboard as he went by. He got out and locked the door. He looked different from last time. No tracksuit today. But then he didn't need it. Today there was no one at home he had to fool. I watched him go down the basement stairs and out of view. I put a clock on him, making a note of the exact time of entry and exit. Old habits die hard. When his jaunty little bone head surfaced out from the staircase it had been fifty-three and a half minutes exactly. Hardly worth the money really. But then, of course, she had a schedule to follow, had them stacked up like planes at Heathrow. It wouldn't do to have them colliding on the runway. The watching gave me an idea. I wasn't going to get mad. I had already decided that. I would use the encounter as a chance to talk to him. But that didn't prevent me from giving him a bit of a fright first.

He walked swiftly down the road towards his car. I was standing on the other side watching. He didn't see me. He was too busy thinking of other things, reliving his greatest moments. He got in the car and was about to start the engine when I waltzed up to the passenger window and gave it a smart little knock.

He looked up, startled, and for a second he didn't recognize me. When he did, he went grey. I watched the colour fading out from under his skin, like a long slow blush in reverse. He pushed the button and the window slid down. Together at last.

'Colin?' I said, in a deliberately anxious voice.

'Hannah? Er . . . What . . . What are you doing here?'

I gave a quick noisy swallow. 'I'm on a job. What about you?'

'I . . . I . . . was . . . er . . . visiting a friend. I . . . We had a meeting, a breakfast meeting.'

'Hmm. I know you work hard, but this is impressive,' I said, opening the door and sliding myself into the passenger seat. 'What is it? Another merger or takeover?' His face changed colour once again, moving from grey to a chalky white. 'You don't mind me getting in for a few minutes?'

'Er . . . No. So what are you doing here at this time?' He said, evidently so rattled that he'd forgotten he'd asked already.

'I'm on a surveillance job. I'm watching a house.'

'Watching a house?'

'Yes. For a client,' I said gesturing to the other side of the road from where he'd come. 'I'm keeping a record of everyone who comes in and out.'

'Really?' And you could see he wanted to ask so bad that it hurt. I let him sweat for a while. But it didn't give me quite the pleasure I had anticipated, so I let it go.

'Actually I'm really glad to see you, Colin,' I said. 'I've been wanting to talk to you about Kate. She seemed in such a state when I saw you both over the weekend. I wondered – are things OK now?'

'Um. Yeah. Listen, I'm sorry, Hannah, but I can't talk now. I'm afraid I'm late for work. I have to go.'

So much for the intimate, honest approach. 'Another meeting, is it?'

'Yes.'

'Another friend?'

'Yes – no. No. Just work.'

'Number 34.'

'What?'

'Number 34. Is that where your meeting was?'

'Er, yes . . .'

'Has she got a gym in the basement, then?'

'What?'

'A gym. Isn't that where you tell Kate you're going? When you leave the house three times a week at 7.10 to drive over here?'

'Jesus Christ.' And at last he put it all together. It hit him so hard I could almost hear the thump. 'Jesus Christ, have you been watching me?'

'No,' I said. 'Not you. Just number 34. And all the men that go in and out. You know you're not the first this morning?'

He stared at me in a kind of paralysed horror. And for one delicious moment it was clear that he really believed me, thought it was business rather than personal. Then he thought again. Well, he may be a lot of things, Colin, but he's not stupid. 'My God, you're incredible, Hannah. You really are incredible. What the hell do you think you're doing? What right do you think you have to spy on me?'

'What right? Oh, that's a nice one, Colin. Let's talk about rights. Have you looked at her recently? Have you seen what's happening to her? She's out of her head with anxiety. She's screaming at the kids, she must have lost half a stone. She's so fucking lost and scared about you and what's happening to the two of you that she can't even think straight. While you're out "exercising".'

'God, you stupid . . . Does she know you're doing this?' In place of fury now read panic, I could feel it, churning up and over. 'Does Kate know about –' and he broke off.

'Know about what? Number 34 three times a week? No, you're all right, Colin. I'm the one with the suspicious mind. She's too busy making excuses for you. How hard you've been working. How the children have separated you, how maybe she's the one who's at fault. I must say –'

'Shut up. Just shut up.' And for a man with zero charisma he'd done some work on the voice. It pinned me to my seat more successfully than a blow would have done. He was shaking with rage. 'Now you listen to me, Hannah. You and I have never liked each other. But we've had the decency to keep out of each other's way. You know nothing about Kate and me. Nothing, do you hear me. You may think you do, but you don't. You're a stupid, prejudiced woman who's never had a real relationship of your own and never been able to recognize anybody else's. What I'm doing here is my business and no one's but mine. And if you breathe a word of it to Kate, I'll personally come round and . . . and . . .'

'And what, Colin? Slap me about a bit? Just like a good husband should. Don't threaten me. I'll tell my sister any goddamn thing I want. You don't deserve her. You never did. I'm just astonished you've got the balls to be doing this at all.'

He grabbed hold of my arm and pulled me towards him. For a second I thought he was going to hit me. Which would have been OK because then I could have hit him back. But instead he just flung me back against the car door. Then he lunged past me and connected with the door handle, flinging it open.

'Get out,' he said in a voice that was definitely shaky. 'Get out before I shove you out.'

I looked at his face. It was rigid with fury. 'OK,' I said quietly. 'I'm going.'

My exit wasn't that dignified. But I made up for it in the walk away. I took it slowly, not looking back. Across the street I was almost knocked over by a man in a suit hurrying past me. He was clearly late for something. Late or eager. He went scuttling down the stairs to the basement flat a few doors on. I had, of course, seen him before, though it would be a first for Colin. I turned to see if he had spotted him. But if he had, he wasn't looking any longer. Through the windscreen across the road I saw his head bowed down on to the steering-wheel. And I saw his body shaking. Well, well, my brother-in-law was sobbing.

It upset me more than I anticipated. When I got back to

my car, to my surprise I found that my hands weren't all that steady, either. I grabbed the portable phone out of the glove compartment. I even got as far as dialling Mum's number, but then pushed the button before it connected. Shit. I was damned if I did and damned if I didn't.

The drive to West London was full of heat and traffic. The encounter filled my head, Colin's anger like a chainsaw ripping through my thoughts. So much for not getting mad. Ah well, what had I expected? In the eight years of their marriage he and I have barely managed one conversation that hasn't had spikes in it. If it wasn't business, it was politics. If it wasn't politics, it was personal. That bullshit about not knowing a real relationship . . . If he was an example of one, God save me from them. But under the fury I was feeling bruised. Stupid not to admit it. Well, it was too late now. That's the point about anger. It helps you break the rules. Sometimes they need to be broken. What would he do? He'd have to tell her. He couldn't possibly risk letting me do it first. At least it would be out in the open. It couldn't be worse than it was now.

The Beauty Centre in the Chiswick High Road was one of a chain. It had a blue smoked-glass shop front with a picture of an implausibly long-legged woman reclining in space air-brushed on to it. I was so glad of an excuse to change topics that I was almost pleased to see her.

Inside it was familiar stuff: lots of young things in white uniforms hard at work with their witch-doctor creams and chemical scrubs. It was the kind of place where a private eye's card would cause quite a flurry. It would also protect me from being treated like a client. I flashed it at the receptionist. She was duly flustered. The manageress was checking the waxing rooms, but she made it short for me.

She was tall and fair, with too much makeup. So what's new? I was already bored looking at her. I followed her to her office, one of a dozen cubicles off a rabbit warren of a corridor, where no natural light penetrated. Smart thinking. Under the right artificial light all skin looks younger. It struck me that in all our encounters I had never seen Olivia Marchant in direct sunlight – that afternoon in the rain the face had been framed by the raincoat collar and hood. Maybe the sun would shrivel her. The image of the monkey returned. I shook my head to get rid of it.

'I'm afraid the records of our employees . . .'

Blah blah blah . . . She was making a passable imitation of a beauty salon manager, but I'd seen it all before and I had run out of patience. I'm afraid the meeting with Colin had seriously eroded my charm levels.

'Listen,' I said. 'Don't give me that crap. You don't have a choice. If you don't tell me, you'll have to tell the police within the next twenty-four hours, anyway. So why not accept the inevitable? All I want to know is what reason Lola Marsh gave for leaving here three months ago, and if you have any details on her records by which I might trace her.'

She stared at me for a second, then said, 'I have no idea who you're talking about.'

'Let's try again,' I said, barely keeping myself under control. 'She was small, plump and quiet. She worked here from June last year till late January. And you gave her a glowing reference which got her a job at Castle Dean in Berkshire. Ring a bell now?'

'What did you say her name was?'

'Lola Marsh,' I repeated, as if it was an enunciation lesson from *My Fair Lady*.

'I'm sorry. I've been manageress for over a year and in that time there has been no beautician of that name working here.'

'But her reference was written on your note paper. I saw a signature.'

'Then, whoever she is, she must have stolen the paper and forged it,' she answered, not without a certain pleasure. 'Now, if you'll excuse me, I have a busy day ahead of me.'

*   *   *   *

Back in the car I gloated over what I'd found out. So Lola Marsh was not just a saboteur, but a liar and a forger. From such minor felonies serious crimes can grow. But why? Not looking like Olivia Marchant was hardly enough of a reason to go and kill her husband. I was about to give it some further thought when the phone beeped. The connection was a little rough, but it was hard to tell if that was the battery running flat or her voice shaking. Either way it was becoming something of a habit, Carol Waverley distressed in my ear. She was whispering, as though afraid someone might be listening in. She said that the police had arrived at Castle Dean half an hour before. They had asked if they could have a look at Olivia's car and take some samples from her apartment. Olivia had been in it at the time, having arrived back with Carol late last night. When she refused, they had made it clear that they could always come back with a search warrant.

'Who do you mean by "they", Carol?' I said as I backed the car down a side road to get myself pointing in the right direction for the motorway.

'The two who interviewed me yesterday. Inspector Rawlings and a younger man –'

'Grant.'

'Yes. Grant.'

'Did they say what they were looking for?'

'No. Just that it was part of their inquiries. When I spoke to them yesterday . . .' But the line was cracking up again.

'Listen, I'll be there within the hour. I'll talk to you then. Put Olivia on the line, will you?'

'I can't. She's with them. She doesn't know I'm calling. Please, come soon. I think they think –'

To save the battery I switched her off. When will you learn, Hannah? Some machines are like people. If you don't feed them, they don't work. Anyway, I already knew what they thought. It had crossed my mind, too.

That they were back again so quickly meant that they knew more today than they had yesterday. And were taking it seriously. Maybe forensics had come up with something juicy. Or the janitor's eyesight had improved along with his memory and he'd fingered a good-looking woman with raised cheekbones.

With the sudden rush of summer, even Berkshire looked green and pleasant. I disturbed its dull Englishness with a few violent thoughts. I put a surgical knife into Olivia Marchant's hand and watched her plunge it into her husband's turned back. Then I saw her straddle his body and dig out his eyes. The first was an easy image, the emotion and the blood conjured out of a million bad movies. The second was rather more troublesome, but it was hard to know if that was because she hadn't done it, or because I hadn't ever seen it done.

I tried the scenario again with little Lola Marsh wielding the knife. Same problem. I decided to wait until I knew more.

Castle Dean looked lovely in the sun. God, I could do with a massage. I parked in the staff car park, next to Grant and Rawlings. At least they'd had the decency not to put themselves in the guest bays. I went in through the back entrance. Carol was in main reception. She looked awful, but then having your boss implicated in a murder charge would be bound to have a downside when it came to future job prospects. I followed her through the door marked 'private'. I remembered it well. When I was last here, Maurice Marchant was still making women beautiful and himself rich. What a difference a week makes.

We talked as we walked. 'Has anything happened since you called me?'

'Well, the young one . . . er . . . Grant, he came in to see me and asked me some questions. He wanted to know if I could remember what Mrs Marchant had been wearing when she got back that evening from London.'

'And could you?'

'Yes. I told him it was her Nicole Farhi culottes and her black Joseph waistcoat.'

Well, that must have knocked his British Home Stores socks off. But whether or not it was what he wanted to hear I had no idea.

'And then he asked if I'd seen her wearing a long black mac and hat. And I told him I had. It had been drizzling when she went to London in the morning and she'd had them on then.' The black mac. Of course. It certainly was a distinctive little outfit. The kind you wouldn't easily forget. Not her, not me. And presumably, not someone else, either. 'I was right, wasn't I? I mean to tell him?'

'If that is what she was wearing, then yes, you were right.'

'He seemed to think it was important,' she said, and I don't think I'd ever seen her quite so uncomfortable.

'Yes. Well, then it probably was.'

'Can you help her?' she asked anxiously.

'I think that depends on what she's done.'

And for the first time I could remember Carol Waverley didn't have anything to say.

*   *   *   *

They were coming down the back stairs as I was going up them. They were like a little posse: Olivia and a woman police officer with the sheriff and his deputy bringing up the rear. She was looking so old I almost didn't recognize her. Or maybe it was the daylight. For once she was a woman not in control of her lighting. 'Hannah?' she murmured as she saw me, and the voice sounded rather dazed.

'Hello, Olivia,' I said cheerfully. 'I've been trying to get hold of you. I need to talk to you. Could we have a quick word?'

I addressed it to the female police officer, who obviously had no idea what to do.

'Get out of the way, Miss Wolfe. If you don't mind.' Rawlings at his most polite. No wonder women get on so badly in the force. Always letting the men do the talking.

I ignored him and nodded at Grant. 'Thanks for calling,' I said. 'I got here as fast as I could.'

Well, at times like this you take pleasure where you can get it. And the look on Rawlings' face as he turned to Grant was pleasure indeed. Grant shook his head quickly. To him and to me. 'Hannah, don't make this any more difficult than it is already.'

'What's difficult? I assume you're not arresting her?'

'No. Mrs Marchant's just helping us with our inquiries.'

'Fine. Then I'd just like a quick word with her. She is my client.'

'Ex,' said Rawlings.

'Wrong,' I said fiercely. 'I'm still working for her. And I want to talk to her.'

'Listen, girlie –'

'No, you listen, *Rawlie*. I'd like to speak to my client, Olivia Marchant. She's not under arrest, she's not been cautioned, and she can talk to whoever she likes. You have no right to deny her access to me and you know it.'

He opened his mouth to launch a salvo, but Grant got in before the blast.

'Constable, why don't you take Mrs Marchant to the office? Miss Wolfe? Let's you and I have a word.'

In retrospect I think it probably represented a great step in his career. One of those Hollywood moments when a man does what a man has to do and everyone realizes that he was – well – a man all along, and no longer just a junior partner. Olivia and the police officer went off down the stairs. Grant turned to Rawlings. 'Five minutes, sir,' he said. 'I'll sort this out.'

Rawlings blew and snorted, then said: 'You'd better, Mike. You'd better. What is this? Fucking amateur's night out?' He stomped off, and you could tell that the swearing had made him feel better.

Well, now the bad language has started . . .

'Hannah –'

'You bastard. I gave you every scrap of information I had, saved you days of donkey work, co-operated absolutely, and you do this.'

'Hannah, officially I don't have to tell you anything.'

'So why the fuck did you promise that you would?'

'Listen –'

'Or more to the point, why did you lie to me?'

'I didn't lie.'

'Looking for a black mac and hat, are we? What happened? Did the watchman undergo hypnotherapy or did some other mysterious witness come forward at the last minute?'

He sighed. 'When we talked to him yesterday afternoon, he wasn't sure. He is now.'

'Bullshit. Did you find the mac?'

'No. And how did you know about it?'

'Not from you, that's for sure,' I said tartly. 'Where does Olivia say it is?'

'She doesn't have it. She says she thinks she must have left it at Marchant's consulting rooms Tuesday afternoon.'

'Which Carol Waverley can back up. She saw her come home without it.'

'Which only means she wasn't wearing it. But somebody certainly was at around 12.30 a.m. The janitor is willing to swear that the person he saw leaving the building had it on.'

'Yeah, but then with his eyesight it would hardly stand up in court, would it?' I said sweetly.

He gave an apologetic little shrug. 'He can see fine, Hannah.'

'Really. You astonish me. Still, I suppose it has occurred to you that you still don't have a shred of proof. Whoever murdered him could have found the mac in the office and put it on just to get out of the building. Which would be an altogether simpler explanation as to why she doesn't have it now.'

'Maybe. But then there's the problem with her alibi.'

'What do you mean?'

'I mean she can't prove she was here that night.'

'Don't be ridiculous. Carol Waverley and half the staff saw her come back.'

'She could have gone out again.'

'Yeah, and Detective Inspector Rawlings could be a Buddhist. Where's your proof?'

'The call she never took.'

'What call?'

He hesitated. And it was clear he thought I already knew.

'What call?' I said again.

'The one that came through from Maurice Marchant just before 11. I thought Carol Waverley would have told you. She was in the office working late when the phone rang. He said he'd been trying to get hold of his wife but she wasn't answering her direct line and he wondered if there was a fault on it. So Carol plugged it through from the main switchboard herself. She still didn't answer.'

Poor Carol. Everywhere she stood in this plot she put her foot in it. Anyone would think she was out to screw her employer. I stuck that one in the 'to be thought about later' file. 'Maybe she was asleep.'

'And maybe she wasn't there.'

'You've tested the line?'

'It works fine.'

'So maybe she was in the shower. Or she didn't want to talk to anyone. Have you thought of that?'

'Oh, come on, Hannah, we already know she had a flaming row with him about another woman.'

'Oh, don't be such a ditz head,' I said crossly. 'I was the other woman. He clocked me when I came to visit him that lunchtime. He knew I was some kind of snoop. When she saw him that afternoon, he accused her of trying to wreck the business by employing a private detective to check up on old clients.'

He stared at me for a second then gave a kind of nasty laugh. 'Oh, yes. You have been hard done by, haven't you, Hannah? Told us everything, while we just shafted you.'

'I'm sorry,' I said. 'It slipped my mind.'

But for the first time I had also surprised him. I could tell he was thinking back to the receptionist's testimony, seeing if it would fit one interpretation as well as another. Obviously well enough to give him room for pause. 'How do you know for sure?'

'Because Olivia told me. And,' I said before he could interrupt, 'because it fits. It was clear he was suspicious of me at the time. He even mentioned Olivia to me to see what impact it would have. Anyway, you haven't found any other evidence of a lover, have you?' He shrugged. 'Oh, come on, Michael. By now somebody must have checked the Amsterdam flight reservations for possible female names that might connect?'

He smiled just a fraction. 'All right. Yes, and no. As far as we can tell, he was travelling on his own.'

'See.'

'But in which case why didn't she tell us about the row?'

'I don't know, maybe that clutz Rawlings doesn't say please enough. Listen, the guy had had someone threatening him.'

'That's only what she says.'

'What? You really think she tried to sabotage her own health farm, and sent a set of anonymous notes to her husband herself?'

He shrugged. 'Put it this way. It wouldn't be the first time.'

'Is that how you do it? Find a similar crime and solve it that way. What is it? A new kind of cost-efficiency saving?'

'Hannah . . .'

'I suppose you've checked the handwriting?'

'It's not the same. But we're having it analysed.'

'How about forensics?'

'Well, Olivia Marchant's fingerprints are all over his office, but,' he said before I could get in, 'that doesn't mean anything. We've taken scrapes from her apartment and we're going over the car. We'll know soon enough if there's anything there.'

For 'anything' read blood on the upholstery or bits of eyes on her clothes. In which case, bye-bye Hannah, hello lawyers. He was right. They would know soon enough. Though, of course, that was no guarantee they would tell me. It had to be said that things weren't looking exactly rosy for Olivia. And she wasn't helping. 'But what I don't get is why she isn't sticking up for herself more. What does she do during these interviews?'

He shrugged. 'Not a lot. She just sits there looking blank. Very calm, very far away. Weird.'

'She needs a doctor.'

'She's seen one. She's in mild shock, but nothing bad enough to stop her answering questions. Listen, Hannah, nobody's out to screw her. It's just there's stuff building up against her and she isn't that interested in denying any of it.'

'So let me talk to her. Maybe I can find out why. It might save you some time in the long run.'

He made a clicking noise. 'Rawlings'll have me back on traffic duty.'

'Yeah, yeah,' I said. 'I can see that he scares the living daylights out of you. Let me see her just for one minute. It's going to look dreadful on your record, harassing the wrong woman.'

Chapter Seventeen

I got what I wanted. I took Olivia into Carol's office, where we had sat five nights before, where she had been so lovely in the night glow and so very certain of herself and her cause. Now, with the daylight streaming in, it was something of an illusion exposed. The face was still impressive, although a little ironed out around the eyes. But the sunshine was crueller to the neck: look closely and you could spot the tell-tale rings, a few dry puckered little creases. It was the contrast that made it so unsettling. Had her face not seemed so young, you probably wouldn't have noticed, would have thought her an attractive woman growing old gracefully. Maybe necks are harder to keep young. Or maybe there had been limits to Marchant's powers after all. Now I realized that in all our other meetings she had worn some kind of scarf or polo neck. It seemed she no longed cared. Oh, Olivia. What are you going to do now he's gone? Who's going to iron out life's wrinkles and pin up those jowls? But she had other things on her mind.

'They think I did it,' she said at last.

'Yes, they do. But then you're not telling them any different.' She shrugged. 'Why didn't you answer the phone Tuesday night when it rang?' I said sharply.

She sighed. 'Because I'd taken a sleeping pill. I was tired and upset and I didn't want to be disturbed.'

'But you didn't tell *them* that?'

'I said I was asleep. They weren't interested in knowing any more.'

'And what about the row that the receptionist overheard at

the office that afternoon? Why didn't you tell them it was about me? If you don't tell them, they don't know.'

'They don't want to know. They just want quick answers.'

'Christ, Olivia, what is wrong with you?'

She stared at me with a slightly puzzled look on her face. 'Why should you care, anyway? I thought you weren't interested any more. I thought we had to "leave it to the police".' She shook her head slightly. 'Does this mean you're still working for me after all?'

'Only if you didn't kill him,' I said to see what kind of response it got.

She gave a bitter little smile. 'See. Now you think it too.'

'I don't think anything, Olivia. Except that if you didn't do it I can't believe how a woman of your intelligence can be so stupid, however much pain you're in.'

The remark stung her, as I intended it to do. She looked up at me. 'You wouldn't understand if I told you.'

'Why don't you try me?'

She looked at me for a moment. I had seen that look once before in this room, when she was staring at Lola Marsh, watching, waiting, trying to define the malice in the motive. Then eventually she spoke.

'You want to know if I killed my husband, right? Let me tell you about Maurice and me. I was twenty-nine when I met him and for as long as I can remember I had been ugly. My mother used to say – what was her phrase? – "that I'd been ruined by a trick of nature", inheriting her body but my father's face. I don't remember him well – he died in a car crash when I was nine – though he never struck me as ugly. She was right about me, though. D'you know what I looked like? – one of those women from the Habsburg dynasty after centuries of inbreeding. We had a portrait once in the gallery I worked in. A Spanish duchess, she was. I couldn't even look at her. It was like looking in a mirror.

'Then I met Maurice. He was just starting out in reconstructive surgery. He was interested in me right from the beginning.

It was at an opening and I'd been working late. He came up and started talking to me. He said he'd been looking at me across the room and did I know that I had the most lovely eyes. I thought he was laughing at me. But he was absolutely serious. Then he told me what he did and how easy it would be to make my eyes light up my face. Those were his words. I remember them exactly. I was so embarrassed I was rude to him. He didn't care. He was excited. For him it was a challenge. He was so sure, he even offered to do it for free, wouldn't take no for an answer. He came back the next day, took me out to dinner, and asked me again. Three weeks later he did the first work on my jaw.

'It took four operations in all. Step by step I didn't notice the difference. Then one morning I woke up, the bruising was gone and there I was, a Habsburg no longer. And he was right. I was beautiful underneath.

'A few months later my mother died and my father's money came to me. There was quite a lot of it. We used it to set up in business. His first clinic and a small health club in the city, before such places became fashionable.

'And that's how we started, Maurice and I. Not exactly the most conventional way to fall in love. But the only way I know about. And that's how it's been ever since. A sort of partnership. I've looked after him and the business, and he's looked after me. Kept me from my Habsburg past. Maybe it was need as much as love, I don't know. But whatever it was, it worked. Gave us both what we wanted.' She shook her head. 'Even now every time I look in the mirror I see him reflected in my face. Killing him would have been like killing a bit of myself.'

Life stories. You hear a lot of them in this job. For this one read Pygmalion with a touch of Faust. But being extra-ordinary doesn't necessarily make something untrue. And for what it's worth, it didn't feel like she was lying. By compari-son my own love life made thin dramatic gruel – sporadic moments of passion or obsession followed by long retreats of boredom and regret. On the other hand at least I didn't find myself emotionally decomposing in the aftermath. And not just emotionally. Maybe there's something to be said for not being that touched by a man.

I wondered briefly why they had not had children. Together twenty years – they must have thought about it. Maybe the physical ravages of pregnancy had always outweighed the passion and joy that any child might have brought. Theirs was, after all, a relationship of priorities. I looked at her. Beneath the left eye the skin on her cheekbone twitched a little – an involuntary movement, as if the strain of the hidden construction was beginning to take its toll. I had a sudden flash of a suspension bridge, tight and majestic, all the weight borne on a few shimmering steel cords. What happened if they snapped? It didn't bear thinking about.

'So,' she said, 'are you still working for me, or do I have to wait until the scientists prove me innocent?'

'They might be more help to you than I am,' I said. 'I'm not exactly getting very far.'

She looked at me for a moment. 'Perhaps that's because you don't know enough,' she said quietly. 'I'm afraid there's something I haven't told you. At the time I didn't think it was important, but now . . . well . . .'

Clients, always the same. Always a little added extra hidden away in the back of the brief. Just because they pay you, they think it's their prerogative. I tell you, you need to be a mind-reader to do this job properly. I looked at her. Sex, I thought. It's got to be sex. 'I'm listening.'

'About six months ago, after we'd bought Castle Dean and I was living here full time trying to get it started, Maurice came to me and told me that he was having an affair with a patient.'

Yeah. Bingo.

She gave a wry smile. 'I already knew, of course. Well, cosmetic surgeons can be very powerful figures in women's lives – as I know better than most. In the past there had been maybe one or two that had ended up in bed with him. But he was always very careful, and it was never serious. That was part of the deal between us. But this one was different. He told me it had started out casual, but that she'd become very involved and now she was threatening to go public over the affair if he didn't agree to leave me and live with her.

'He said he was scared of alienating her. That he wanted to finish it, he just didn't know how. It was typical of Maurice, really. Getting carried away with the power of his own creation, then expecting me to bail him out. Only this time I didn't. I suppose I was angry he'd let it go so far. So I told him it was his problem. That if he wanted to leave me, I wouldn't stand in his way, but that I wasn't going to humiliate myself getting involved with some crazy woman who thought she'd found a way of blackmailing him for a meal ticket.'

'What did he say?'

'Nothing. But a week later he came back and told me that it was over. He didn't say any more and I didn't ask. He even brought me a present. A holiday in the Bahamas. While we were there, he asked me to give up the health farm and come back to London to live with him full time. To keep him from temptation, no doubt. In the end we compromised. I brought in Carol to run the place so that we could spend more time together in London.'

'And is that when he did the last face-lift?' I asked, somewhat appalled by my cruelty, but needing to see her reaction.

Once again she surprised me by not being offended. 'What do you want to know, Hannah? Whether or not the knife was a substitute for sex between us?'

You bet, I thought.

'The answer is no.' She paused and gave just the ghost of a smile. 'Although maybe it was occasionally another way of showing commitment. Does that make any kind of sense to you?'

I gave a little shrug. Not really. But if I began to worry about ideology again, she might find herself without a private

184

eye. And right at this moment she needed one. 'What about the other woman?' I said after a while.

'She disappeared out of our lives completely. He never said who she was and I never asked. Months went by and everything was fine.'

'Until the letters started to come,' I said softly.

'Yes.' She paused. 'Until the letters started to come.'

'Is that why you didn't show them to him?'

'No. It never occurred to me they were connected. Not at first. I mean it was all in the past. He never mentioned her. No, I didn't show him because I really didn't want him disturbed.'

'Olivia,' I said quietly. 'Either you tell me the truth or I leave right now.'

She stared at me, then closed her eyes. 'I swear I didn't know they were from her. How could I? But yes, I suppose I didn't show them to him because I didn't want to take the risk. Whoever wrote them was obviously desperate. If it was her, I didn't want him to feel responsible.'

'So what about me? Why didn't you tell me?'

'Because it was nothing to do with you,' she snapped. 'Because whatever had happened between us before was private and unimportant,' she continued fiercely. Since it seemed so important for her to believe it, I didn't contradict her. Or at least not with words. She shook her head. 'Anyway, from something he'd said at the time I was sure that the relationship had started when she came back to complain about some treatment or other. I thought if you were any good at your job you'd be able to find her from that description. And if it wasn't her, if it was a genuine crank, then it was most likely to have been an angry patient anyway.'

Maybe, I thought, maybe not. I let her stew in it for a bit.

'Well,' I said at last, 'is that it?' Because, of course, I was pretty sure it wasn't.

'There's one more thing. The afternoon before he died, when we had the row about you coming to the clinic –'

'You showed him a copy of the letter?'

She nodded, suitably impressed by my deduction. I decided not to tell her it hadn't been that hard. 'He was so furious at the idea of you spying on him that the only way I could get through to him was to tell him the whole story.'

'And he recognized the handwriting?'

'Yes. I saw it immediately in his face. But he didn't say anything. He just told me that if any of this got out, it would ruin the business, and that I'd been stupid to get you involved. He said I should get rid of you immediately and that he'd handle it. He told me it had nothing to do with me and I wasn't to worry. That he'd sort it out . . .' She hesitated. 'I started to tell you that morning at the flat after . . . but you didn't want to hear. You said you couldn't work for me any longer and we should leave it to the police. But they were already looking for a reason to accuse me. If I had told them about the affair, they would have just twisted it against me.'

And there was some truth in that. Still . . . 'Well, you've not exactly convinced them of your innocence now by not telling them.'

She shook her head, and I watched that subtly older neck swallow a few wild gulps of saliva as she tried to keep back the tears. They had come out of nowhere, surprising her as much as me. She dropped her eyes and I waited while she struggled to regain control. At last she spoke again, but so quietly that I had to strain to hear her. 'Maybe they're right. Maybe I did kill him. I mean I was the one who showed him the letter. Maybe if he hadn't seen it, he would never have . . . I mean he might still be here now.'

'Maybe,' I said deliberately, resisting the emotion. 'But he isn't and you are. And you don't strike me as the kind of woman to let someone else destroy it all without fighting back.'

She looked at me and I thought I caught something of the old spark in her eyes.

'Anyway, if you don't tell them, I'll have to. Otherwise I

risk getting done for withholding evidence. And I can't afford that.'

She opened her mouth to protest, then closed it again. 'All right,' she said. 'I'll tell them.'

'Fine.' I got up and went to the door. 'Last question, Olivia. And I strongly suggest you tell me the truth. Do you have any idea who this woman was?'

She looked at me. Maurice had been right – she did have lovely eyes. The kind you could fall into. She shook her head. 'I know it doesn't make any sense, but I keep seeing Lola Marsh in front of me. When she came to me that day and said that she wanted to work with Maurice, well, it was clear she knew all about him and the business already.'

'She'd never been a patient, though.'

'No. And I even checked her handwriting before you came in that night. It wasn't the same at all. But I keep remembering her manner. That barely contained fury. Maybe you were right about that night. Maybe I shouldn't have just let her go.'

'So why did you?' I said, though I already knew the answer.

'Because in the end it couldn't have been Lola.' And she laughed. 'Just think about what she looked like, poor squat little troll. Not his type at all. No, believe me the only infidelity that Maurice would have allowed himself would have been a beautiful one.'

Chapter Eighteen

Grant, of course, was waiting outside for me. He'd obviously put himself on the line, letting me see her for so long, and he needed to know it would pay off. So I told him she'd made a confession, then counted to five before I added that it wasn't quite the one he was looking for.

He was so eager to get back to questioning her that he didn't bother to make sure that I had left the building. We didn't even banter any more. But then that was all right with me. I always lose interest when the plot picks up. Must be something to do with displaced adrenalin.

I didn't even get a flutter when I bumped into Martha in the car park, all dressed and ready for work: white shoes, white tights, white uniform. Positively virginal. Except for the smile. 'Well, well. The private detective – back so soon. How you doing?'

'Not bad,' I said.

'I hear I got the wrong girl. Sorry about that.'

I shrugged. 'It was an easy mistake. At least you got the right room.'

'Seems a bit irrelevant now, though, doesn't it?'

'A bit.'

'How is she?'

'Mrs Marchant? Upset.'

'Rich, though.'

'Yes,' I said. Hmm, add that to the list of motives and you could see how tasty the police must have found her. 'I suppose she is.'

'They took away her car, you know.'

'Yes.'

'They must think they can find something.'

'Maybe.'

'She's in trouble, isn't she?'

I was interested in how sure Martha sounded. 'Well, you obviously think so.'

She looked at me and for that second I thought she was going to say something else, something that would turn it all around, deliver it to me on a plate. Ah, the fantasies of private detectives. Instead she just laughed. 'What do I know? I'm just the hired help.'

'Oh, I'm not so sure. I hear they left you in charge for a while.'

She grinned. 'Yeah, can't you tell? The place is running better already. Your shoulders are still in a bad way, though.'

'Worse,' I said. 'Much worse.'

'Well, the offer still stands.'

'Thanks. By the way, what did you make of Lola Marsh?'

She laughed. 'Thumbelina of the face-packs? Well, she had me fooled.'

'So I should keep her on my list?'

She shrugged. 'I thought he was stabbed in the back.'

'He was.'

'She'd have had to stand on a chair then, wouldn't she?'

'I suppose she would.' I smiled and opened the car door. Castle Dean would miss her, no doubt about it. 'Oh, by the way, did you hear about your job?'

'Yeah. I got it.'

'Congratulations. So when do you go?'

'Er . . . I haven't quite decided.'

Interesting. Maybe she'd got a taste for Carol's power. Or maybe she'd just found a new playmate. I rather hoped it was the latter. That way at least somebody in this mess would be having a bit of fun. She gave me a wave and headed off to her G5 sponge heads.

I played with the idea of Lola Marsh all the way up the motorway. But although every which way she threw up more questions than I could answer, she still didn't make my nerves tingle. Maybe I was just falling into Olivia's trap, equating beauty with substance. But I don't think so. Somehow, Lola just didn't seem big enough to have done it. And I didn't just mean size. I slid her back on to the B list.

At the end of the motorway I stopped for petrol and a sandwich. The girl at the service-station counter was painting her fingernails, each one a different colour. Not Castle Dean style at all. I watched her as she used one hand to pull through the credit-card form, and wiggled the fingers of the other to dry her nails in the breeze. She was marvellous. Big and punky with tatty jeans, a skimpy T-shirt and methodically tousled black hair. Her body had that lovely plumpness that some young women get in their early twenties, a puppy-dog quality to the flesh, rich and generous. As she pushed the form across the counter to me, the open-armed T-shirt exposed a flash of a ripe breast. She grinned and hoisted her shoulder strap up a little higher. After so much worked-over flesh it was a pleasure to see somebody so unselfconscious about her body. But then, of course, it was presumably her own. Would Maurice Marchant have fancied her? I wondered. Those perfect natural curves? Or was his lust, as I suspected, more narcissistic than that?

Interesting how the mind wanders when left to its own devices. Visual clues – the subconscious' way of letting you know it's still there.

On past experience I reckoned the portable had life in it for one more phone call. I was about to pick it up when Carol Waverley beat me to it, a woman desperately trying to keep abreast of the plot. 'Where did you go? I expected to see you afterwards.'

'Sorry, Carol. I had an appointment.'

'What happened with the police? What did Olivia say?'

I gave her a resumé of the story so far, leaving out the infidelity. Its absence put more emphasis on that 11 o'clock phone call that Olivia never answered. It had obviously been causing her grief too.

'I tried to tell you about it this morning, but we got cut off. I told the police that she had been exhausted and was obviously asleep, but I knew they'd twist it around.'

'It's their job, Carol,' I said. 'It's called detecting. Listen, you know the best thing you can do?' I added, acutely aware of the state of my battery.

'What?'

'Keep an eye on her and let me know if you find anything that might help. OK?'

'No, don't hang up. That's what I'm trying to tell you. I have found something.'

'What?'

'Well, you remember how before Maurice's death you asked us to check out which of our clients had been referred from Castle Dean to his clinic? To see if any of the names matched?'

I remember that I had asked Olivia to do it, yes. But then obviously computer filing was beneath her dignity, and she had passed it on to someone of worthier status. 'Yes?' The line crackled ominously.

'Well, after I'd done it, Olivia suggested that I hold on to the malpractice list, just in case any of the names should come up again. Anyway, this afternoon I did some work, just to take my mind off things. We send out a mailing shot every two months or so. You know – special offers, discounts, new treatments, that kind of thing. It was already overdue and Olivia had asked me to see to it. The mailing list is on computer. It includes all previous guests, of course, but also anyone who's written in for a brochure or made an inquiry over the last six months. It's just a way of following them up really.'

'And?' Even intimately cradled between my shoulder and my ear, she was fast beginning to sound like an early Marconi recording. If she didn't get there soon, she never would.

'Anyway, I was going through the addresses to check if there was anyone I could discard when I saw the name. I was sure I'd seen it before, so I checked the other list. So I told Olivia, and she said I should call you.'

'Who was it?' God, a girl (and a battery) could die waiting for the punch-line.

'Belinda Balliol?'

Some people call it coincidence, some people call it *Zeitgeist*, some people even call it morphic resonance. Me, I don't have a name for it, I just know that when it happens I get this little shiver up and down my spine. 'Let me get this right. You're saying that someone called Belinda Balliol rang in with a request for a brochure and details of the health farm?'

'Yes, that's right.'

'When exactly?'

'April 24th. It's on the file.'

A little over a month ago. Just before all the trouble started. 'Great. But as far as you know she never came there?'

'Well, if she did, she didn't leave her real name, or she'd be on the other file. But I've been thinking about that. I mean we do these special one-day visits. Most people pay by cash for those and she could always have filled the form in wrongly if she hadn't wanted us to know who she really was. What's more they include a facial and a face massage. I checked the back rotas. On most of the day visits Lola Marsh was doing those.'

See what happens when you let a private eye loose on a profession. Everybody gets the bug. 'It's certainly possible, yes. Listen, d'you want to give me the address that you sent that brochure to?'

'I've got it here. Care of the Majestic Casino, London. Does that help?'

'Yes and no,' I answered. 'Thanks, anyway.'

'Hannah?'

'Yeah.'

'Is it important? I mean – should I tell the police too?'

'Are they still there?'

'They've just left. Olivia said I should tell you first.'

I looked at my watch. After 3. Given their resources, if she told them today I wouldn't stand a chance. Well, they'd already had two early mornings this week. They'd probably appreciate an evening off. I told her no just as the line went down. I think she heard me.

       *   *   *   *

This time I didn't bother with cover stories. Just showed the guy at the desk my card. My other card, that is. He wasn't that impressed. Maybe it was just part of the culture: private eyes in private clubs. I asked for the manager, but he hadn't arrived. The owner was around, though. But then for him business was obviously its own kind of pleasure. Though he was a good deal less Confucian second time around.

'Mr Aziakis. What a surprise.'

'For you maybe, not for me.' The handshake was firm; old bones, but still capable of putting on the squeeze. 'I hear you're looking for Belinda Balliol? What happened? Have you spent the money already?'

'No,' I said. 'It's under my mattress. Why? Is that a problem?'

'Not at all. The only "problem" was you following her into the staff area afterwards.'

My, my, the all-knowing eye. And I had tried so hard to be discreet. 'How did you know?'

He shrugged.

'She didn't do anything wrong,' I said firmly.

'Yes, that's what she said.'

'What else did she say?'

'Nothing. She refused to discuss the incident.'

'But you didn't sack her? I mean the man at the desk said she was on holiday.'

'Miss Wolfe, I don't like private detectives. In my experience they only ever come into my business when there is trouble. You want to tell me one good reason why you should be any different?'

Maybe it was the accent that made him sound wise. Take that away and he was probably just an old thug. I sighed. 'Because I didn't cheat you out of any money,' I said. 'And because trouble is what you've got with or without me.'

So I told him. Version one, that is: the unhappy client with a grudge to bear. Interestingly he didn't think much of it.

'You want my opinion?'

'Very much.'

'I don't think Belinda Balliol was unhappy with her body . . .' He left a pause. Timing. It can in some circumstances be mistaken for wisdom. 'Though she used to be.'

'What does that mean?'

'When she first came here nine, maybe ten months ago. She was unhappy about herself then. Very unsure. But gradually she became different.'

'Physically, you mean?'

'Physically, mentally. In all kinds of ways. It was most interesting to watch. The breasts, the face – the nose and cheekbones in particular, I think. All this changed.'

'You notice a lot,' I said.

'I like women.' He shrugged. 'I'm just a little too old for them to like me.'

Oh, I don't know, I thought. I bet you score higher than any woman of your age. Power – stuck on top of a pair of testicles it's worth a dozen face-lifts. Maurice Marchant used to be living proof of that.

So Belinda had not stopped at the chest. Nose and cheekbones as well, eh? Maybe that had been Maurice's way of compensating for the hard silicone. Or maybe he'd just found in her another Olivia: someone ripe for the changing. And the bedding. Until he decided to get out, leaving her looking great but feeling bad.

'And when did all this take place?' I asked.

'Last year. Not long after she came. The summer, I think. She was very happy then. Lots of smiles and charm.'

'And then?'

'Then I don't know. Something changed. She was more attractive but also more difficult.'

'How "difficult"?'

'More above it all. Withdrawn. As if we all owed her a living. It caused some resentment among the other girls.'

Boy, this guy really knew his staff. What do you bet he put the make on all of them, just in case? 'So why didn't you get rid of her?'

'Because in this profession you don't kill the goose that lays the golden eggs. The Majestic customers liked her. There was something about her looks and her rather cold confidence that made them want to play at her table. Each casino has a honeypot. For a while she was ours.'

'For a while?' He nodded but said nothing. 'So what happened the night I came?'

'Perhaps you should tell me. She was quite angry, that much I know. When I called her in and asked her what had happened, she wouldn't say a word. She told me to mind my own business. I pointed out that nine hundred pounds *was* my business, but she still wouldn't speak. I made it clear that if she refused to tell me, I'd have to ask her to leave. I gave her a day to think about it. As it happened, she had two weeks' leave due, anyway.'

'Mexico,' I said.

He frowned. 'Maybe. I don't remember. Anyway, I asked her to call me before she went.'

'And?'

'And she never did. I haven't heard from her since.'

*   *   *   *

He turned out to be so helpful that I felt guilty about not offering him his money back. He gave me the key to her locker and, as I was leaving, pressed into my hand a slip of paper with Belinda's address and telephone number. Sometimes there's a lot to be said for being a woman – even if his fingers did linger a little too long in mine.

The locker was a severe disappointment. Just a spare purple chiffon dress, a carton of Lil-lets, a copy of *Time Out* and of *Vogue*, and a paperback of *Tess of the D'Urbervilles*. Unfortunately she wasn't the kind of girl to write her name in the flyleaf. I turned to the cosmetic ads in *Vogue*.

She hadn't been interested enough to biro any of them. A cursory flick through the *Time Out* revealed an article on the dangers of cosmetic surgery. I checked the cover. It was dated six weeks ago.

Aziakis was standing behind me. I rolled up the magazine and slid it deep into my bag, keeping my back between him and the locker. If I had stopped to think, I probably wouldn't have done it. Well, whichever way you cut it, the magazine was evidence. But what Grant and Rawlings never saw, they could never miss.

The telephone number Aziakis had given me turned out to be the same as the one I found in the file on her. I called from the casino. I didn't expect her to be in, but it was worth checking. The answering machine clicked on. Sorry, can't take your call. The same jaunty voice. The same jaunty message. Good. That left the address.

It was a small street a stone's throw away from West End Lane, lined with little thirties-style semis, some neater and more cared for than others. No. 22 was one of the better ones. There was a red Labour sticker in the top window for an election that was already over. Funny. I didn't have her down as a political animal. I rang the doorbell just to make doubly sure she wasn't there. She wasn't.

But somebody else was. He looked much more the Labour-sticker type, and he'd never heard of Belinda Balliol. He was sub-letting the house from a mate who'd gone to Saudi on a job. As far as he knew, the mate had been living there for about six months. He didn't know who'd been there before or where I might find them. In the car I looked at Belinda's phone number again. As she had kept it after moving, I assumed she must still be living in the area, but I couldn't tell much else until I had had a look at my trusty British Telecom code book. It was time to go home.

The light on my machine was blinking welcome. I whirled back the tape and listened as a gruff male voice told me his name was Patrick Rankin, that he was still in Majorca, and could be reached at the following number. I wrote it down, but couldn't get excited about it. I'd long since crossed him off my list.

I made myself a cup of coffee and ate a packet of custard creams. The sugar rush was better than the caffeine. From my bag I dug out the *Time Out* article, just in case. But I'd seen it all before: exploding tits, sucked thighs, over-stretched faces. It read like the synopsis of a David Cronenberg film.

I was turning the page as I caught sight of my face in the mirror above the table. For a second it shocked me. Caught in repose I looked older than I remembered, the skin around the eyes a little worn, a definite droop to the corners of the mouth. Intimate moments of a private eye. How much would it worry me, no longer being young? I pulled back my cheeks to see what kind of drop we were talking about and my face jumped up a couple of centimetres. I batted my eyelashes and tried to smile. It wasn't a pretty sight. I let gravity re-establish control.

From above my right eye the scar winked at me, its glossy stretch of skin catching the light. I gave a big grin back. Little lines exploded everywhere. Behind every last one of them there was a history – a recurring gesture, a joke, a story, a moment of pleasure or even pain. Take the lines away and who would I be? Not someone younger, that's for sure. I picked up the phone and went back to work.

Chapter Nineteen

With the A–Z open at page 43 I closed my eyes and dive-bombed my biro on to a square. J7. I picked out one of its streets. The British Telecom code book, which comes free to every happy subscriber, had already helped me locate the 328 prefix as an area where West Hampstead meets Kilburn. Now I had an address to go with it. I was about to dial the operator when a call came in. It was the other crime in my life. The domestic one. As soon as I heard her voice, I felt bad. But that could have been my guilt at managing so many hours without thinking about her. 'Hi, Kate. How's it going?'

'You remember home. Nothing much changes here.'

'Yeah, I gather the video recorder hasn't made it to Kent yet. Amy left a message on my machine, asking me to collect yours and drive it down for her.'

'Did she? The little monkey. Well, you know Mum. She still thinks television makes your eyes go square if you watch too much of it. She's trying to interest them in jigsaws.'

There was a pause. The engineers on the 328 exchange would be busy going home. I needed to be about my business. But then so did she.

'Hannah?'

'Yeah?'

'Have you – have you seen or spoken to Colin at all since I've been gone?'

I took a deep breath. 'Why do you ask?'

'Um . . . It's just that he called today. He wants to see me. He's coming up tomorrow and we're going out for a meal.'

'It's a weekday,' I said.

'Yes. He's taking time off work.'

'Is he ill?'

She had the grace to ignore it. 'Listen, he asked me if I'd talked to you at all.'

'He did?'

'Yes.'

'What did you say?'

'I said I'd mentioned that we were having some trouble. He was furious. He said that you'd always made it your business to undermine him, and that wasn't what we needed right now. I told him you'd been very sympathetic, but he made me promise not to talk to you again until he'd seen me.'

'So what are we doing now?'

'Well, I suppose . . . I just wanted to check. I know how you two feel about each other and I didn't want you . . . er . . .'

'Going round and shouting abuse through his letter-box?'

She laughed, evidently relieved. 'Something like that.'

'No,' I said. 'Don't worry. I've no intention of seeing or speaking to Colin before you do.' Technical truths. Not the same as emotional lies. 'What do you think he's going to say?'

There was a silence on the other end of the line. 'I don't know,' she said at last.

But you've missed him, I thought. You've missed the scumbag, I can hear it in your voice. And that means whatever he tells you, you'll give him a second chance. Erring men and forgiving women. They were coming at me from all angles. Ah well, what did I know about true love? Or even untrue love for that matter. But I tell you, I was learning.

'Thanks,' she said. 'I'll . . . I'll give you a call when we get home.'

Can't wait. I went back to homicide. The British Telecom repairs operator for the 328 area took a while to answer. I was so worried I'd missed them that when I did get through I had trouble sounding like a bored engineer.

'Yeah,' I said. 'I'm checking fault lines on this prefix. Can you plug me through to routing and records please?'

The line clicked, rang and connected again. A man's voice answered, crisp, busy. 'Yep, R and R.'

'Hi. I'm working on a fault on 328 9999.'

'Yeah, and I'm going home. What's your problem?'

'The problem is it's not the line. I think it must be in the house. Can you confirm the address for me? I've got 17 Cotleigh Road,' I said, lifting up my finger from its resting place in the middle of square J7.

'Hold on.' He punched the number up on his computer and came back to me. 'No. You're way out. It's Fairbray, on the other side of the Kilburn High Road. No. 22. Who gave you Cotleigh?'

'Obviously somebody who's working for Mercury,' I said, but I'm not sure he got the joke. 'Thanks, anyway.'

'No prob. Didn't know we had a woman working on this sector.'

'Positive discrimination,' I replied. 'It's the only way forward.' And I blew him a kiss down the line.

I didn't bust a gut to get there. Well, if she had been doing something violent on Tuesday evening, she wasn't likely to have stayed around to answer questions. She might even have been telling the truth and be sunning herself in Mexico. Nice place if you can afford the ticket.

Outside it was airless, a heavy sky creating an early dusk. A city on the edge of a thunderstorm, so leaden and forbidding that people already had their lights on.

I used the drive to make up some stories about Belinda Balliol. First I started with the facts. As part of a self-improvement campaign, she'd gone to Maurice Marchant sometime last summer and bared her chest to him. He had done his stuff but she hadn't been satisfied with the result.

From here on fact turned to fiction. Or possibly faction. If she was the lady I was looking for, then during the next couple of breast examinations his hands wandered (or had been guided) further south and the result had been a new body both for Belinda (free offer?) and for Maurice. The lovelier she became, the more infatuated he was with his own work. Until, that is, she started asking for more than new body parts. Then came Olivia's ultimatum, his rejection and her cold withdrawal. Six months ago, Olivia had said. Which was the same time as Belinda started to behave oddly at work, moving house and failing to give anyone her new address. A couple of months after that Marchant started getting letters, while Belinda made inquiries about Castle Dean health farm, perhaps even went there to meet the dour Lola.

Hardly surprising then that when I appear on the scene asking questions, she freaks out, going out of her way to lie about the operation and avoid seeing me again. The following afternoon Olivia shows Maurice a copy of the anonymous note. He recognizes the handwriting and calls her number. She does or doesn't reply. Either way he ends up with an eye operation he didn't need, while she loses her job and disappears into the blue yonder.

Well, you have to admit it did have a certain swing.

Which was more than can be said for Kilburn. Rumour has it that it's an upwardly mobile area now, but then rumour can be a dangerous thing. As far as I could tell, it hadn't changed since the last time I crawled through its traffic jams and walked its littered High Street.

On the other hand Fairbray Road certainly took me by surprise. The houses there turned out to be very nice indeed. Double-fronted most of them and worth a good few bob. Even renting you'd be in need of a good income. Bigger than hers would have been, that's for sure. Unless someone had given her a down payment.

Number 22 looked pretty shut up to me. The curtains upstairs were all drawn and the windows locked tight. The air would be foul in there. It was foul out here.

I rang the bell, keeping my finger hard down while I sang an entire verse of 'Heatwave'. Nobody came to join in the chorus. The glass panels in the door were wired and the street busy with people coming home, so I decided to go round the back.

Things were a lot easier there. It was quiet, not overlooked, and the back door was flimsy; old wood and older glass. I wrapped my jacket round my forearm and gave it a smart backhand. I didn't even cut myself finding the lock inside.

The passage inside was dark. And I was right about the air. It was foul, but with more than just heat. A sickly, rotting smell rose up to greet me, as if someone had left some meat out too long. It was the kind of aroma to make a private eye nervous, especially in an empty house with a missing suspect. I pinged on a hall light and let my nose do the detecting.

It took me as far as the kitchen. It was seriously fetid in there, though the fridge was empty and the work surfaces clean, just as you'd expect of someone who'd gone to Mexico. I finally tracked the stench down to under the table where a cat's bowl had been pushed to the back of the wall. It could easily have been overlooked in any last-minute departure. There was half a tin of food still in it. Or, to be more precise, trying to get out. I recognized the seething movement. They were becoming something of a feature in this story, maggots. Some clues come wriggling.

It made me sure of one thing. I should be wearing gloves. I dug out a pair of thin plastic ones from my bag and stretched them on. My hands were now the same colour as the maggots. I picked up the bowl, slammed it in the sink and turned the hot tap on full. The water came out scalding. They writhed and squirmed their way down the plug hole. I threw the bowl in the dustbin, checked the two reception rooms and made my way upstairs.

The smell persisted, curling its way around the banisters, hovering like mist in the air. There was still no sign of any cat. Maybe it had gone to a cattery. I certainly couldn't remember seeing a cat flap anywhere.

On the floor above I started with the main bedroom. The double bed was made, but with a slight indentation in the cover, as if someone had lain on it afterwards, and there was a towel on the floor near by. On the bedside table were a glass and an empty bottle of pills. Nembutal, prescribed on the 5th of April, according to the label. Maybe her conscience had been keeping her awake. In the wardrobe I found a set of tasty-looking clothes neatly pressed and hung up. Underneath was a suitcase. It was empty, but then she might have had two.

Across the landing there was a sparsely furnished study. On a desk sat an Amstrad computer. I thought about all those computer-printed notes to the health farm and went through the drawers looking for disks or bits of paper that might connect one to the other. Nothing. The place looked as if it had been cleaned out. I had to make do with the waste-paper basket. I was lucky it was made of metal, otherwise it would have been more than the papers that would have burnt. Fortunately for me she'd made a bad job of it. Either she'd been in a rush or not come back to check. The sheaf of pages had been so tied together that there had not been enough oxygen to carry the flame.

I lifted out a couple of half-charred sheets. They were letters, written in a long loopy hand on plain white paper. I held one of them up to the light. A blackened edge had eaten into the words:

... like I do. You must know that by now, Maurice. Every time you touch me, we both know it. I love you. More than she does, whatever you may say. You don't owe her anything. You must realize that. I can make you happy. I can't bear to think of you living there like this. In the end it can only ...

The rest of the sentence was gone, not burnt this time but cut away with a pair of scissors. What word would you have put next? Hurt? Damage?

Outside, the sky moaned with distant thunder and the

trees shivered with the prospect of rain. I picked another letter out of the bin. There was an awful monotony to the text: love, need, exhortations to leave. Other people's love letters – nothing so private, nor so painful. Especially these, since their presence here all together must mean that the man they'd been written to had given them back. But when? Only one date had survived the flames. October 24th. Just weeks before Maurice had admitted he was having an affair. I looked again, this time studying the words for their shape rather than their meaning. The *m*s and the *a*s. I found the word 'me'. It was, of course, already familiar. A tall swoop – up down, up down – and a tightly curled little *e* hanging on for dear life.

My, what a poetic shock it would have been if he *had* opened them himself, to read what had once been words of love regurgitated into hate. I dropped them back into the bin.

And as I did so, I heard a noise – a rasping kind of sound, fierce and frantic, coming from somewhere across the landing. I moved out of the room. There was another closed door on the other side of the bedroom. I walked up to it and stopped. Silence.

'Hello?' I said, scaring the shit out of myself with the sound of my own voice. In response the wood shook a little.

I put my hand on the handle and turned quickly. As the door opened two things hit me at the same instant. The first was the cat, teeth bared, flinging itself out with all the strength that its little body could muster. Poor little sod – it looked hungry enough to eat the maggots. The second was the smell. First rotting food and now faeces – the perfumes of neglect. The animal didn't stop to complain. It went streaking down the stairs, yowling its hunger to the world. I stepped into the darkness left behind it.

The air inside was damp as well as rank. I took a few steps in search of the light and put my foot into what I knew from its consistency had to be a pile of cat shit. I flicked on the switch. It started a fan whirling somewhere near by, but still it was dark. I opened the door as wide as I could. The light from the landing splashed its way in, picking up more little deposits on the floor, then a pile of what looked like clothes next to a laundry basket. I fumbled my way in over them, past a shower unit, to the bath. Over the sink I found a light that worked. Except there are some things that should best remain in the dark.

At least I knew why the cat hadn't died of thirst. On the contrary he would have had more than enough to drink, although it might have been a little off-putting to the taste buds. The water in the bath was a murky dark colour. My brain short-circuited to a certain Marks & Spencer's buyer, except the dying here didn't have the same spelling.

She was lying with her body almost completely submerged, the tops of those designer breasts peeping up from the surface. They didn't look so good now, though this time you could hardly blame Maurice Marchant. Her eyes were closed, that lovely face already a sallow, greyish hue, puffy, slightly overblown. Water preserves of course, but from the look of her she'd been there for a couple of days at least and in this heat things would be starting to curdle inside. My eyes were drawn back down to the breasts. Where the water met an armpit I spotted the tiny, delicate ridge of a scar. Did he run his fingers over it as they made love, admiring his work, checking its progress, contrasting the feel of the surface with what was inside? Maybe simple caresses were an anti-climax after such bizarre intimacy? Even the thought of it made me feel sick. On the edge of the bath behind her lay a dinky little razor-blade, the kind that women use when they can't stand the thought of the wax, and next to it a half-empty bottle of whisky and a glass.

I braced myself and plunged a hand down into the icy water until I found an arm. It was cold and squishy to touch, almost too heavy to lift. As it broke the surface the hand fell limply backwards, white as white can be, except for a jagged slash of black across the main artery of the wrist, through which a life had washed away. Tremendous. I'd come looking for a murderer and found a suicide. Question is how were the two related?

A crack of thunder like a cannon-shot hit me from behind. I dropped the arm back into the bath and the bloody water splashed me. I jumped away, and for that second it got to me. I stood wiping my hands on my trousers with a Lady Macbeth kind of energy. Too many cuts. This whole damn thing was full of too many cuts, and too many women with not enough respect for their own flesh.

I could feel my stomach turning. I grabbed a wad of toilet paper. Something came out, but it was more spit than vomit. At least it was out. I steadied myself and turned my attention to the bundle of clothes, picking them up by an edge of fabric so as not to disturb anything. I didn't need to look far. It must have been a classy sweater once, a cream-cotton weave, soft as soft. Except for the hard black stains all down the front, and the spray of black spots over the sleeves. The trousers were the same, blood and stuff all over them too. Underneath I found a handbag, one of those sack affairs in which women carry their lives as well as their car keys. I opened it up carefully. In the bottom I saw a purse, a credit-card wallet and a makeup bag tubby with contents. Nestling next to it was a long, nicely proportioned surgical knife, half wrapped in bloody tissues. Of course – the missing letter opener. A nice irony, given the mail it would have opened.

Back in the bedroom I stood by the window, face into the storm, swallowing down long, greedy breaths. London rain had never tasted so fresh. Enough now, Hannah, I heard Frank's voice harsh in my ear. Enough. It doesn't belong to you any more. Close the window and call the police. Don't touch anything else. It's over.

The phone was by the bed. I was dialling the number when I noticed the second cord going from the wall into the back of one of the drawers. I put my finger down on the receiver and followed the wires. In the bottom drawer I found the answering machine. Of course. That bright little voice that had always been there even when its owner wasn't. Next to the recording head the light was blinking furiously. I pressed the button and heard the high-pitched scrunch of voices rewinding. Then I pressed 'play'.

I listened, transfixed as my own voice came over the airwaves, a private eye somewhat overplaying the role of curious journalist. Monday morning, a million years ago. Then came a beep, and another voice I recognized. An old man anxious not to lose his casino's honeypot. 'Hello, Belinda. This is Christo Aziakis. It is Tuesday afternoon at 1 p.m. I'm still waiting to hear from you.'

Then came a beep with no message, then another followed by a blast of a lively acoustic but no words: me in the Majestic reception area this afternoon, checking? No Maurice. But then, of course, this was only the machine. Chances were that if he had phoned her on Tuesday evening, she would have been here to take the call. The machine clicked off. So did something else, except the sound came from downstairs. Boy, for an empty house this place was positively jumping. The cat trying to crow-bar its way into the Kitekat tin? I listened but all I could hear now was my own heartbeat. I picked up the phone and dialled the emergency number. As the ringing tone connected, I heard it again. This time it was more definite. So definite that I knew what it was immediately. Footsteps. Someone was moving about downstairs.

I slipped the receiver down on the bed and moved softly to the open door, snapping off both the lights in the hall and the one in the bedroom at the same instant. The night had slipped in under cover of the storm and the house turned to black under my fingers. Downstairs once again the noise stopped. But to my horror I was now paralysed. An invisible hand plucked at my gut strings. How come I'm such a baby in the dark these days? Blame it on Joe, still the only man to make it regularly into my dreams. Below me the sound of steps started again, but quieter this time – soft footfalls on carpet, across to the bottom of the stairs. Then the unmistakable sound of the first tread upwards.

I slid my way behind the door, pulling it close to me, my face brushing into something cold and oily as I did so. Across the room the telephone was talking to the bed cover. 'Hello. Hello. This is the emergency services. Which service do you require? Hello, is there anyone there?'

The footsteps were nearing the top of the stairs. I imagined the figure reaching the last step, standing in the hall, ears and eyes alert in the darkness. A street lamp was throwing a dirty light through the bedroom window, but it didn't reach to the bed. 'Hello? Hello?' They'd be trying to trace the call now. But even when they have an address the heart attack victim is usually dead by the time they arrive. A lot can happen in twenty minutes. Like now.

The figure moved into the doorway. Through the crack all I could see was a dark blur. I started to shake, my brain slipping back a cog into the memory of dark country air and a man's fist. I picked up the image and hurled it like a mental discus far, far away from me. I watched it spin and shimmer into the distance. Then I braced myself, ready to jump the instant the figure entered.

But before I had a chance the door was wrenched away from me, with a sharp brutal movement that left me exposed. I took the oily thing with me, lifting and flinging it in the direction of my attacker. It covered the face and much of the body, obscuring any vision long enough for me to deliver a savage kick to beneath the knee. A man's voice yowled. I rammed him with the full force of my body weight and he went over, but not before a hand had shot out to take me with him.

I let out a banshee scream of anger as I came down on top of him, using the corner of my elbow as a sharpened mallet to smash into his chest somewhere under the rib-cage. I heard him groan. 'Ha . . .!' I hit out again and I heard another yelp. But I wasn't listening any more. Or counting. The blood was up and singing in my ears, the sweet sound of heart and body pumping in unison. Don't mess with me . . . The words came howling through me from below, from a past dark with panic and pain.

''Annaa . . . Oh, Christ.'

Don't mess with me . . . I come from a place where fear is its own muscle and fury an endless fuel.

''Annah. Stop . . . Hannah.'

Hannah. Me. I registered the name in the shout at the same time as an arm shot out to deflect a further blow. He used the leverage to pull me sideways and throw himself on top of me. He was heavy. Heavier than he looked. 'Hannah,' he shouted again. 'It's me, Grant. It's OK. You're safe'

'I know it's fucking you,' I said, as I smashed into him again, at the same time arching my back violently to throw him off. 'I know. I know.' And as I said it, I realized I was screaming too.

Still it took a while to stop, the message in the brain not the same as the one in the body. But when he pinned my arms down to the floor, suddenly it all went out of me. I felt it go, a great whoosh sluicing through my system, almost like a rush of urine when you can't hold it any more. I fell back against the floor, feeling its hard wood against my back, gulping in air, looking up into his silhouetted face. 'God, Hannah,' he said, half laughing, half coughing, 'you've got some punch.'

The violence passed. It took us both a while to find our breath, me below, him above. The mood changed. The picture stilled. Slow mo – the biggest cinematic cliché in the book. He relaxed his weight back further on to his hands, his head coming fractionally closer to mine. You could almost hear the music. Here we go. The bit in the movie where you kiss her. Come on, you know the rules.

Hard to know if it was the film buff or my body talking. I heard myself laugh. It was a mad sound. He frowned, his lips parted in a kind of bewilderment. 'Hannah?' he asked quietly.

'I wouldn't try it,' I said, louder than I intended. 'I'd probably bite your tongue out.'

'What?' He laughed in astonishment.

God, was I in some trouble. Maybe Colin wasn't so wrong about me after all. Maybe Joe had inflicted a more lasting damage than the eye. No time to think about that now. I shook my head frantically, looking to cover my nakedness with the plot. 'I've found her,' I said, and it struck me later when I tried to remember the moment that I may have been crying, but I'm still not sure. 'She's in the bath. She slashed her wrists. There's blood everywhere.'

And so it was only afterwards, after he had helped me up and held on to me for the longest shortest time to check I was OK, that we both realized that the oily cape we were lying on was, in fact, a full-length PVC black raincoat.

Chapter Twenty

I called Olivia to tell her the good news when I finally got home early the next morning. She was groggy, but at the right end of the sleeping pill to hear the phone. She didn't say a lot, but then I suppose there wasn't that much to say.

It still took the lads from the lab to really get her off the hook, though. Just Rawlings' way of being nasty to the end. I can't tell you how threatened he had felt, finding Grant sitting in the car with a new partner. I had to take a bollocking for all the things I'd touched, even though I had worn gloves. But by then I had recovered and took it like a woman. After all, we both knew it wouldn't affect the final outcome. As indeed it didn't.

When the reports came in thirty-six hours later, they showed that while Olivia's car and apartment were forensically spotless, bits of the inside of her husband were to be found all over Belinda Balliol: on her clothes, in her shower, on the mac and in some tasty little stains on the upholstery of her car. Even more importantly her fingerprints were all over Maurice Marchant's office.

According to the PM, she died around 3 a.m. that morning, having taken enough Nembutal to knock herself out a couple of hours before. The phone company's records showed that she'd made a call to Marchant's office earlier that evening and spoken for five minutes, while a neighbour who had been out walking his dog said that he had seen her car drive off at around 11.10. Her body showed signs of bruising around the upper arms, commensurate with a struggle.

It was her car that clinched it. The ageing janitor turned out to have had the eyes of a cat. (And Grant the honesty of a weasel). Not only had he seen a tall woman in a raincoat leaving the premises just before 12.30 a.m., but he'd also spotted a vehicle driving away into the night as he ran out after it. Far too dark and too quick for anything as sophisticated as a whole registration number (although he thought he'd seen a Y), but he had once been a car mechanic and certainly recognized a newish Ford Fiesta when he saw one. Popular little women's car. Perfect for the about-town health farm manageress. Which was, of course, another reason why the police had been quite so full of themselves when it came to Olivia Marchant's guilt, especially when they discovered her Fiesta's number plate had a Y in it.

Indeed so convinced was Rawlings they'd got the right woman that he showed little interest in investigating Olivia's alternative story, at least until forensics told him any different. So it was Grant who took the files home that night from Castle Dean, and Grant who found Belinda Balliol's interesting enough to call at her place of work. Mr Aziakis, of course, had been expecting him. Not only did he tell him all about her body work and how she hadn't been there since Monday night, but also, under Grant's questioning, revealed that for the last six months or so she'd been driving to work regularly in a Ford Fiesta.

From there it was just a question of using police short cuts to put an address to a telephone number and to get hold of the letting agency. The house had been on lease, six months' rent paid in advance. The lease had begun in November, which was the month in which Maurice had given her the push and which, by further coincidence, was also when Belinda Balliol had bought the year-old Ford Fiesta, whose registration number included a Y . . . And all on a croupier's salary? It didn't take a genius to work out that someone had given Belinda a helping hand. But was it a pay-off or blackmail? Either way, according to her current bank statements, she needed more money. Because not only was the bank getting worried, so was the letting agency. They had already sent a letter threatening her with a notice of quittal if next month's rent wasn't forthcoming. The police found it at the back of a drawer in the study. It perhaps goes without saying that nowhere in the house, the car or her bag was there any sign of any ticket or travel document for Mexico.

And the sleeping pills? Well, they came from a doctor she had seen seven weeks before, complaining of nerves and insomnia. When pushed further, she had talked of personal problems. He had assumed a matter of the heart and pre-scribed her only ten, just in case. She must have used them sparingly.

Now all the bits were in place, I checked them against the fantasy of my car journey. It wasn't a bad fit. Except maybe the fact that she had used her precious savings to fund the sabotage. That seemed a little profligate, though she'd obvi-ously thought it worth the money. But then given the pay-off six months before, she was probably right. At least it showed the Marchants that she meant business. It must, then, have given her the fright of her life when I turned up out of the blue asking questions. Maybe she thought he – or even worse they – had put me on to her. Either way she had little time to think about it. When Marchant called, she must have been more than ready. I saw her at her cupboard, picking out the right clothes, standing in front of the bathroom mirror, making up that lovely new face so she might prove irresistible to an old lover. She'd already gone out of her way to show how suitable she could be. Nice house. Same car. Maybe she had been trying to turn herself into Olivia so he wouldn't be able to tell the difference. Apart from the rings around her rival's neck. And the ones Olivia had hooped around his soul.

But it hadn't worked. We were back in that consulting room in the middle of the night. Except now there was no one to tell us what had gone on. The silence of death. Nothing quite like it. According to the pathologist's report, the woman who had killed him must have been either pretty strong or pretty angry. The first blow had severed an artery. I watched the blood spurt out all over that gorgeous cream sweater. Maybe he had told her there was no more money and she had just lost her temper.

I thought of Joe, and the violence I had found in myself once the right button had been pressed. But violence is one thing. Mutilation another. She must have loved him a lot to hate him so much. I had said as much to Grant, as we sat together in the car waiting for the sirens to roll in.

He shrugged. 'I don't know, Hannah. You should have seen as many corpses as I have. You'd be amazed by what people can do to each other in that moment, then not remember a thing about it afterwards. Defence mechanism, I suppose. Particularly for women. Anyway, what is it they say? Hell hath no fury . . .?'

And I smiled, because that was one of Frank's favourite quotations, too. A case of the sentiment fitting in with prejudice.

'What's so funny?'

'Nothing. It's just for a moment there I'd almost forgotten you were a policeman.'

Which brought us to the aftermath and what happens when the fury dies away. But there even the forensic boys couldn't help, couldn't turn the facts into feelings. I thought about her leaving the building, shaken and shaking, her bloody clothes encased in Olivia's long black mac. That would have been a bonus, finding something to cover the mess she was in. Did she realize how it might look: a tall woman in the same coat, driving away in the same make of car? Maybe there had been some method to her madness after all. The possibility of setting up her rival and watching the whole family implode. Except she decided not to stay around to enjoy the show.

I imagined her, a young desperate woman, the adrenalin long gone, arriving home reeking of her lover, only this time the smell of blood rather than sex. I saw her push her way into the bathroom, strip off and fling herself into the shower, leaving that vicious little pile of clothes behind her. But there are some things that hot water can't wash off. Just as there are some words that don't burn, despite the ashes. I saw the towel on the floor and the indentation on the bed cover, the empty glass of whisky and the pills. Maybe she had thought that she'd find some peace in sleep, only to realize that sleep would mean dreams, and that in the end it would be easier to choose that other tunnel of forgetfulness. Just a question of not being able to live with what you have done.

*   *   *   *

The day after the official reports came through, I got a letter from Olivia Marchant. It read:

There are no words with which I can thank you, Hannah. I think you probably saved my life. Now I have to learn to live it without him. If I had had your confidence and sense of self when I was your age, perhaps things could have been different. As it is, I must own it for what it is. The only thing I regret is that I never met her. It would help me to have known more about her. Detective Sergeant Grant told me she was young, just twenty-eight years old. And when I asked him, he said she was beautiful. I would assume that Maurice had had something to do with that. When I try to imagine forgiving her, I think that maybe she couldn't bear to lose him either.

Yours in gratitude,
Olivia Marchant

Nicely turned, I thought. And generous. In more ways than one. Tucked inside the envelope was a cheque for a thousand pounds. The amount didn't surprise me. I was getting used to being overpaid. The real problem was how it didn't make me feel any better. God, I hate this bit. I hate it when it's all over, but you still feel as if it isn't. What I needed was something to earth it, to let it go.

So I drove down to the Nag's Head. Well, a promise is a promise and the money was already burning too many holes in my psyche. My windscreen washer man was there at the traffic lights, sitting having a fag, a stack of the *Big Issue* next to his bucket and sponge. I rolled down the window and called him over. He gave me a grin and ran up with a copy.

'Hi, Hannah.'

'Hi.' I took it from him and in return handed him two fifty-pound notes. He stared at them with stunned disbelief. 'I used you in a bet,' I said. 'They could afford to lose it. Have fun.'

I drove off before he could ask further.

In a dozen other circumstances it would have made a perfect end. But my malaise was too deep for a corny philanthropic gesture to cure, and anyway we all know this isn't really the end. For some time now this has been a story of two marriages, two sets of infidelities in need of resolution, and only one of them had come to rest.

Two evenings ago Colin had taken his wife out to dinner in the country to try and patch up their relationship and prevent her from finding out the truth. I went home and waited for my sister to tell me about it.

Chapter Twenty-One

She took her time. Three days, to be exact. I sat through a long weekend, then finally lost my patience and called my parents. It was early evening on the Kent–Sussex border and my mother had been out dead-heading the roses. I think that was where I first encountered violence, in my mother's gardening. Her and her shears. The plants used to tremble as they heard her opening the shed doors. I could see her now, hair caught up in an old-fashioned roll, wisps escaping as she pulled off the gardening gloves to pick up the phone.

We talked weather and saucepans and my father's angina. Then she told me all about the lovely visit they'd had from Kate and the family, and how they had gone home the day before and what a marvellous man Colin was, the way he worked so hard and cared so much for his family. I suppose every girl sets out to make herself in the image of what her mother isn't, but in my case you can probably appreciate now that it was a matter of survival. I put the phone down, got out my stash and rolled myself a joint.

And so it was that I was not entirely in control of all my faculties when half an hour later the doorbell rang. I looked out of my open window to see Kate standing below on the door-step, a bottle of champagne in one hand, a pot plant in the other and no kids hanging round her skirts. No doubt they were at home with Daddy playing happy families. I took a few deep breaths of fresh air and went downstairs to greet her.

She looked a little guilty, no doubt about that. But she also looked happier. Younger even. Reconciliation: cheaper than a face-lift. But was it less painful? She smiled at me. How mean was I going to be to her?

'Kate, what a surprise. Mum must be baby-sitting.' Very mean was the answer to that question.

'No. We're home.'

'We?'

'Yes. We all came back together last night.'

'I see,' I said and held out my hand. 'And those are for me.'

When I was little, I could be so cruel to her; even though she was the elder, I was always the one who could make her cry. Once I told her a ghost story that had her sobbing with fright. I felt guilty about it later, but it didn't stop me at the time.

I took the bottle and the plant. 'Thank you. You don't mind if I don't invite you in. Only I'm quite tired.'

'Hannah . . .'

'Don't worry, Kate. You don't have to say anything,' I said firmly. 'It's got nothing to do with me, remember.'

She looked at me for a moment. I smiled. I thought I did quite a good job, but then we're talking Kate here. She sighed, then put out her hand and took the champagne back. I was so surprised that I let it go. 'It's not a present, Hannah,' she said quietly. 'It was a way of getting you to speak to me. If you don't want to talk, you can't have it.'

'What?'

'You heard. You can keep the pot. Mum says it doesn't need a lot of water, but you have to dead-head the old blossoms. Give me a ring when you're not so tired.'

And she turned on her heel and walked down the path. Well, when I say I used to be the cruel one, I did, of course, have to learn it from someone. Some responses just take you right back to childhood. 'All right,' I said. 'But I still don't think it's fair.'

We sat around the table. It was good champagne. At least it was better than most of the stuff I've drunk, but then that wouldn't be difficult. She had sniffed at the air a bit as she

218

got out the glasses, but didn't say anything. In fact she didn't speak until the bubbly was poured and we were sitting down.

'You stoned?' she asked.

I laughed. 'Not really. Your arrival seems to have sobered me up. How did you know?'

'How do you think?' She paused. 'We were sitting in opposite seats last time.'

'What?'

'When I was here last. I was sitting there, with a cup of coffee. You were here.'

'Yes.'

'I don't think I've ever been so unhappy, you know. Or not that I can remember. You were so good to me. I can't tell you how grateful I was that you were here.'

'I – er . . . it was nothing,' I said.

'I really thought it was all broken up. I kept wondering how I would cope, bringing them up on my own. What I'd do for money, how they'd be without a father. So many people do it, don't they? It must be possible.'

'Yes,' I said. 'But you're lucky. You don't have to do it after all.'

'No. No, I don't.' She fell silent. I didn't push it. That's the thing about dope. Even the silences are OK. Although long.

'We're all right, Hannah,' she said after what seemed like an hour and a half. 'Colin and me. We've talked about it. I wasn't imagining it. There was something really wrong. A reason why we've grown apart, why he'd become so distant. The business has been in trouble. Serious trouble, much worse than he'd ever admitted to me. Eight months ago the bank threatened to foreclose on the loan because they'd fallen behind on payments. He even thought about selling the company, but he was advised that he wouldn't get enough to cover the outstanding debts. He's been worried sick for the best part of a year, but didn't tell me because he didn't want to burden me with it. He's always felt that work was his responsibility, his half of the relationship, and he couldn't bear for me to know he'd failed. Isn't it crazy? That in the 1990s a man like him should still feel so ashamed of something like that?'

I grunted. 'Well, he's always been a traditional kind of chap,' I said. Nice one, Colin. Make her feel sorry for you and then anything that comes after is forgiven in advance. I wondered who would mention the skirt first, her or me.

'I was so angry with him. But then I kept thinking about his father and how nobody had ever said anything to anybody in that family. It was a big step for him. Telling me. You should have seen him,' she said quietly. 'He cried. He said he felt that somehow he was betraying himself as a man, not being able to support the family. That if he'd told me he knew I would have helped, agreed to sell the house or go back to work to bring in extra money. But that would have broken his side of the bargain.'

I thought of Kate sitting in her nice Islington kitchen awash with children and toys and chaos, against the odds so enjoying it all, happy to have a career behind her. Colin was right. Of course she would have coped, but it would also have been the death of a kind of innocence between them, a breaking of a promise. Not the only one, though.

'And what about the other money?' I said at last. 'The two or three hundred pounds he was taking out of the joint account every month. Did he tell you about that?' What had he said? That he was siphoning off private funds to pay the public debt. Very clever, Colin. Who says you're not fit to run a business?

'Oh, that . . .' She hesitated. 'Hannah, I'm sorry, but I mean . . . if I tell you, will you promise me not to tell anyone else. I mean I know how you feel about Colin, but if Mum or anyone – it's not for my sake, but Colin –'

'Kate, it's me, Hannah, remember. I'm the one who stopped talking about my life to Mum twenty years ago. You really think I'm going to tell tales on yours? I wouldn't say a word to a living soul. Was it a woman?'

She nodded and her face broke out into a sudden grin. 'Yes. It was.'

'Who was she?' I said, the dope pushing me into an amazed smile in reply to her laughter.

'She was a therapist.'

'What?'

'A therapist.'

I would have laughed too had my bottom jaw not fallen so far away from my top one. Colin and a therapist?

'Isn't it incredible? When things started to go so wrong and he couldn't tell me because he was so scared it would break up the marriage, he began to feel ill. He couldn't sleep, then he started having panic attacks. So he went to his doctor and she suggested he should see someone and referred him to this woman in Kentish Town who deals with short-term crisis patients. She was wonderful apparently. Really helped him to think it through. When she heard that I had taken the kids to Mum, she told him that he had to tell me the truth. He came the very next day. He just walked into the room and burst into tears. Luckily Mum had the kids in the garden. Oh, Hannah. I felt so awful. That I hadn't known, or hadn't even tried to understand. He's been through such pain, stupid bloody man.'

I was grateful that she kept on talking. That way I didn't have to say anything. My mind was spinning like some astronaut who'd snapped free from the space cable. A therapist. Jesus Christ. I ran it all back again: the monthly bills, the early mornings, the nice residential street, the basement flat, the fifty minutes on the clock, the next client in a suit and the unexpected ordinariness of the woman who had opened the door to me. And finally, the sight of Colin sobbing into his steering-wheel. Look at it one way and you had infidelity, look at it another and it was crisis management.

Much though I would have liked to disbelieve it, I knew immediately it was true. God, no wonder he'd been so freaked when he saw me. And so beside himself with worry and with rage. Poor old Colin. A man weighed down under the burdens of masculinity. It might have been better if she had been a hooker. Well, I know what to buy him for Christmas. The latest Pete Pantin album.

I was lucky I was stoned, really. That way I could just roll with one thought into another, enjoy the journey, not have to take responsibility for the meaning, or my part in it. But dope can be a dangerous ally in such circumstances. Pleasure to paranoia is an easy step. When I got there, it hurt more than I care to admit. My God, among the many ways in which I have fucked up in my life this was a real beauty.

Except for one thing. When she'd sat here a week ago weeping into her coffee cup, he hadn't been the only problem in the marriage. She had been doing a little retreating herself, sexually as well as emotionally. Not any more, it seemed.

'And what about you, Kate? What about your doubts? Or are you ready to patch it all up?'

She gave a little frown as if the reference embarrassed her. As well it might. Maybe they'd already sorted out that bit, making the bedsprings sing in mother's spare room. In which case they'd got more nerve than I ever had.

'We'll work it out,' she said quietly. And then, as if she knew it wasn't enough: 'It's who I am now, Hannah. I don't know how to be anybody else. Even if I wanted to.'

And I knew that was all I was going to get. I looked at her, this sister of mine who had occupied such a powerful place in my childhood and my life. And I realized again the one single fact that always caused me trouble. That she actually loved this man, that against all the odds of his pomposity and conservatism, there was something in him that had touched her. Something in his steadiness and reserve and his old-fashioned notions of life and marriage that made her feel safe and free. And although what had happened would no doubt shake those easy choices, make them have to redefine each other anew, it wouldn't entirely obliterate their relationship.

Kate needed Colin. She might be lovely and bright and sassy enough to have a hundred others, but Colin and Ben and Amy were what she wanted. And I couldn't keep pretending that she didn't – like some women want bigger breasts and younger faces because they think it will make them feel good, because they want to fight the world in their way, not mine. And just because it wasn't my choice, it didn't give me any right to refuse them theirs, to assume that it automatically made them stupid or damaged. Face it, Hannah, you can't make the world in the way you think it should be. You just have to accept it for what it is.

Dope. Don't you just love the philosophical depths into which it plunges you? I took a slug of champagne and climbed back into the ring. After all there was still a conversation going on.

'. . . if you feel you can handle that?'

'What? Sorry. I was still thinking about Colin.'

'Hannah!' She laughed. 'You don't think they're right, do you?'

'Who?'

'The people who say marijuana rots your brain?'

'Nah,' I said. 'They're just jealous. What were you saying?'

She poured the rest of the champagne into her own glass and took a gulp. 'That we want you to come to supper next Saturday.'

'We?'

'Yes. Colin too. He says if we're going to turn over a new leaf, then you might as well be included. That it's time you and he stopped behaving like a couple of school kids.'

'Well, he can –'

But she got in before me. 'He knows that I talked to you. He knows that you know. I really think this is his way of trying to make peace.'

Either that or I'm going to be the dinner; chopped and fricasseed in that big shiny Habitat wok of his and served with a cheeky little red from Oddbins. Except, with Colin's financial problems, it would probably have to be Safeway from now on.

But the joke was on me, really. He held all the trump cards. And given the depth of my guilt, it would be altogether easier to believe in his charity. Or his therapist. Maybe I should get her name. Maybe she could turn me around too. After all he wouldn't be needing his 7.30 appointment any longer.

'Thanks,' I said. 'I'd love to come, but maybe I could take a rain check? This last job finished in blood and tears and I need to get away for a bit. Maybe in a couple of weeks, when I get back . . .' I paused. 'I promise.'

She nodded and didn't push it. She left quite soon afterwards. Well, even the new Colin needed some help to put the kids to bed. But she had one more gift for the giving. As she dug around for her car keys, she came across it.

'Oh, look, I almost forgot. This is for you. It was in one of the drawers at home. I thought you could put it on your notice board. For dart practice.'

She handed me a photograph, worn and yellowing, with little whitish triangle marks at each corner showing that it had once been in an album. It was taken in the garden on that hideous swing settee that my mother had got with a trillion Green Shield stamp books about a hundred years ago. She and my father were sitting in it together, with Kate and me cross-legged in front of them, desperately trying to look older than our eight and nine years.

They were holding hands. My mother's hair was permed in that Heddi Lamarr way that forever divides fifties parents from the following decades. Her face seemed firmer and plumper than I ever remembered it. Olivia Marchant was right. My mother had once been much younger. I thought of her now – wrinkles like dried-up little tributaries feeding into the thin line of her lips, and the more generous spread of her stomach and thighs. Maybe that was the real reason Olivia had never had children. Whatever pleasure they might bring to the soul, their growing-up would have been too savage a reminder of her own ageing. Or perhaps, even worse, she feared they would have become competition. I was suddenly glad that my mother wasn't part of the generation that longed for eternal youth, that she at least had the maternal courage to show me how to grow old. Mind you, the way I'd treated her over the years had probably hastened the process. Even in the photo I was snarling.

'Don't you love it?' Kate said. 'Look, you're the only one not smiling. Mum told me she remembers it being taken. You wanted to wear a mini skirt and she made you put on a proper dress, and you had a huge row about it and didn't speak to anyone for the rest of the day.'

We both laughed, and then she grabbed hold of me tight and hugged me to her. I hugged her back. Sisters. Could be they're the only good thing to come out of families.

After she left, I wrote a letter to Colin. Well, it was better than doing it face to face. It came out a little rambling, but was truthful and had a good deal more humility than I realized I had in me. I was pretty sure he would accept it. And then maybe I'd feel OK about going to supper.

I was on my way to bed when the phone rang. There was a policeman on the other end of the line. Maybe he could smell the dope. I blew some smoke down the receiver just to make sure. But he didn't arrest me.

'I thought you'd like to know that the inquest is provisionally set for the 13th. You'll need to be there, of course. Can you make it?'

'Probably,' I said. 'I'm thinking of going away for a while, but I should be back by then.'

'Yeah, takes it out of you, doesn't it?' Pause. 'How you doing?'

'Great,' I lied.

'How's the arm?'

'Fine,' I lied again. The bruise from his fingers was already a study in purple. 'How about your knee?'

'Bloody painful. As is my chest. I've sustained less damage on a GBH charge.'

There was a little silence during which no doubt we both thought about our time on the floor together. Do I fancy you? I thought. Will I ever fancy anyone again? You don't know till you try, Hannah. How bad can it be, fucking a policeman?

'I wondered if you wanted a drink sometime?' he said casually.

'Is this official?'

'Yeah, a double date with Meredith Rawlings. Does it sound official?'

'Er . . . I don't know,' I said. 'I'm a little off beam still.'

'OK. Well, I just rang to check. Look after yourself, Hannah.'

'Michael . . .'

'Yes?'

'Maybe when I get back . . .' I paused. Oh well . . . I could always blame it on the dope later. 'How about Sunday night?'

And he laughed. 'Should I wear a uniform?'

Now that's what you might call an ending. Except, of course, it still isn't one.

*   *   *   *

The next day the weather broke with the morning and I looked out on a leaden sky, the wind whipping up the crisp packets, and children in duffel coats on their way to school. Another English summer reasserting its right to perversity. Maybe going away hadn't been such a dumb idea after all. A way out of a bad date and a break before an even worse inquest. Could be just what I needed, as well as could afford, for once in my life. I did a quick piece of addition. Olivia's varying moments of generosity came to just under two thousand quid, even after I had paid the windscreen man and the car pound. Well, I had earned it.

Belinda Balliol's *Time Out* was still sitting where I had left it on the table five days before. Nothing so out of date as an old listings magazine, except for the travel ads. Because it was still technically evidence, I had found myself unable to throw it away. Remind me to stick it in a cupboard if Grant ever ends up in my sitting-room.

I made myself a cup of coffee and flicked through to the back of the mag. In my imagination I was already halfway to Tuscany and that heart-aching early evening light that makes everything rosy, both in landscape and in life, when my eye was caught by something else on the page. A box ad that had been ringed in careless blue biro. Zenith Travel: the best prices to North America. And by the side of it a name scribbled in that loopy little hand I had grown to know so well. 'Richard'. Richard?

So I rang the number. Well, it was just a phone call. No time, no trouble. Just a way of closing the book. Richard had just walked into the office. I could hear him drinking his cappuccino as he said good morning, slurping his way through the froth. I told him I was a friend of Belinda Balliol's and that she'd recommended him to me.

'Balliol?'

'Tall girl, blonde, good-looking?'

'Oh yeah. Booked about six weeks ago. Picked up the ticket herself. How's she enjoying Chicago?'

'Chicago?' I said, quietly putting my own coffee cup down on to the table.

'Yeah,' he said. Then it unfolded like a flower before me. 'Let me see. I can usually get this in one. Wednesday 28th, afternoon British Midland flight to Amsterdam, then catching a KLM connection to Chicago that evening. I could have got the same price for her flying straight out of Heathrow, but that was the route she wanted. How's that for memory, eh? So. Where can I do you for?'

Chapter Twenty-Two

I said I'd get back to him. I don't know whether he heard me or not. I was having some trouble with my ears, the sound of my own blood pumping too hard through the inside of my head. Chicago via Amsterdam. A long way from Mexico and exactly the same travel itinerary as someone else in this story. Although neither of them made their planes. What was it his secretary had said when I tried to book in for an appointment? 'I'm sorry. He's not available from Wednesday. He'll be in Amsterdam and Chicago.'

So Belinda was going to the same places as Maurice? Although not scheduled to reach Amsterdam at the same time. Of course, I knew that already. Grant had checked the passenger list. But then people would, wouldn't they, I mean if they were suspicious? At least some people. Probably better to be safe than sorry. But Amsterdam to Chicago? Could be people hadn't thought of checking that one.

KLM had, though. With a little persuading they gave me a list of their no-shows for the 773 evening flight out of Schiphol last Wednesday. And guess what? Both of them were on it, pre-booked into adjoining club-class seats. I suppose, of course, it could just possibly have been a further planned persecution. Possible, but not, when you think about it, probable. Because if that was so, how come we didn't find her ticket? Tickets aren't like love letters. There is nothing painful or emotionally humiliating to hide there. No point in destroying them. On the contrary. Might even be there was something to celebrate in keeping them. They would certainly have packed an emotional punch even after death.

I sat for a moment trying to take it all in. I tried to see her house again, to call to mind all the places I might have missed in it, but the picture kept fading. Instead I was sitting in my car in a Kentish Town street, watching a man going into a basement, seeing another following him. Then meeting a rather cautious woman in an ordinary skirt and top with some hastily applied mascara. Finding infidelity where there was none. Putting one and one together and making eleven. Easy mistake when you know. It's not what you see, it's the way that you see it. Or the way that you *want* to see it. What had Colin said? 'You're a stupid prejudiced woman . . . and you don't have the first clue about what is happening here.'

On the desk I saw my own scribbled sums, totting up Olivia Marchant's considerable generosity to me. I thought of how slowly but surely I had become more involved in her story. I dug out Belinda Balliol's file and read it again. And again. I saw the number for the casino scribbled in the margin, and realized how it had been the perfect short cut to her. I thought some more about her car and that coat and her life over the last six months. And gradually, in the same way that staring long enough at a negative allows you to invert the image and see the positive picture, I started to see things from Colin's point of view, and to conclude that maybe this was a traditional detective story after all.

I spent the rest of the day visiting a few places and talking to a few people. Then I came home and wrote everything down. Well, it wasn't easy and there were a lot of details I had to get right. The most important thing was that it all fitted, it all made sense. Except, that is, for one character, Lola Marsh – the girl of the grudges and the face-packs. Come to think of it, she'd never really been properly accounted for, anyway. Stubborn in more ways than one. I went into the kitchen to refill my coffee cup and, as I waited for the water to boil, I saw the family snapshot grinning out at me from the board. Two little girls, one scowling, one smiling. One following in mother's footsteps, the other desperate to get away. Family dynamics. Maybe it was always like that – the rebel and the acolyte.

Shit. It was so long ago I had almost forgotten them. The roly-poly bodies, the thick and thin thighs, the new marble stone. And the two sisters, one fair-headed, one red. If one didn't hold a grudge, that didn't necessarily mean the other had forgotten. I scrabbled about in my notebook. First I rang the Chiswick beauty salon, where I was much nicer to the manageress, and she in turn was much nicer to me, especially when I called her plump red-headed ex-employee by the right name. Then I rang the girl herself. Or rather the place where I thought she might be. And sure enough, a young female voice answered. You could almost hear the sunshine in the background.

'Hello,' I said. 'Is that Cilla Rankin?'

'Yes?'

'Hi, Cilla, how's the weather? Better than here I bet. What happened? Did you go straight from Castle Dean to Majorca? Good idea to get away. Your dad must have been pleased to see you.'

'Who is this?'

'It's OK. I'm a friend. We've met before.'

There was a silence. 'I know who you are. Farah said you'd been to see her too. I didn't have anything to do with his –'

'I know you didn't. No one's accusing you of anything, Cilla. Honestly. You were just in the right place at the right time, that's all. But I do need to ask you a few questions. Is that all right?' There was a silence on the end of the line. I heard a man's voice in the background. 'Or maybe I could have a word with your dad about it all. Though he's probably trying to put it behind him.'

'No. Not Dad,' she said quickly. 'Wait a minute. Let me go to another phone.'

And after that I didn't really need a holiday. There was too much fun to be had at home.

*   *   *   *

I called Castle Dean to tell them I was coming. Or rather tell one of them. It took me a while to track her down because she wasn't in her office. But that was because, strictly speaking, it wasn't her office any more.

'I'm glad you called. I was going to ask Olivia for your address, to write to you. To say goodbye.'

'Goodbye?'

'Yes. I'm leaving tomorrow.'

'Why? What happened?'

'You'll have to ask Olivia about that. All I know is what she said to me. That she wants a fresh start. To put all the unpleasant stuff behind her. It seems that I remind her of the unpleasantness.'

'Oh Carol. I'm sorry.'

'Oh, it's all right. The place is being shut down for a couple of months anyway. She's doing some refurbishment. Expanding it apparently. I'll get a good reference, she's made that quite clear. And she's been very generous about the redundancy money.'

Yeah, I bet she has. But then it was something she was good at, paying off her employees. And she could afford it now. 'Still,' I said. 'After all you've done for her, you must feel rotten. Do you know who'll be taking over?'

And before she had answered, I wrote a name down on the pad in front of me. It was the right one. Well, it wasn't that hard. After all she had all the right qualifications: competence, intelligence, ambition. Except if you really thought about it, you could see it was none of those qualities that had actually got her the job. I remembered that meeting in the car park, the day they towed Olivia's little Ford Fiesta away, and the feeling I had had of something left unsaid. Not any longer. Martha's elevation was, you might say, the cherry on the top of my cake.

We chatted for a little longer, and then I wished her goodbye and good luck. And asked her to do me one small favour before she went. It took some coaxing to get her to agree.

It was late afternoon when I arrived and the sky had cleared. Not exactly Tuscan, but nice nevertheless. The guest car park was only about a quarter full. Maybe the shut-down had already started. Either that or murder and sabotage had wrecked the business. I went round the back to where Olivia's car was snuggled back into its parking bay, about fifty yards away from the girls' quarters. Nifty little vehicle. Get you to London and back in good time if you put your foot down and there wasn't much else on the roads.

I went in the back way, up through the garden and in through the side door. In the lounge tea and dried biscuits were being served. I could still remember the taste. I went through to the atrium. There were a few women lolling about on deck chairs or in the pool, but the Jacuzzi had been pumped empty, its peeling blue bottom exposed to the world. I looked at my watch. It was 5.20 p.m. The final shift would be back at any moment. I slipped into the massage room, slid the screens around the bed, took off my clothes, arranged my equipment and lay face down on the towel.

She came in a few moments later. I could hear her opening a cupboard, then washing her hands at the sink. She moved towards the screens and smartly snapped them back. I gave her, I think it is fair to say, the fright of her life.

'Hello, Martha,' I said. 'I've come for that massage.'

She stared at me, then gave a funny little laugh. 'Hannah? Carol told me it was –'

'I know what Carol told you. But then she's pissed off about losing her job. And it wasn't a complete lie. I did especially ask for you. After all . . . you did promise.'

'Does . . . does Oli – Mrs Marchant –'

'Know I'm here? No, but I don't think she'd begrudge me a free session, do you? She owes me quite a lot, after all. So, do you want me on my tummy or my back?'

'Er . . . that's fine. That's fine as you are. I'll . . . I'll just go and get some oil.'

'You don't need any oil, Martha,' I said firmly. 'From what I remember your hands do just fine without it.'

She hesitated for a second, then decided to do what she was told and came and stood by my side. I smiled at her, then put my head down on the table. I could hear her breathing, trying to steady herself. After all, this is what she was good at.

I felt the flat of her palms come to rest lightly on my back, the right one down near where it met the cleft of my buttocks. I thought about the last time I had felt those hands on me, and the wary, delicious confusion they had brought with them. It was a shame there would be no time to explore that further. But then I had a date with a man tomorrow night. And anyway, I don't like being made love to by people whose ambition is more important than their morality.

You could tell she was nervous. She started off on the shoulders and her opening strokes were neither quite so sure nor so steady. But the longer I was silent the more confident she became, the more those talented little fingers pushed and probed, hitting the knots, finding the tensions, coaxing them out, smoothing them away. Halfway down the back she hit a particularly tender little spot, and I groaned. Her hands hesitated, then moved over it again, working it skilfully, easing it from pain into pleasure. I relaxed, my body playing truant from my mind for a moment. She must have felt it, because now the hands started to move further downwards, gentle, loving, until they found themselves back where they had begun, teasing their way around the start of the cleft, then round over the curves of the buttocks down on to the thighs below.

And I let myself go with them, just for a while. There would be time enough for retribution. And sometimes a girl needs to relax. 'Oh, that's good,' I said slightly breathlessly. Because I wanted her to feel secure and because it was. Flesh.

This story was all about flesh and how important it was to make sure somebody loves it. And when you come to think of it, I had something to learn from that too.

So I let her play around my upper thighs for a while, caressing, suggesting, exciting, until with an expert little flick her fingers slid under and in, into the mouth of me, where no one had been for what felt like such a long time.

But I was already saving myself. 'Congratulations, Martha,' I said suddenly, in a very matter of fact kind of voice, not at all mussed up by sex or desire. 'I gather you got the job.'

Her hands froze, and the fingers withdrew themselves swiftly.

'What happened? Did she like your way with the customers, or was it more to do with the things you saw while you were on night duty?'

She still wasn't speaking. I flipped myself up and over on the bed, removing her hand from my legs as I moved. I saw a face caught between guilt and defiance. Familiar Martha stuff. She had probably spent much of her life perfecting it. She opened her mouth. 'I don't know –'

'Shove it, Martha,' I said. 'I've had it with lies. Yours and everybody else's. If you were in any other establishment, what you're doing now would have already got you the sack. But not here, eh? Here it gets you a promotion. Now why could that be? It certainly wasn't what Olivia Marchant had in mind the last time I talked to her about you. But then that was before Tuesday night, wasn't it? So what's changed? How shall I put it? Maybe now it's a question of I'll keep your secret if you keep mine. Is that it? How much did you need the job, Martha? Enough to perjure yourself? You know it makes you an accessory, don't you, not telling the police?'

'I don't know what you're talking about. I got the job because I'm good at it,' she said, but she sounded much less sure. 'I'm a good manager.'

'I'm sure you are. But that's not why you got it. You got it because you have something to sell. And because Olivia needed to buy it. It was the car, wasn't it? You saw her car.'

'I –'

'Didn't you?'

My voice was so loud and so hard that it even hurt my own ears to listen. I didn't realize I was so angry. But then she was paying for both of them. She stared at me, then slowly she nodded her head. But I needed more than a nod. 'Tell me.'

She swallowed. 'I was going back to my room that night.'

'The night of Marchant's murder?'

'Yes.'

'What time?'

'It must have been sometime after 3. I heard the noise of a car coming up the drive. It was coming in through the back way. I was worried someone might see me, so I hid in the doorway.'

'But instead you saw her?'

She nodded. 'She parked in her usual space and got out. I saw her let herself in through the back of the house and close the door. Then I went to bed.'

'What about the woman you were with?'

'She'd gone back to her room before. I stayed to clear up. It was only me who saw her. I didn't even think about it till the police came that day to take the car away.'

The day I had met her in the car park and she had been so sassy and sure. 'So when did you break the news to Olivia?'

'That evening, after I'd seen you.'

'And what did she say?'

'She asked me if I was sure I could recognize the figure. I told her I was. She said she'd just been out for a drive, because she couldn't sleep. And that it was perfectly innocent, but that it wouldn't necessarily look like that.'

'And you agreed.'

'I didn't say anything. Then she asked me if I would stay on, that she'd been thinking of doing some work on the place, putting some more money into it, and she'd be looking for a new manager.' She looked up at me. 'I'm more than good enough for the job,' she said fiercely. 'I deserve it.'

'Yeah,' I replied. Then I slipped my hand underneath the side of the couch and ripped off the little tape recorder I had put there. I switched it off. 'It's just a shame you won't get it. Now maybe you'd better tell me where she is.'

Chapter Twenty-Three

I knocked on the door, although I felt more like kicking it in. It struck me that I had never been in her Castle Dean apartment. That every time we had met here it had either been in Carol's office or across a midnight swimming-pool. There was music coming from inside, a thudding underbeat and some talentless double-tracked voice over the top. It sounded like Olivia Marchant was dancing. But then she had a lot to dance about.

She opened it and for the first instant I didn't recognize her. She was wearing a shiny bodysuit, one of Castle Dean's best, and from the look of it the body inside had been working out. It was still in great shape, no doubt about that, tuned and pumped and exercised to within an inch of its fifty-year-old life. But it wasn't the body that had stopped me in my tracks. It was the face.

At first I thought I was just seeing her without the makeup, the film of sweat and lank hair pulled back under a nylon headband taking the polish off that perfect visage. But when I looked more closely, I noticed something else. On the left-hand side, high up around the cheekbone where the twitch had been, something was definitely happening to the skin.

'Hannah?' she said. And as she saw me, she brought up a towel quickly to her face, as if nursing a bruise. 'I . . . You should have told me you were coming. I'm afraid I'm –'

'Busy? Oh, I'm sure you can spare me a few moments, Olivia. After all, if you remember I'm the one who saved your life. Can I come in?'

She looked at me and I think it was clear, even then, that

she knew what I was talking about. She let the door fall open and walked in ahead of me. I closed it behind me.

'I'll go and get changed,' she said.

'I wouldn't bother,' I answered coldly.

'No,' she replied quietly. 'You wouldn't. But I would. Maybe you could wait in the other room.'

Client, servant. Sometimes it's hard to break the pattern. I did as I was told.

The place came as a bit of a shock. It was full of pictures of her. They were everywhere, on the walls, on the tables, even in the fireplace: studio-type jobs, with backdrop and lighting, like a private portfolio on display. Or a shrine to past triumphs. There was only one of Maurice, sitting at his desk, those clever hands crossed in front of him. But then, of course, something of him was in all the other photos, anyway. I looked more closely at a couple. No doubt about it. Olivia's face had been a great success story, especially when younger. There was one black and white photo taken amid a haze of cigarette smoke, like those film noir publicity shots of the forties. She was half turned to the camera, her mouth slightly open, cheekbones like a rockface. Lauren Bacall. Muriel Rankin would have died to look like that. Come to think of it, she had. I heard a noise behind me.

Olivia was standing in the doorway, her usual elegance restored: a long diaphanous silk dress over leggings, a scarf back in place around the neck. But short of a paper bag over her head there was something she couldn't conceal. The rest of the face was its own perfectly constructed memory of youth, but that left cheek was no longer included. I thought back to the image of the suspension bridge. But this was more a natural disaster, a kind of landslide, the cheek slipping downwards leaving the skin lumpy and pitted. The cruel fact was that the left side of Olivia's face was caving in. In her eyes I saw the pain it was causing her, more than two deaths had ever done.

'What happened to your cheek, Olivia?'

'I – there seems to be some problem with the skin.'

'Yeah. It's the mini face-lift.'

'What?'

'Maurice's latest success. Marcella Gavarona had the same problem. She complained and he redid it, but it caved in again three weeks later. After that he just sent her home to Milan saying she was a freak case. She was planning to sue. But I don't suppose that's an option open to you now. How long has this one been?'

'Six months,' she said quietly.

'Six months. Of course. The last-ditch attempt to keep him. Except it didn't quite work, did it? Because he wasn't as keen to give her up as you suggested. In fact, if you hadn't come across the love letters in the first place, I bet he never would have told you about her at all.'

If my words surprised her, she didn't show it. Instead she sat herself down on the settee, taking a little while to arrange her skirt around her, suddenly fastidious, distracted almost, like some heroine out of a Tennessee Williams play. Then she put up her fingers to probe a little into the collapsing cheek. 'He promised me it would last four or five years,' she said quietly. 'And that he'd be there to do the next one. He lied.' She paused. 'But as it turned out, he lied about a number of things.' Then, suddenly: 'Are you recording this?'

'No, Olivia,' I said. 'This one's just between the two of us. A private consultation.'

And to prove it I took the little tape recorder out of my pocket and put it on the table in front of us, both its reels silent and still. She smiled at the gesture, but only the right side of her face co-operated, the left dragging down her features as if she were a stroke patient. It made my little scar seem like a positive asset. She felt her skin and her fingers fluttered up again. But each touch revealed only more damage. It was almost enough to make you feel sorry for her. Almost.

'What happened, then, Olivia? Did he agree to give her up but find he couldn't do it? He did try, though, didn't he? Or maybe he just knew you were watching, staying in London, hanging on his every move, checking his phone calls, making sure there were no diversions on his way home or into work. He certainly never went near her house all that time. Or if he did, he made damn sure none of the neighbours saw him. But even you couldn't be with him every minute of the day. As you once told me – such a busy man, such a ferocious schedule. Up early every morning to go into the office or the hospital before the day's operations. His day starting just around the time hers finished. And you know what they say about doctors' couches. That they see more action than most beds. Not to mention the fingerprints left all over the place.

'How long did it take you to realize, Olivia? Did you follow him to work one day? You must have known you didn't stand a chance the minute you saw her. Not just because she was younger, but because she was his. Because Maurice had fallen in love with a woman he had created. Just as he'd created you twenty years before.'

'No.' She spat it out. 'You're wrong. She wasn't anything like me. You met her, you saw her. She wasn't that lovely or that special. The jaw was good, I'll give you that, but the nose was awful – vulgar, cute, no real character at all, the kind of thing he used to despise. And the breasts, well they were just crude, all size and no shape. Cowboy standards. No. Maurice didn't fall in love with her because of his own brilliance. He fell in love with her because he was getting sloppy and he couldn't tell the difference. You must have noticed it going through the files. There were more complaints in the last two years than in the preceding ten. He'd got lazy, stopped trying. And he just wanted to be with someone who wouldn't remind him of that.'

'And was that enough to kill him for?' I asked quietly.

'I've no idea,' she said, her voice smooth again. 'But presumably you have a view on that.'

Despite myself I smiled. I like her more like this: the original Aeyesha rather than the whimpering monkey secon time out of the flame. Give me them sassy every time. But then she knew that about me. Knew I would fall for that kind of bait.

'All right,' I said. 'I'll tell you what I think happened. I think you could just about bear the idea of them together until you found out about the trip. Found out that Maurice was taking her to the conference in Chicago, that he was using her as his advertisement just as he had once used you. That was what you couldn't handle. And that's when you decided to kill them.

'I must say you went to a lot of trouble over it, but then I suppose you always were the business end of the partnership. Still, it took some planning – using her love letters to write the anonymous notes to him, faking a request for health farm details, even targeting your own business to make the threats look serious. Using Lola for the sabotage – now that was clever. She could never be traced back to you, but you knew for certain that she would respond. Because you knew that Lola was really Cilla Rankin, the daughter of one of Maurice's more disastrous failures, herself out for a bit of revenge after her mother's death. What happened? Did you follow up her references and find out she never existed?'

She shrugged. 'I didn't need to. She looked just like her mother. She was already going to fat. Thighs and upper arms. Carol didn't want me to take her, said her references weren't good enough, though of course she meant her looks. But I knew she'd come in useful. She was such an angry little soul. Better to have her inside than out. I knew she'd bite. And I knew if you were any good at all you'd manage to track her down.'

Me. Yes. This was where I came in. 'Thanks,' I said. 'And which phone book did you pluck me out of?'

'Does it matter?'

'No, I suppose not. Except, when you think about it, you were looking for a particular kind of person. Someone

241

independent enough to try and solve the case on their own, but suggestible enough to be controlled.'

She didn't say anything.

'So, first I find Lola for you, then I'm flattered and spoilt enough by your attention and money to see if I can get to the mastermind behind the threats. You're a great help of course. All those files, all those suspects. Just a question of narrowing them down for me, and making Belinda's complaints look a bit more desperate, adding a phone number to make sure I'd know where to find her, basically making sure she made it to near the top of the pile. Which, of course, she did. I saw her early on. As you knew, when you called on Tuesday morning. Which meant you also knew that when the time came I could vouch for her being difficult and nervous.

'So now you had it all mapped out. Maurice was leaving Wednesday morning first thing, so you could be sure he'd be working late in the office the night before. You planned to see him in the afternoon, so you could tell the police later that that was when you showed him the anonymous note and he recognized the handwriting. But it didn't quite work out like that, did it?

'How nearly did I blow it for you, Olivia? By going to see him against your orders? Because of course he recognized me immediately. Belinda must have given him my description from the casino. The minute I walked in and he spotted the scar, he knew I had to be employed by you. And that really freaked him out, didn't it? Because then he knew you were up to something. What happened in your row, Olivia? Did he tell you the truth? That not only was your relationship over, but it had been for years and this time no pleading or threatening would stop him from leaving you.'

She stared at me. Her left eye twitched, as if more subterranean activity were about to take place, slipping her face another few centimetres back towards ugliness.

'What did you do? Beg him to think about it one more time? Say you'd call him that night to talk about it further?

Except by the time he was trying to get in touch with you, you were already on your way somewhere else, weren't you? Having put yourself to bed in front of the whole of Castle Dean, you were already out again, halfway to Fairbray Road. What did you tell her? That you knew everything and that you'd come to meet the woman your husband loved more than you, to have a drink and make your peace and send them on their way with your blessing?

'She wasn't that bright, was she? God, she must have been petrified of you. Did she notice how much dope you'd put in her drink? Or did you have to force some of it down her throat? Upper torso bruising, commensurate with a slight struggle. You must have been grateful for all those work-outs. Then, as soon as she starts to fall asleep, you go into her bathroom, take out some dirty clothes from her laundry basket and put them on over your bodysuit. You leave your car where you've parked it a couple of streets away, then take her keys and drive her Fiesta to Maurice's office.'

I paused. She was all concentration now, eyes fixed on mine, body rigid, but whether from anxiety or memory it was hard to say.

'He must have been surprised to see you,' I said quietly. 'What did you do? Tell him that you'd come to make peace with him too, then once he was off his guard kill him and take his eyes out to make sure he'd got the message? After that it was easy, just a question of covering your tracks. You wore your own coat out of the building, making enough noise to rouse the janitor into seeing a figure and at least a glimpse of a car. Back at her flat you showered, left her clothes on the floor, put her in the bath and started the blood flowing. You wiped off any fingerprints, erased Maurice's last message to her on the answering machine, and burnt just enough of her letters so that her handwriting could still be identified. Then you drove home and got to bed in time to be woken by the news of your husband's murder.

'And from there on it fell into your lap. You just played

243

the grief-stricken widow, too poleaxed even to defend herself against the police accusations, knowing that as long as I was out there rooting for you it was only a matter of time till you could help and guide me – and them – back towards Belinda Balliol, thereby letting you off the hook. Long-suffering, loving wife, jealous, abandoned mistress. Textbook stuff.'

It was only when I stopped talking that I realized I was shaking, the retelling rekindling the rage and reminding me of all the ways in which I had been used and manipulated by her. She must have seen the anger in my eyes. But she sat absolutely still, watching me carefully as if I and not she were the dangerous one. But her fake serenity was cruelly undermined by a series of violent skin shudders. Not cruel enough, some would say.

'I owe you an apology,' she said evenly. 'I never meant to insult your intelligence. I rather thought you'd be, well, pleased. That it might be a kind of triumph for you, getting to Belinda Balliol before the police did.'

'Yeah,' I said. 'It was great. Particularly her rotting body in the bath. I'll treasure that one for a long time to come.'

She swallowed slightly and dropped her eyes away from mine. Now, finally, it seemed as if she were in some kind of pain which was not directly connected with her own appearance. I felt the need to make it hurt even more. I thought of Belinda's swollen face, her mushy skin, the colour and smell of the bath water around her. Then I thought of Maurice. After the violence comes the clean-up. The more scientific cuts of the pathologist, the quick-freeze and the neat plastic bags, all the blood and ooze carefully washed away. A clever mortician might even be able to put his eyes back. I decided to dig them out again. What had Michael said about killers not remembering what they'd done? Maybe they just didn't get the right kind of reminders.

'Tell me, how difficult was it, Olivia? Stabbing your husband in the back and then gouging out his eyes?'

244

She didn't reply immediately. And when she began to talk she didn't open her mouth fully, as if afraid she might trigger off another seismic tremor. 'It was his own fault,' she said so quietly I had to strain to hear it. 'He turned his back on me. Turned away from me while I was still talking. He said he didn't want to hear any more because there was nothing more to say. He was going and I had better make the best of it. He even suggested I'd benefit from the "fresh start". Fresh starts. Of course Maurice was an expert at those: cutting out the dead wood, making it all smooth and new again.' She laughed. 'You know, the only one he didn't transform was himself. You should have seen him naked: the flab and the sag starting everywhere. But of course on him it didn't matter. Because he was the designer, the one with the knife – until, that is, I picked it up.' She stopped for a second. 'You should think about it, Hannah. I only did to him what he'd done to others. I even left the messy bits till he was dead and couldn't feel the pain. He didn't hurt that much, anyway. I'd say that on balance I'd suffered more hurt over the years than he did. Lost more blood. And more flesh.' She shook her head. 'He should have listened to me. He knew the rules. We wrote them together twenty years ago, the price of his fingers under my skin. I just took what was mine.'

'Your pound of flesh,' I said quietly. 'And what about her, Olivia? What rules did she break?'

'I don't care about her,' she answered with a sudden fierce clarity. 'She was a silly little opportunist who knew a good meal ticket when she saw it. She probably would have left him, as soon as she could have been sure of his money. I would never have touched her, if he'd stayed with me. He made the choice. They could both be alive still if it wasn't for him.'

And it was clear, for what it was worth, that she actually believed that. I found myself as much disappointed as disgusted. I suppose somewhere I'd hoped that as a woman she might feel more remorse than a man, suffer more sense of horror at discovering the violence in herself. But maybe there are some ways in which we're more equal than we'd like to believe.

As for poor old Belinda, well, even her death was just a footnote in someone else's love affair. Her real sin was less to do with being an opportunist, than not understanding the passions she had walked into, the small print of the contract she had helped her lover to tear up. Of course her punishment had not fitted the crime, but then that's the point about victims – they get what they don't deserve. At least this way she'd never need more cosmetic surgery. Unlike the woman sitting in front of me, whose face was coming apart at the seams. The face, but not, it seemed, the mind.

'You do realize, of course, that you can't prove a word of all this,' she said quietly, straightening her back and smoothing down her skirt. Fresh starts. It wasn't just Maurice who was an expert. 'That all you've got is a good story, while the police have all the conclusive forensic evidence.'

It was the least I expected. I leant over to the little tape recorder, and pressed the play button. Well, if she felt no guilt then why should I? She started for a moment, thinking I had fooled her all along, but when the voice came out it wasn't hers. It was mine. Followed by Martha's.

'The night of Marchant's murder?'
'Yes.'
'What time?'
'It must have been sometime after 3. I heard the noise of a car coming up the drive. It was coming in through the back way. I was worried someone might see me. So I hid in the doorway.'
'But instead you saw her?'
'She parked in her usual space and got out. I saw her let herself in through the back of the house and close the door. Then I went to bed.'

I switched off the machine. She stared at it for a moment. The silence grew louder and longer. She turned her attention to the back of her hands and started stroking them gently, running her fingers along the line of the veins. And you know the strange thing was that, in spite of the surprise, she didn't seem that upset.

'I don't suppose you're interested in money?' she said after a while, and the voice was almost gay, as if she knew what the answer would be.

I shook my head. 'Sorry, I've tried it. It doesn't seem to make me happy.'

She smiled. 'Nor me. Though it did for a while. And you know what? Neither does the beauty. Not really. Not any more. Not without him.' She paused. 'I didn't lie to you about everything, you know, Hannah. Not about the important things. Not about Maurice and me.'

What had been her words? 'Killing him would be like killing a part of myself.' I thought back to her grief that morning after in the apartment. Even with her skills not all of those tears had been crocodile ones. 'No,' I said. 'I didn't think you did.'

'Tell me. Have you ever loved anyone like that?'

I shook my head.

'I didn't think so. Just as well, really – it only brings you pain in the end. Well, I suppose you'd better call your young policeman now. You know, I don't believe he's even noticed your little scar. Or if he has, he finds it quite attractive.'

'You sure you don't want to make the call yourself?' I said quietly.

She shook her head. 'I don't see how it could make that much difference, do you? Not in the long run. No, I think I'll go and get myself ready. See if I can't repair this "damage" with a little makeup. I wouldn't want to miss my Gloria Swanson moment, would I?'

And as she spoke, I realized how much I was going to miss her. All that cunning intelligence. God, what could she not have done, had she not been so in thrall to the image in the mirror.

I sat for a while after the door had closed. On the sideboard the Lauren Bacall picture winked at me. 'So you're a private detective. I thought they only existed in books, or else they were greasy little men snooping round hotel rooms.' The only woman who could really answer Philip Marlowe back. But it still didn't make her a heroine. Just a more poignant kind of victim.

I don't know when I began to realize that Olivia had been away too long. The bathroom light had activated a fan and it suddenly struck me that its noise might have conveniently covered up any other. I stood up and went into the hall. The door was shut. I didn't bother to knock.

Luckily the lock wasn't a serious one. It gave at the first kick, the bolt splintering and tearing out of the wood. The tiled bathroom behind, lit by a harsh halo of bulbs around a makeup mirror, was empty. At the end stood another connecting door. This one I didn't need to kick in. It was already open.

The bedroom beyond was airy and elegant, dominated by an enormous double bed. She was sitting in the middle of it, her back propped up on a bank of pillows and fancy cushions. They looked like they had taken some arranging, as did she, lying there, silk flowing over those perfect long legs, hands clutched to the left side of her chest as if she was cradling something to her.

As I burst through the door, her head snapped up to greet me and I registered a single wild second of terror in her eyes.

I was halfway to the bed when the call of her name was blown away by the sound of the gunshot. Her body jolted forward, then back, as if convulsed by a massive electric shock, arms thrown back on to the cover. And there, under her breast where the hands had been, was a shining dark hole the size of a fifty-pence piece, pumping blood like a newly burst pipe.

I grabbed one of the pillows and slammed it down on to her chest, stuffing it hard into the hole, holding it there as I screamed out her name. But even as I did, I knew it was useless. Whatever her faults Olivia Marchant was a woman who knew about bodies – a woman who knew exactly where her own heart was.

I let go of the pillow and stood for a moment steadying myself, watching as the blood slowly seeped its way up through the soft folds, the contrast of the red and white spectacular and appalling. In the curl of her palm lay a small but squatly efficient pistol, the kind rich women can buy without a permit if they know where to look. She must have hidden it well for the police not to have found it. At least she had had enough sense not to use it as the murder weapon, though it would have made for a kinder, swifter death than the one she'd reserved for her husband. And a prettier one. Trust Olivia to pick the more aesthetic way of blowing herself to oblivion.

I looked up at her face. In the profound stillness of death even the cheek seemed better now, softer, almost lovely again. Only the eyes were disturbed – that final terror frozen in their lidless stare. I did my client a last service and closed them. The skin was still warm. She'd make a great-looking corpse. And as she would have known better than most, it was in Billy Wilder's interest that Gloria Swanson should look particularly old in those closing shots.

I stood vigil over the body for a while longer, then turned and walked out, closing the door behind me. Back in the living-room her perfect face stared out at me from a dozen pictures. I picked up the phone and dialled the number of a policeman I knew.

Well, every first date has to start somehow. To my surprise, now it was all over, I was quite looking forward to it.

READ MORE IN PENGUIN

In every corner of the world, on every subject under the sun, Penguin represents quality and variety – the very best in publishing today.

For complete information about books available from Penguin – including Puffins, Penguin Classics and Arkana – and how to order them, write to us at the appropriate address below. Please note that for copyright reasons the selection of books varies from country to country.

In the United Kingdom: Please write to *Dept. EP, Penguin Books Ltd, Bath Road, Harmondsworth, West Drayton, Middlesex UB7 0DA*

In the United States: Please write to *Consumer Sales, Penguin USA, P.O. Box 999, Dept. 17109, Bergenfield, New Jersey 07621-0120.* VISA and MasterCard holders call 1-800-253-6476 to order Penguin titles

In Canada: Please write to *Penguin Books Canada Ltd, 10 Alcorn Avenue, Suite 300, Toronto, Ontario M4V 3B2*

In Australia: Please write to *Penguin Books Australia Ltd, P.O. Box 257, Ringwood, Victoria 3134*

In New Zealand: Please write to *Penguin Books (NZ) Ltd, Private Bag 102902, North Shore Mail Centre, Auckland 10*

In India: Please write to *Penguin Books India Pvt Ltd, 706 Eros Apartments, 56 Nehru Place, New Delhi 110 019*

In the Netherlands: Please write to *Penguin Books Netherlands bv, Postbus 3507, NL-1001 AH Amsterdam*

In Germany: Please write to *Penguin Books Deutschland GmbH, Metzlerstrasse 26, 60594 Frankfurt am Main*

In Spain: Please write to *Penguin Books S. A., Bravo Murillo 19, 1° B, 28015 Madrid*

In Italy: Please write to *Penguin Italia s.r.l., Via Felice Casati 20, I–20124 Milano*

In France: Please write to *Penguin France S. A., 17 rue Lejeune, F–31000 Toulouse*

In Japan: Please write to *Penguin Books Japan, Ishikiribashi Building, 2–5–4, Suido, Bunkyo-ku, Tokyo 112*

In Greece: Please write to *Penguin Hellas Ltd, Dimocritou 3, GR–106 71 Athens*

In South Africa: Please write to *Longman Penguin Southern Africa (Pty) Ltd, Private Bag X08, Bertsham 2013*

BY THE SAME AUTHOR

'Make way for Hannah Wolfe, one of the best private eyes, either sex, either side of the Atlantic' – *Daily Telegraph*

Birth Marks

Life's tough for a lone, broke, female private eye on the wrong side of thirty. But not as tough as it must have been for talented dancer Carolyn Hamilton, progressing down a chain of seedy dance studios to the bottom of the Thames, with stones in her pockets and an eight-month-old foetus in her womb. It was an unusual grand finale.

So unusual that even a woman like Hannah Wolfe finds it hard to put the pieces together. She follows the detour to France, and the very different world of super-rich war hero Jules Belmont: a man who's running out of time to buy his immortality . . .

'The suspense rating reaches high voltage levels. Make it a must' – *Guardian*

'Dunant's barbed observations of life and men and things that go wrong are a delight. Intelligent, extremely well written and compassionate' – *The Times*

Fatlands

Hannah's latest brief is to mind teenage rebel Mattie Shepherd, the daughter of a top research scientist. It was never meant to be a day to remember, but what began as a Knightsbridge shopping trip ends in an act of explosive violence . . .

'Action and mystery which is pacy and top-class. It is, though, style which carries *Fatlands* so far above most other current crime novels' – *The Times*

'What Dunant does brilliantly is to use the thriller as a vehicle for the novel of ideas, without ever letting ideas get the better of pace or plot . . . What she does even better is create a fictional voice that is as barbed and wise-cracking and lucid and laid-back as Chandler's' – *Sunday Times*